Under the Wings of Shadowlight

Destinies Entwined in Shadows book 3

__Under the Wings of Shadowlight__
Book Three of Destinies Entwined in Shadows
© 2025 Everett Vale
All rights reserved.

No part of this book may be reproduced, stored in a retrieval system, or transmitted in any form or by any means—electronic, mechanical, photocopying, recording, or otherwise—without the prior written permission of the author, except in the case of brief quotations used in critical reviews or scholarly articles.

This is a work of fiction. Names, characters, places, and incidents are the product of the author's imagination or used fictitiously. Any resemblance to actual persons, living or dead, events, or locales is purely coincidental.

Interior formatting by Edward Freeman

__First Edition: October 2025__
ISBN: 979-8-89965-103-8
Published by __Staten House__

Available on Kindle, major online bookstores, and at:
books.by/freeman-vale

Dedication

To those who have walked through the shadows and found beauty in their depths.

To those who have faced fate with defiance, even when the path was written in blood.

And to those who understand that the darkest truths often reveal the most brilliant light.

This story is for you.

Table of Contents

Introduction

The road to fate was never meant to be straight. It twists, it bends, it fractures beneath the weight of those who dare to walk it. And in the end, it always demands something in return.

This is the third book in the Destinies Entwined in Shadows series, and though the faces change, the battle remains the same. Anira and Ashric's journey led them through war, through prophecy, through the slow, aching realization that their lives were not their own. Aelina and Dorian uncovered the echoes of the past, the remnants of a war long buried, only to find themselves standing at the threshold of something greater—a war not of kingdoms, but of the very fabric of existence.

Now, the focus shifts once more.

Eira has spent her life wielding a power that was never meant to be tamed, a magic that whispers to her in the voice of something both ancient and forbidden. Shadowlight is neither wholly dark nor wholly light, but something caught between—something like herself. And in a world where prophecy shapes the bones of fate, Eira will learn what it means to be caught in the middle.

She will learn what it means to betray.

Rhys, a man who has already lost everything, walks a path that is neither redemption nor ruin. He has seen the truth of the prophecy, the way it turns the choices of men into inevitabilities. He knows how this ends. But knowing does not make it easier.

This book is not about heroes or villains. It is not about victory or defeat. It is about the choices made in the gray, in the places where right and wrong no longer matter—where survival is the only truth.

The threads of fate have tightened. The players are in motion.

And by the end of this book, one of them will fall.

This is *Under the Wings of Shadowlight*.

The war is not over. It has only just begun.

Prologue:

The Weight of What Came Before

The city of Vaelwyth was dying.

It had been dying for centuries, its bones crumbling beneath the weight of time, its streets twisting beneath a sky that had long since forgotten the warmth of the sun. Once, this place had been a sanctuary, a kingdom carved from stone and magic, its towers reaching toward the heavens as if to challenge the gods themselves. Now, it was nothing more than a relic of something broken, a whisper of a past that refused to fade.

The ruins stretched endlessly, swallowed by creeping mist and the thick, thorned vines that had grown through shattered temples and collapsed bridges. The ground was littered with remnants of war—bones stripped clean by time, rusted blades buried beneath the earth, the sigils of forgotten houses weathered beyond recognition. And beneath it all, something still stirred.

Something that had never left.

Deep within the heart of the city, where the air was thick with the scent of damp stone and dying magic, a presence watched. It was not human, nor was it beast—it was something older, something waiting, something bound to the echoes of a war that had never truly ended. The ruins were its prison, and yet, the prison was failing.

A figure moved through the empty streets, their steps slow, deliberate.

A woman.

She was cloaked in deep black, the fabric tattered from travel, her hood drawn low over her face. But the shadowlight that coiled at her fingertips, barely visible beneath her gloves, betrayed her identity.

Eira had come to collect a prisoner.

A man who should have died long ago.

The wind howled through the broken archways as she pressed forward, the weight of this place settling over her like a second skin. She did not fear the city. She did not fear the whispers that curled through the air, remnants of the past that had been sealed here, waiting for a new host to listen.

What she feared—**or perhaps, what she refused to admit she feared—**was the man she had come to find.

Rhys.

Once, his name had been a warning spoken in hushed voices, a symbol of devotion twisted into something violent, something cruel. A Shadowborn zealot. A betrayer of kings. But now, the Shadowborn were crumbling, and the war that had shaped him was slipping from his grasp.

She had been sent to retrieve him because no one else would dare.

She tightened her grip on the dagger at her side, its hilt worn, the leather wrapping soft from years of use. She would not trust him. She would not pity him. He was not her ally. He was a means to an end.

And yet, even as she told herself that, she could feel it—the shift in the air, the slow tightening of something unseen, something inevitable.

The prophecy had already begun to turn.

And by the time she left this city, it would have claimed one of them.

Chapter One:

City of Dying Gods

The city of Vaelwyth was not just ruined; it was devoured. The remnants of its greatness stood like jagged bones against the sky, crumbling under the weight of time, forgotten prayers, and the decay of something much older than war. Eira had read of this place in texts buried deep within the vaults of the Arcanum, in tomes that whispered of gods who had turned their backs on the living, of temples where men had once bled for favor, of power that had been locked away not for protection—but for fear. But none of those words had prepared her for the sight before her now.

The streets were swallowed by mist, curling in thick tendrils over broken stones, seeping into the empty doorways of shattered buildings as if the city itself still breathed. The air was damp with the scent of rot and old magic, thick enough that Eira could taste the metallic tang of it on her tongue. Every step forward was met with the slow groan of an earth that had forgotten how to be walked upon, as if even the ground resented her presence. She had never been afraid of ruins before—she had spent her life hunting knowledge in places like this, uncovering lost truths and stolen secrets. But Vaelwyth was different.

She pressed forward, her dark cloak dragging against the damp cobblestones, shadowlight coiling lazily at her fingertips. It had always been there, just beneath her skin, waiting, watching. But here, it pulsed. It recognized something, something hidden beneath the layers of ruin and regret. It knew this place.

That was not comforting.

At the edge of the square, half-buried beneath the weight of fallen stone and creeping vines, stood the remnants of a temple. Its pillars were cracked, leaning toward each other as if trying to hold themselves up, as if even stone could mourn its own decay. This was where she would find him. Rhys. The traitor. The zealot. The man who was supposed to be dead.

Eira did not believe in fate. She believed in choices, in consequences, in the inescapable price of power. But as she stepped over the broken threshold of the temple, she could feel the weight of something unseen pressing against her ribs, something inevitable. As if the path she was walking had been carved long before she set foot on it.

Her fingers flexed against the hilt of her dagger as she took in the ruin before her. A single shaft of pale, dying light streamed through a shattered archway, illuminating the figure chained to the far wall. He was exactly as she had been told—half-starved, his once-gilded armor reduced to rusted fragments, his face shadowed beneath tangled dark hair. His wrists were bound in iron, but not ordinary iron—sigil-marked cuffs meant to suppress magic.

Yet, despite it all, he smiled.

Eira's grip on her blade tightened.

"You're late," Rhys said, his voice hoarse but edged with something sharp—something that did not belong to a dying man.

Eira did not return his amusement. "You should be dead."

Rhys tilted his head, golden eyes gleaming in the dim light. "Many people have tried to make that happen." A pause, a slow curl of his lips. "You can be the next, if you'd like."

Eira exhaled through her nose, stepping closer. He was dangerous. Even bound, even weak, she could feel it radiating off of him. The way he watched her, the way his body remained loose, unaffected by the chains—this was not a man who had accepted his fate.

Good. She didn't need him to be broken. She needed him to talk.

"You know why I'm here," she said, her voice even. "The war is shifting. Your people are gone, scattered or dead. The last of the Shadowborn's influence is unraveling, and yet you're still alive. That tells me something." She tilted her head. "It tells me you still have a part to play."

Rhys chuckled, low and dark. "And you think you get to decide what that part is?"

She stepped closer, lowering her voice. "I think you already know you don't have a choice."

His smile faded just slightly. Not enough for most to notice. But Eira noticed everything.

Outside, the mist thickened, curling at the edges of the broken archway. Something was shifting. The city had noticed them.

And it was listening.

Eira took another step forward, letting the weight of her presence settle into the room like a slow-building storm. The air inside the temple was thick, suffocating, as if the very stones had absorbed the suffering of the people who had once worshipped here. Rhys watched her approach, unmoving, that same infuriating smirk pulling at the corner of his mouth, but his golden eyes flickered—assessing, calculating. He was already deciding how much of himself to give away.

She would not let him have that advantage.

"You may not have a choice," she repeated, her voice cold, measured. "But you do have an opportunity."

Rhys exhaled a short laugh, tilting his head. "That's a pretty way of telling me you're about to make a threat sound like a gift." His chains clinked against the stone as he shifted. Even bound, even weakened, he still moved like a predator—controlled, deliberate, like he was waiting for the right moment to strike. "Tell me, shadow-weaver, what is it you think I have that you want so desperately?"

Eira clenched her jaw at the name. Shadow-weaver. It wasn't inaccurate, but coming from him, it felt like something else. An insult wrapped in curiosity. A warning that he already knew what she was.

"You have knowledge," she said, ignoring the way his gaze sharpened at the word. "The kind of knowledge that doesn't belong to the living."

Rhys chuckled lowly, his head falling back against the stone behind him. "Ah," he murmured. "So you're finally admitting the truth—you don't want me. You want what's inside my head."

Eira allowed herself a slow blink. "Your head is the only thing keeping you alive right now. Keep that in mind."

Rhys let the silence stretch between them before exhaling, his smirk fading into something more thoughtful. He studied her then—really studied her, as if seeing past the cloak, past the reputation, past the control she so carefully wielded. It was unsettling.

"You don't trust me," he finally said.

"No," Eira answered without hesitation. "Should I?"

Rhys smiled again, but it was different this time. Not amusement. Not arrogance. Just quiet, knowing. "No," he admitted.

The admission sent a flicker of something uneasy down her spine, but she didn't let it show. Instead, she took a slow breath and let the words that mattered fall between them. "The Shadowborn are moving again. Their numbers are weaker, but their purpose is not. If we don't stop what's coming—"

Rhys cut her off, his voice turning sharp. "What's coming has already begun."

Eira hesitated, and that was all the confirmation he needed. His golden eyes gleamed, recognizing her uncertainty, and he seized on it like a blade pressed between the ribs.

"You don't know what you're fighting," he continued, his tone softer now, but no less dangerous. "You think you do, but the moment you stepped into this city, you became part of something you weren't ready for."

Eira's fingers twitched at her side, the shadowlight beneath her skin pulsing in warning. She hated how he spoke, how he made it sound like she was already caught in a snare, like the war she was trying to prevent had already made its decision.

"Then enlighten me," she said, voice steady. "Tell me what I don't know."

Rhys watched her, his golden gaze flickering to her hands, to the subtle glow of magic waiting just beneath her fingertips. And then, after what felt like an eternity, he leaned forward as far as his chains would allow and whispered, "Unbind me, and I will."

Silence crashed between them, sharp and suffocating.

Eira didn't move. She didn't breathe.

Because in that moment, she understood—this was not a negotiation.

It was the beginning of something far, far worse

Eira did not move.

The words hung between them, thick with the weight of something far heavier than simple choice. Unbind me, and I will. It was an offer, yes, but it was also a demand, a gamble, a test. The moment she reached for those chains, the power dynamic between them would shift—perhaps not entirely in his favor, but enough to make a difference. Enough to make her question whether she would regret it.

Her fingers twitched at her sides, shadowlight curling faintly in response, sensing her hesitation. Magic was not patient. It never had been. It wanted answers, certainty, action. But Eira had lived long enough to know that certainty was a luxury, and answers were often the sharpest weapons of all.

Rhys watched her, golden eyes glinting in the dim light, unreadable. He didn't speak again, didn't try to convince her, didn't push. And that was the most dangerous part. Because he didn't need to.

The decision was already working its way into her bones.

Eira exhaled slowly, letting herself assess him like she would a battle map, like she would a locked door she needed to open without triggering the trap hidden inside. She had seen men like him before—men who carried their sins like second skins, men who learned long ago that survival was an art, not a right. Men who smiled even when bleeding.

He had been a Shadowborn once. A zealot. A soldier of their faith.

And yet here he was, left to rot in a forgotten temple, his own people having abandoned him to fate. That meant something.

"You understand what you're asking," she said finally, her voice even. "You understand that I don't trust you."

Rhys tilted his head. "I'd be more concerned if you did."

Her grip on her dagger tightened. "I don't need you alive."

"Ah," he murmured. "And yet, here you are."

Eira's throat tightened, but she didn't let the flicker of irritation show. She wasn't sure if he was always like this or if imprisonment had sharpened his edges into something more reckless. Or perhaps he simply did not care anymore. That, too, was dangerous.

"Let's say I unbind you," she continued, tilting her head slightly. "You walk out of here, and then what? You run? You fight me? You show me just how much of the Shadowborn is still left in you?"

Rhys let out a slow breath, his gaze shifting to the chains at his wrists. For the first time since she arrived, something unreadable crossed his expression—something quieter. "No," he said simply. "I show you what you came here to find."

Eira inhaled sharply, her magic rippling faintly at the weight of those words.

Because that was the problem, wasn't it? She had come here for him. And not because of what he was—but because of what he knew.

The war was shifting. The prophecy was unfolding. And Rhys held a piece of it inside him.

The rational part of her screamed against it. Do not unbind him. Do not give him power. Do not mistake necessity for control.

But she had made her choice long before she set foot in this ruined city.

Eira took a slow step forward.

Rhys did not move, but she saw the way his body tensed, the way his breath steadied, like a man who had been waiting for something inevitable.

Her fingers hovered just over the chains, the sigils etched into them flickering faintly beneath the touch of her magic. They were powerful. Strong enough to hold a man like him, to keep his abilities sealed away, his connection to the Shadowborn severed.

But all magic had a cost.

"You betray me," she murmured, her voice quiet, steady, "and I will not kill you quickly."

Rhys smiled again—but this time, there was no arrogance in it.

"Then I suppose we're both taking a risk."

Eira exhaled.

And then she unbound him.

The moment the final sigil flared and cracked beneath Eira's touch, the chains loosened with a groan, their iron seeming to sigh as they released the weight they had carried for far too long. The glow faded slowly from her fingertips, the shadowlight sinking back beneath her skin like a creature reluctant to leave the surface. Silence followed, heavy and expectant, as if the city itself was holding its breath.

Rhys didn't move at first.

His wrists were free, the thick cuffs now clattering to the floor, their enchantments spent, nothing more than cold iron and forgotten promises. He stared at them for a moment—not as if he were surprised, but as if he were remembering something lost. Then, with a slow exhale, he stood.

There was no staggering. No hesitation.

His movements were controlled, fluid, and too composed for a man who had just been unshackled. As if the chains had been a formality, not a prison.

Eira stepped back instinctively, her posture tense, shadowlight coiling up her spine like a warning. Rhys didn't look at her right away. He stretched first, rolling his shoulders until they popped, the long silence broken only by the soft crack of bone and the creak of old armor plates shifting with him. The motion was slow, almost deliberate, like a man reacquainting himself with the concept of freedom.

Then his gaze found her.

And everything changed.

There was no hunger in his eyes. No rage. No mockery. Just quiet calculation, deep and steady, like a storm waiting behind stained glass. He didn't thank her. He didn't gloat. He simply took a single step forward, and Eira felt the air ripple with something that had been dormant until now.

Shadowlight.

But not hers.

It moved through him in a different way—older, colder, more controlled. Where hers burned with chaos, his seeped, slow and sure like ink spilled into water. This was not a magic borrowed or barely restrained. This was a magic claimed.

She didn't let her expression shift. She had known, somewhere deep down, what he was. But seeing it now, unfettered—it was a different thing entirely.

Rhys took another step. "You were expecting something more dramatic, weren't you?"

Eira didn't answer. Her fingers hovered near the hilt of her dagger, but she didn't draw it. Not yet.

He looked around the temple slowly, his gaze sweeping over the moss-choked stone, the broken statues, the high, open archways where birds once roosted and prayers once echoed. "This place is still listening," he said. "It remembers what we did here."

Eira's voice was calm, but her pulse betrayed her. "What did you do here?"

He smiled faintly. "I broke something I was never meant to touch."

And then the ground trembled.

Just once. Barely more than a breath. But the light filtering through the shattered ceiling shifted, and far above, something moved—a ripple in the dark, a breath not taken in centuries.

Eira turned sharply toward the sound, her instincts roaring to the surface. "What did you wake?"

Rhys stepped past her without fear. "Not me." He glanced over his shoulder. "Us."

The tremor passed through the temple a second time, more deliberate now—less a shiver of stone and more a pulse, like a heart beginning to beat after centuries of stillness. The faint glow of shadowlight along the fractured walls intensified, tracing the lines of ancient carvings that had once been dull and inert. Now, they bled with colorless light, sickly and alive, as though Rhys's release had stirred the very bones of the place.

Eira's breath stilled as the air grew dense, electric with something old and watching. The statues along the outer wall, cracked and eyeless, shifted almost imperceptibly. Dust rose where no wind passed.

"Rhys…" she warned, stepping to his side, her magic already rising beneath her skin, pulsing in defense.

He didn't answer immediately. His eyes were fixed on the far side of the temple where an altar of black stone stood crumbling yet defiant, the moss that covered it now sloughing off like it had been burned away. He exhaled slowly. "It's not a creature," he said. "It's a response."

Eira's heart pounded harder. "A response to what?"

"To me," he said grimly. "To us."

The altar cracked with a thunderous snap that echoed like a scream. From the stone fissures, a thick darkness poured—not shadowlight, but something older, more instinctive. It writhed across the floor like smoke soaked in venom, and from it rose a figure.

It had no face—only the impression of one, featureless and smooth, like obsidian worn down by centuries of grief. Its form shifted constantly, long-limbed and whisper-thin, a construct of despair given shape. Where it moved, the ground died. The floor beneath its feet blackened, stone crumbling into ash.

Eira stepped back, pulling Rhys with her, though he resisted the gesture with a grim smile. "It remembers me," he said. "This place. This thing. We're part of each other, in ways I've tried to forget."

The creature moved, slowly at first, its head tilting like it could hear their thoughts, like it knew them better than they knew themselves. Eira raised her hand, the light burning at her palm flaring to life. The being hissed—not in fear, but in pleasure.

"Run," Rhys said, voice suddenly cold, certain.

Eira didn't question him. She turned and ran, her cloak snapping behind her as her feet pounded over ancient stone. Rhys was at her side, his stride effortless despite the time spent in chains. Behind them, the sound of breaking pillars filled the space—the temple collapsing around the thing that had awakened, no longer content to watch.

As they burst through the shattered archway and into the street beyond, the sky above them darkened unnaturally, the light dimming like the city itself was mourning. The mist thickened around them in churning waves, trying to pull them back into the temple's grasp.

"We need to keep moving," Eira said through clenched teeth, glancing back only once. She saw the creature at the edge of the ruin—not pursuing, but waiting. Smiling with no mouth.

"It won't chase us," Rhys said, breath steady, "not yet. It just needed to see that I was free."

Eira stopped in her tracks. "Why? What is it waiting for?"

Rhys turned his face to the shadowed sky, and something in his expression hollowed. "It's not just me it wants anymore," he said. "It's you."

They didn't stop until the mist thinned and the broken skyline of Vaelwyth softened into a shadowed grove, its trees gnarled and silver-leaved, untouched by time or decay. The air here was still strange—too still, too silent—but it was better than the feeling of being watched. The temple had vanished behind them, swallowed whole by the weight of what had awakened within it.

Eira slowed first, one hand pressed against the rough bark of a twisted tree, her other clutching her side. Her breath came in sharp bursts, the cool air cutting against her throat like knives. The magic inside her still seethed, not settled, not quiet—alive in a way that frightened her more than the creature they'd fled.

Rhys said nothing for a long time. He stood a few feet away, leaning against a half-fallen stone pillar overtaken by roots and moss, his head tilted back to the canopy above. He looked untouched. Too composed. And that angered her more than anything.

"Is this where you pretend nothing just happened?" she snapped, her voice raw with exhaustion and fury. "Or are you just waiting until I'm too tired to question you again?"

He didn't move. Not at first. But when he did, he turned toward her slowly, his expression unreadable. "I'm waiting," he said, "because I know what you're about to ask, and I don't know how to answer it."

Eira stared at him, the ache in her chest growing sharper. "You said it wanted me."

Rhys's jaw tightened. "It did."

She stepped closer, her magic pulsing again, crackling faintly along her skin. "You brought me here. You knew what that place held, what it would wake. Don't pretend you didn't."

"I didn't know you would wake it," he said, eyes darkening. "I thought... I thought it would respond to me."

"It did," she said. "But then it looked at me."

A tense silence fell between them. The sounds of the forest seemed to withhold breath, the trees listening. Eira stared at Rhys, her pulse heavy in her ears, and for a brief moment, she didn't see a prisoner or a weapon or a threat. She saw a man carrying something he never meant to share.

"I don't want to be part of your prophecy," she whispered.

Rhys looked at her then, really looked at her, and for the first time, there was no mask. Just a raw honesty that scraped at her soul. "Neither did I."

Rhys's gaze drifted away from hers, his jaw clenched as if fighting words that didn't want to surface. For a long moment, he was silent, staring past her toward the tangle of trees where mist still lingered like a fading bruise. Eira watched him carefully, her anger giving way to something colder, heavier. This wasn't just deflection. It was fear. Not the kind that made a man tremble—but the kind that lived in his marrow, that made him build walls no one could climb.

"I was there," he said at last, voice low and without embellishment. "Not when the prophecy was first spoken. That was centuries ago, passed in fragments and riddles like all curses are. But I was there when the Shadowborn tried to bend it."

Eira's breath hitched, but she didn't interrupt.

Rhys continued, each word deliberate. "They thought they could use it. That if they deciphered it, they could shape it. That by controlling the people it named, they could control the war to come. I was part of that effort. One of the chosen few to dig through the old texts, to find the symbols hidden in bloodlines, in ruins, in songs no one had sung in generations."

"You were a scholar?" Eira asked, disbelief edging her voice.

Rhys let out a soft, humorless laugh. "No. I was a weapon with a mind sharp enough to understand what it was being pointed at."

She looked at him, really looked, and for the first time, she saw the weight behind his eyes—not just regret, but shame. Bone-deep.

"Did you find anything?"

His shoulders shifted. "Pieces. Names. Symbols. One of them matched me. I was meant to carry a portion of the prophecy's burden—like a vessel. I let them mark me. Let them fill me with knowledge I wasn't meant to survive."

Eira's brows knit. "You were a vessel?"

Rhys met her eyes again, and there was no fire in them now—only the steady burn of endurance. "They carved the words into my bones, Eira. And now they're waking up."

The forest felt suddenly smaller, the air tighter. Eira took a slow step back, her magic instinctively rising to the surface. "Why didn't they kill you?"

"They tried," he said. "But the prophecy had already chosen me. And prophecy doesn't let go that easily."

A hush fell again, this one filled not with silence, but with understanding. Terrible, inescapable understanding.

Eira looked down at her own hands, the faint trace of shadowlight still dancing along her fingers. "Then what does it want from me?"

Rhys didn't answer immediately.

Then: "I think… it wants you to finish what it started."

Eira sank onto a moss-slick stone, the cold of it seeping through her cloak, grounding her more than she cared to admit. The revelation hung between them like fog—dense, quiet, impossible to escape. He had let them carve prophecy into him, let himself be made into a vessel of knowledge that should never have lived inside a single man.

And now that knowledge was bleeding into the world again, one fractured truth at a time.

She looked at him—not as an enemy, not even as an ally, but as someone terrifyingly familiar. They were both touched by shadow, both shaped by forces that didn't ask permission.

Rhys remained standing, arms crossed loosely over his chest, his posture deceptively casual. But his eyes were watchful. Not predatory. Not defensive. Guarded, yes—but only because the walls he'd built around himself had been made for survival, not cruelty.

"You're not what I expected," she said, voice quiet.

He raised a brow. "Because I didn't try to kill you?"

She didn't smile. "Because I thought you'd want to."

That startled something out of him—a laugh, rough and tired, like it hadn't been used in years. "I've wanted a lot of things. Most of them don't survive past the first hour of being hunted."

Eira's gaze fell to the earth, her voice lowering. "I've never been hunted. Not until recently. But I've always been... watched." She flexed her fingers, letting shadowlight flicker along her palm. "Like it was waiting. Like it was mine before I ever asked for it."

Rhys tilted his head. "That's what it does. It waits. It watches. Then it chooses."

"And now it's chosen both of us," she murmured.

He didn't correct her. He didn't need to.

The silence stretched, not uncomfortable, but heavy. Weighted with recognition. There was no point pretending they didn't see pieces of themselves in the other now. Not after the temple. Not after what it had shown them—that the prophecy didn't just connect them. It required them.

"You should rest," Rhys said eventually, his voice softer than it had been before. "We'll need to keep moving by morning. This place might be quiet now, but it won't stay that way."

Eira nodded, but didn't move. Her gaze remained on the dim trees, her thoughts deeper still. "I don't know if I trust you."

"You shouldn't," he said, without hesitation.

She looked up at him, startled by the honesty.

"But I think," he added after a pause, "that's the only thing we have in common worth building on."

Their eyes met. And in that shared, broken truth, something bound them tighter. Not trust. Not yet. But something that might become it.

Eventually.

Eira eventually lay down beneath the low boughs of a crooked tree, her cloak wrapped tight against the damp cold, though it did little to keep it out. The earth was soft, the leaves above pale and quivering, rustling not with wind, but with some breathless awareness of what walked beneath them. Her eyes remained open for a long time, tracing the pattern of branches against the darkening sky, as if answers might be written in the stars she could not see.

Across from her, Rhys sat with his back against a stone, one leg stretched long, the other bent loosely at the knee. He stared into the darkness beyond the trees, eyes sharp, golden, and unblinking. He didn't speak again. He didn't sleep. Eira wasn't sure he needed to.

When her eyes finally closed, it was not the silence that carried her into sleep, but the steady hum of her own magic, coiled inside her like a sleeping serpent. She dreamed of the temple again. Of that thing with no face. And of Rhys standing beside her—unchained, watching her with sorrow in his eyes as the world cracked open beneath them.

She woke with a start, the morning air colder than the night had promised.

Rhys was already on his feet.

"Come on," he said quietly, without looking back. "We don't have time to linger."

Eira rose without a word, brushing dirt from her cloak, fingers tingling faintly with magic. The forest before them loomed dense and silver-drenched, its shadows stretching longer than they should, its silence deeper than nature allowed. Somewhere ahead, the path would splinter, and danger would find them again.

She followed him into the wilds of Vaelwyth, where the roots ran deep with forgotten magic and the trees whispered secrets not meant for mortal ears.

Whatever had begun in the ruins was far from finished.

And the road forward would not be kind.

Chapter Two:

Chains and Lies

The deeper they went into the wilds of Vaelwyth, the more the land itself began to change. The trees no longer grew upward but spiraled at impossible angles, their limbs twisted like limbs reaching for something just out of grasp. What little sunlight pierced the dense canopy came through warped, fractured by veils of mist that clung to every surface like breath on glass. The ground beneath their feet was uneven, soft in places where it shouldn't have been, and too dry in others where moss should have thrived.

Eira walked in silence, each step feeling like it pulled her farther away from the known world and deeper into one that remembered her. **The magic in her veins thrummed louder now, as if the shadowlight recognized this place—**not as a stranger, but as a forgotten home. It unnerved her. Even more unnerving was the way Rhys said nothing as the path narrowed and the trees bent lower, forming a tunnel that seemed to breathe with them as they passed through.

She stole a glance at him. He moved like he belonged here. Not in the way one belongs to nature or to peace—but in the way a blade belongs to its sheath. Too calm. Too familiar. Too still.

"You've walked this road before," she said, breaking the silence that had stretched too long.

Rhys didn't look at her. "Many roads. But yes. I remember this one."

She narrowed her eyes. "You remember it, or you were brought through it as one of them?"

He stopped, finally turning his head toward her. The sharp cut of his jaw and the faint scar just beneath his right eye caught the strange light filtering through the canopy. "Both."

The word dropped between them like a stone in water. She didn't ask what had happened here, not yet, but the question hung in the air all the same.

"Why did they leave you alive, Rhys?" she asked, her voice quieter now, her steps slowing as the path narrowed even more. "If they were done with you—if you were dangerous enough to chain up—why not kill you?"

He didn't answer right away. The silence stretched long enough that she wondered if he would bother at all.

"They didn't leave me alive," he said finally, voice low and without inflection. "They just failed to make sure I stayed dead."

Her breath caught. "What does that mean?"

Rhys stopped walking and turned to face her fully. The gold in his eyes burned low, banked like embers. "It means I died once, Eira. Not metaphorically. Not emotionally. I stopped breathing in that temple. I saw what waits beneath the prophecy. And it let me go."

Eira stared at him. "You're saying... you were *let* go?"

His lips twitched in something that might have been a smile, though it didn't reach his eyes. "Or sent back."

The forest around them groaned suddenly, branches creaking though there was no wind. A burst of leaves fluttered down from above like ash, gray and silent. Eira's skin crawled.

"This place isn't just old," she murmured. "It's listening."

"Yes," Rhys replied, voice barely audible. "Because it remembers what we are."

They moved again, quieter now, more aware of the eyes they couldn't see. Eira kept her magic close, just under her skin, but it moved of its own accord now, responding to the air, to the trees, to Rhys. And beneath it all, she felt something else taking shape—a pressure building, a tether tightening.

Their connection, whatever it was, wasn't weakening.

It was growing stronger.

And neither of them had any idea what that meant.

They reached the edge of a shallow ravine by mid-afternoon, though the light above them suggested little more than a dull stretch of endless twilight. The trees parted here, revealing a yawning gap in the earth. A crooked stairway of carved stone descended along the slope—barely visible beneath centuries of overgrowth and moss—but still there, as if someone had left a door open that should have remained sealed.

Rhys stopped at the top of the path, staring down into the hollow below. His shoulders stiffened, though only slightly, the kind of tension that lived in old wounds and unburied memories.

Eira moved up beside him, her voice low. "What is this place?"

He didn't answer at first. Just stared. Then: "A failure."

The word echoed off the trees, caught by the hollow and dropped into silence.

He began down the steps without waiting, and Eira followed, her boots crunching softly over scattered debris—broken twigs, shards of old stone, feathers blackened and split. As they descended, she noticed the air changing again. The temperature dropped, and a strange scent met her nose—not decay, not rot, but something older. Stagnant. Hollow.

At the base of the ravine lay what remained of a ritual site. The stone circle, once precise, was now fractured—some sigils faded, others scorched into the ground as if burned from within. The center was charred black, the earth there cracked open in a jagged ring like the aftermath of a lightning strike.

Eira stepped toward it cautiously. The magic here wasn't just lingering—it was trapped. She could feel it pressing against her senses, desperate, wrong.

"You were part of this," she said quietly, looking at Rhys.

He nodded once. "This is where they tried to sever me from the prophecy. They thought the magic could be drawn out—bled out. Ripped from my body like poison."

"And it didn't work."

Rhys walked to the edge of the blackened center, his boots scuffing ash. "No. It made things worse."

Eira could barely breathe. The shadowlight in her blood ached here. Not with pain, but with memory—as if it knew this place. As if it had been watching, even then.

"What happened to the others?" she asked.

Rhys's jaw tightened. "Dead. All of them. Some by my hand. Some by theirs."

She looked around again. There were no bones. No markers. But she could feel the ghosts in the silence, their pain still woven into the stone. The magic hadn't left—it had consumed them.

And Rhys had survived.

"Why you?" she asked.

His gaze met hers, and for a heartbeat, she saw something unguarded there. Not pride. Not power. Just burden.

"Because I was willing."

The words chilled her.

They stood in silence for a long while. The wind had vanished entirely. Even the trees were quiet. Only the soft, rhythmic pulse of Eira's magic reminded her that time was still moving forward.

"Whatever was done here," she said finally, "it left a mark. On the land. On you."

Rhys looked down at his hands. "Yes. And I'm starting to think it left one on the prophecy too."

She turned to him sharply. "What do you mean?"

He shook his head. "I don't know yet. But something about us… this… it wasn't supposed to happen. Not like this."

Eira felt the weight of those words settle deep in her chest. There was more to the prophecy than they had been told. More than the Shadowborn understood.

And whatever had begun here at this broken ritual site had not ended.

It had just changed shape.

The air grew heavier as they left the scorched circle behind, ascending the crumbling staircase that cut through the ravine like a scar. Every step away from the ritual site felt like dragging a wound uphill—not one of flesh, but of memory, of something carved too deep to be touched by time. The silence clung to them, no birds, no insects, only the steady crunch of boots against stone and the soft rustle of Rhys's cloak catching on thorned undergrowth. Eira didn't speak. Her mind was too full, her magic too unsettled. The energy in her veins still trembled with resonance, a low hum of warning that refused to die down.

At the ridge above, the world opened again, but not into comfort. The trees here were taller, older, their bark a strange marbled gray, their leaves shriveled and dry as paper despite the season. They twisted as they grew, like they had fought too long against something unseen. The forest wasn't just unnatural—it was *resistant,* as though it strained to keep itself from being pulled apart. A narrow path wound through the skeletal wood, and Rhys followed it with the ease of someone who had walked through death and come out the other side.

Eira stayed close, each step deliberate, her eyes scanning the shadows where the light barely reached. She tried to shake the feeling that the woods were leaning in around them. That the trees weren't just growing—they were listening. The sensation of being watched had returned, more focused now, like something that had been patiently circling was beginning to draw near.

Half an hour into their march, she paused, her hand instinctively reaching for the hilt of her dagger. "Did you hear that?" she whispered, barely above breath.

Rhys stopped beside her, eyes narrowed. "No," he said, his voice tense. "Which is the problem."

The wind had stilled completely. No birdsong. No creaking branches. Even their footsteps seemed swallowed by the air. Then, from behind them, a soft *click* echoed—too sharp, too distinct, like bone striking stone. Eira turned on instinct, but the path behind them was empty. No movement. No sound. Still, the chill crawling up her spine rooted deep.

Rhys stepped forward, slow and careful, scanning the underbrush with trained precision. "It's not following. It's flanking."

Eira's heart thudded once—not fast, but loud, like it wanted her attention. She drew her blade, the edge gleaming faintly with the shimmer of shadowlight. "What is it?"

Rhys didn't answer. He turned his head toward the trees just off the trail, gaze narrowed. "We're not the first to walk this path in days. There are prints. Two sets. Light. Human. But there's another—too wide, too deep. Not human."

The words settled in her stomach like lead. Her grip tightened on the hilt. "Tracked by what?"

A low growl answered them—not from the ground, but from above.

Eira barely had time to look up before something dropped from the branches, landing hard in the center of the trail between them. It was wrong—bipedal, but crooked, as if it had learned to walk only recently. Its limbs were too long, its head tilted too far to one side, and its flesh glistened with a slick gray sheen, like old wax melted over bone. There were no eyes. No nose. Only a wide, trembling mouth full of needle-like teeth.

It shrieked once—a sound that didn't come from its throat but from inside its chest, muffled and desperate—and lunged for Rhys.

He was faster than she expected, moving like shadow through smoke. His blade—blackened steel etched with ruined sigils—flashed once, catching the creature across the side. It hissed and reeled back, clawing at the wound like it didn't understand pain. Eira moved to his side without thinking, her shadowlight flaring along her arms, alive and eager. The creature didn't hesitate—it struck again.

This time, it came for her.

She slashed with the blade, then reached with her other hand, releasing a burst of shadowlight that struck the thing square in the chest. It screamed again—louder now—and staggered back into the trees. There was a flurry of movement, a twitching retreat into the brush, and then... nothing.

Silence fell once more.

Rhys exhaled, his chest rising and falling with quiet urgency. "It wasn't sent to kill us," he said slowly, eyes still on the trees. "It was sent to see how far you've come."

Eira's breath trembled. "Then it knows."

He looked at her, something grim settling in his expression. "*They all do now.*"

The path led them into a narrow cleft between two ancient ridgelines, where the trees receded and the air shifted from suffocating to still. The mist thinned here, the sky opening above them like a reluctant breath. Nestled in the crook of the rock face, hidden by time and clever enchantment, lay a structure of moss-eaten stone and collapsed wood—a waystation long abandoned, or so it wanted the world to believe.

Rhys stepped forward first, placing a hand on the rusted sigil carved into the threshold. With a faint shimmer, the illusion that cloaked the front archway peeled back, revealing a shadowed interior and a scent of dry herbs and dust. He glanced back at Eira, his eyes unreadable. "It won't hold long. But it'll be enough for now."

Inside, the small space was cloaked in shadows, but it was dry, warmer than the forest, and—most importantly—quiet. A stone hearth sat cold along one wall, beneath it the remnants of a long-dead fire. The room was circular, lined with carved shelves that had once held supplies, most of which had rotted into disuse. Yet there was still a sense of sanctuary here, a breath carved out of the storm.

Eira sank to the ground near the hearth, her limbs shaking from the adrenaline now draining from her body. She wiped her blade clean with the edge of her cloak, eyes distant, her thoughts caught between the terror of the creature and the sick certainty in Rhys's voice: They all know.

Rhys crouched across from her, lighting the hearth with a flick of flint and practiced ease. Sparks caught, crackling against dried moss until flame curled upward in low, flickering orange. The light danced across his face, casting sharp planes and soft edges—making him look younger, and at the same time, far older.

"I've never seen something like that," Eira said at last, her voice rough, her fingers twitching where they rested on her knees. "Not even in the worst shadow-cursed lands."

"You wouldn't have," Rhys replied without looking up. "That wasn't a creature. It was a remnant."

Eira frowned. "A what?"

He met her gaze. "A sliver of what came before. Not alive, not quite dead. More like... a memory that learned how to walk." He paused, the firelight flaring in his eyes. "They send them to test. To see what you are."

Eira's skin prickled. "And what did it see?"

Rhys leaned back against the wall, stretching his legs in front of him. He didn't answer right away. "That you're farther along than they expected."

She folded her arms, trying to still the tremor she couldn't quite banish. "That thing... it reacted to my magic. It didn't flinch. It wanted it."

Rhys nodded. "Because you're no longer simply wielding shadowlight, Eira. You're becoming it."

Her stomach turned, but she didn't argue. She'd felt it too—that pull during the fight, the way her magic had surged, hungry, eager. It hadn't felt like defense. It had felt like dominance.

"Is this what you meant? When you said it marks you?"

He looked at her, and for once, there was no sharpness in his expression. Just quiet understanding. "Yes. And it doesn't stop. Not until you choose what part of yourself you'll keep—and what you'll lose."

Eira stared into the flames, the heat barely warming her fingers. "I'm not ready to lose anything."

Rhys tilted his head slightly. "Then hold on while you can."

They sat in silence after that, the fire cracking softly between them. Outside, the forest rustled with the sounds of night falling again. The reprieve would be short. But for now, they breathed the same air, shared the same fire, and tried to forget—just for a little while—that they were being hunted by fate itself.

The fire had burned down to a soft glow, its light gilding the rough stone walls in warm, flickering gold. Outside, the forest groaned softly, branches creaking under unseen weight, but the waystation remained untouched—as though the old enchantments remembered their purpose and clung to it with fading determination. Inside, the silence stretched, not oppressive, but heavy with the weight of unspoken truths.

Eira hadn't moved far from the hearth. She sat cross-legged, her cloak draped around her shoulders, but her posture was not one of rest. She was still coiled tightly beneath her skin, still listening for footsteps that might never come. Her eyes glinted with the low light of the fire, shadowlight still lingering faintly at the edges of her fingers, pulsing in rhythm with her thoughts.

Across from her, Rhys leaned with one shoulder against the wall, his head tilted back, eyes half-lidded but watchful. There was a line of tension in his jaw, a stillness in the way he held himself—not like a man at ease, but like someone waiting for a pain that hadn't arrived yet.

After a long pause, Eira's voice slipped into the quiet, low and rough. "Did it hurt?"

He turned his head slowly, his eyes catching the firelight like molten gold. "What?"

"When they made you into this," she said, her voice not sharp but careful, like she didn't want to shatter the moment with too much weight. "The vessel. The rituals. The prophecy carved into your bones. Did it hurt?"

Rhys didn't answer immediately. He looked back toward the fire, the light dancing across the sharp lines of his face, revealing shadows that didn't come from the room. "Not at first," he said finally. "At first, it felt like clarity. Like all the chaos I'd lived through finally meant something. They made it sound like a gift. Like sacrifice would elevate me."

Eira's brows furrowed. "And then?"

His fingers twitched against the hilt of the blade resting near his hip. "And then it started speaking back. Whispering things I didn't remember knowing. Showing me faces I'd never seen. Truths that weren't mine to carry."

She watched him closely, her magic responding to the quiet tremble beneath his words. He wasn't just recounting pain. He was still living in it.

"I can feel it sometimes," she murmured. "Like there's something inside the shadowlight. Watching me. Waiting. I tell myself I control it, but it's always... close."

He met her gaze again. There was something raw there, something rare. "That's because you haven't let it break you yet."

She looked down, the flames catching the edge of her jaw, softening the steel in her features. "What if it does?"

Rhys leaned forward slightly, elbows resting on his knees. "Then you'll crawl back from it. Or you won't. But it won't be the magic that defines you. It'll be the choice you made when it tried to."

The silence that followed wasn't cold or strained. It was something else—a mutual recognition. A tether forming between two souls carrying wounds too deep for light to touch.

Eira let her head drop slightly, eyes fixed on the fire. "I don't want to be part of this prophecy."

Rhys exhaled softly. "Neither did I."

Their eyes met across the dim space, and in that shared truth, something fragile but unmistakably real passed between them. Not trust. Not yet. But the shape of it. The possibility.

Outside, the mist thickened once more.

But inside the waystation, for just a breath of time, they were not weapons. Not curses. Not fate-bound.

They were simply Eira and Rhys.

And for the first time, it almost felt like enough.

The pale light of morning seeped through the cracks in the stone wall, a reluctant gray that made no promises of warmth. It slid over the floor like cold water, illuminating the dust that drifted lazily through the air. Eira stirred before the sun crested the horizon, her body aching with the kind of tired that lived deeper than the bones. Sleep had come and gone in fitful stretches, chased away by dreams that smelled of ash and whispers, of firelight and Rhys's voice echoing with prophecy.

She sat up slowly, pulling her cloak tighter around her shoulders. Across the small chamber, Rhys was already awake, crouched by the dying hearth with one hand outstretched to stir the coals back to life. There was something composed in the way he moved, as though the night had reset him, drawn his sharpness back into place. But Eira could still see the tension in his shoulders, the way his jaw clenched a second too long before he finally spoke.

"Storms moving in from the east," he said without looking at her. "The air's changed."

She rose, brushing dirt from her tunic, her body still heavy but functioning. "You can tell that from the fire?"

Rhys glanced up, his lips twitching faintly. "From the pressure in my ribs. The magic reacts before I do."

Eira moved toward the doorframe, peering through the mist that lay just beyond. The forest was still there—twisted, silver-veined, coiled with silence—but different now. As if it knew they were leaving and had not decided whether to mourn or resent it.

"We won't be able to backtrack easily," she said, eyes scanning the path. "Whatever that thing was, it's not the only one."

"No," Rhys said, rising to his feet. "It was a scout. There will be others. And they won't come for us alone next time."

She turned to him, brushing a loose strand of hair behind her ear. "So where are we going?"

His eyes darkened slightly, the glint of memory surfacing. "West. There's a shrine buried in the cliffs—older than Vaelwyth, older than the war. The last place I remember seeing the prophecy written in full."

Eira narrowed her eyes. "I thought it was all fragments and riddles."

"It is now," he replied, fastening the clasp of his cloak. "But once, it wasn't. The Shadowborn tried to erase the original text after what happened to me. They failed. Some of it survived."

She took a slow breath. "And you think it'll help?"

"I think," Rhys said, shouldering his pack, "it'll tell us why the prophecy changed. Why it's binding us together when it shouldn't."

Eira didn't speak right away. The answer hung between them like fog—heavy, close, and not quite formed. She stepped out of the waystation first, the weight of her magic settling over her like a second skin. Rhys followed, his presence at her back no longer a threat, but not yet a comfort either.

They moved into the forest again, side by side. The trees closed around them, the shadows stretching long and low.

And the prophecy, somewhere deep beneath the soil, turned another page.

Chapter Three:

Beneath the Veil

The forest grew stranger as they pressed farther west, its trees bending not only in form but in memory, as though the land itself remembered something it refused to speak aloud. The terrain twisted in unsettling ways—hills that dipped too sharply, paths that seemed to vanish behind them, and trees with bark like stretched skin, pale and cracked, bearing deep veins of silver that pulsed faintly when touched by shadowlight. The mist followed them still, but thinner now, more curious than concealing, as though it had become an observer rather than a shield. Eira felt it clinging to her boots and cloak, to her hair and her skin, whispering things she couldn't quite hear, like echoes beneath running water.

She didn't speak much. Rhys even less. But the silence between them had shifted since the night before. It no longer pressed like a barrier—it moved more like fabric, draped between them, separating and connecting all at once. The tension had softened into something wary but coexistent. Neither comfort nor camaraderie, but a quiet acknowledgment that they were bound now, in ways even prophecy hadn't been clear about. And though she hated the unknown, Eira had long ago learned that fear never left—it simply changed its name.

By midmorning, the trees thinned into a stretch of cragged land where the soil turned gray and brittle beneath their feet. Sharp rocks jutted from the ground like the ribs of something long buried and desperate to claw free. At the edge of this strange rise, the earth fell away into a shallow basin carved by time and forgotten rituals. The air shifted again, colder, and laced with something faintly metallic. The scent of blood long dried and never washed away. Eira paused at the cliff's edge, her breath catching in her throat, not from exertion—but from recognition.

The basin below wasn't empty. Carved into the far wall of the cliff was an archway of ancient stone, its surface blackened with fire scars, overgrown with ivy that gleamed a sickly green in the weak light. Symbols had been etched above it, deeply scored into the stone, though many had been chipped away—as though someone had tried to erase the language itself. Only one symbol remained unmarred, and it glowed faintly as Rhys stepped forward: a broken circle encasing an open eye, weeping.

Eira's pulse quickened. Her shadowlight surged, restless. The closer she stepped toward the basin's edge, the more it stirred inside her, responding not just to the magic, but to something older. Memory. Not her own—but embedded deep in her bones, or perhaps in the shadowlight itself. She staggered slightly and caught herself on a nearby rock. Rhys noticed.

"It's reacting," he said softly, not as a warning, but as a confirmation of something he'd expected. "You feel it too."

She nodded once, still staring at the ruined entrance. "It's not calling me," she whispered. "It's... recognizing me."

Rhys knelt near the edge, eyes fixed on the path leading down. "This place is where it all began—at least, for the version of the prophecy I was meant to serve. The shrine was supposed to be sealed after the rites failed. But nothing stays buried forever."

Eira crouched beside him, the wind curling around them with soft, breathless sighs. "This isn't just history," she murmured. "It's a wound. Still open. Still bleeding."

Rhys turned his gaze to her, something more serious in his expression than she had seen before. "You don't have to go in."

She met his eyes, steady. "Yes, I do."

They descended together into the basin, the earth shifting beneath their feet as if uneasy with their presence. With each step, the wind died further, until even their breathing seemed too loud. The light faded, not into darkness—but into shadowlight, soft and violet-tinged, rising from the stones as if the ground itself was exhaling ancient memory.

They stopped just before the threshold of the shrine. Eira laid a hand on the scorched stone, and her magic pulsed like a second heartbeat. From deep within the darkness beyond the arch, something stirred—not malicious, not welcoming, but aware.

The prophecy hadn't just led them here.

It had been waiting.

The shrine swallowed them with a silence so deep it felt like stepping into the breath between heartbeats. The air was heavy, weighted with centuries of unshed words and dormant power that stirred as their footsteps echoed along the smooth stone floor. The corridor narrowed the farther they walked, walls lined with sigils half-buried beneath soot and lichen. Eira's fingertips brushed them as she passed, and beneath her touch, the symbols pulsed faintly—responding to her magic like a creature stretching after a long slumber.

Rhys moved slightly ahead, his pace cautious but certain, his steps guided more by memory than sight. The deeper they went, the more the light around them shifted—not from the fire he carried, but from the walls themselves, which began to shimmer faintly with the cold luminescence of buried power. It was not warm or comforting. It was ancient, spectral, cast in hues of bruised violet and fractured silver, a reflection of magic that had once tried to reshape the world and had failed.

At the end of the corridor, the space opened into a circular chamber, vast and still. The floor was carved in concentric rings of runes and mirrored stone, their etchings too perfect to be made by mortal hand. In the center stood a dais of polished obsidian, and on it, a pedestal of bone-white stone that pulsed like a heartbeat beneath thin layers of dust. Eira stopped at the threshold, shadowlight stirring along her arms in thick, restless coils.

"It's here," she said, voice barely above a whisper.

Rhys approached the pedestal with a reverence that startled her. He placed one hand on its surface, and with a low hum, the stone flared to life. Light spread outward from the point of contact, trailing along the etched rings in the floor, illuminating the chamber with a soft, ghostly glow. On the pedestal, symbols rearranged themselves, shifting like water, until a single line of script resolved into something they could read.

Eira stepped closer, breath held.

When the serpent sheds its final skin, and the weaver's flame is undone, the shadowlight shall choose not the strongest, but the broken one.

She stared at the words, heart pounding. "This isn't part of the original texts I've studied. This... it's something new."

"No," Rhys said, voice flat. "It's older. It was struck from the record. Hidden before the rest of the prophecy was ever spoken aloud."

She looked up at him, eyes narrowing. "Why?"

Rhys didn't answer. Because he didn't have to. The truth settled into her bones like ice. The prophecy had never been about heroes. It had always been about sacrifice. About what would remain when everything else was burned away.

Eira reached out and laid her hand on the pedestal beside his. The light pulsed sharply, then faded to black.

And in the darkness, she fell.

Not physically—but inward, as though the shrine had opened a door inside her. The chamber vanished, replaced by a vision.

She stood beneath a blood-red sky, ash falling like snow. The earth was scorched, cracked, alive with veins of molten magic. And standing at the center of it all was herself—but not her. A version of Eira cloaked in flame and shadow, her eyes burning with light that did not belong to her. Her mouth moved, but no sound came—only the shattering of stone and the echo of screams. Behind her, the world split open.

And before her... Rhys, kneeling, his hands bound, eyes full of something between sorrow and acceptance.

Eira stumbled back, gasping as she came to, the chamber spinning around her. Her knees hit the floor, hard. Rhys was beside her in an instant, steadying her with a hand on her shoulder.

"What did you see?" he asked, voice tight.

She looked up at him, her voice a whisper of breath. "The end."

Eira's breath came in ragged gasps, her palms pressed flat against the cold stone floor, as if the solid weight of it might anchor her in the present. But the vision clung to her skin like oil—thick, cloying, and impossible to forget. She could still feel the heat of that broken world, still taste the ash in the air. Her shadowlight trembled violently beneath her skin, not in resistance, but in resonance, as though it too had seen and remembered.

Rhys remained beside her, unmoving except for the slow rise and fall of his chest. His hand rested gently against her shoulder, the contact steady but not demanding, a silent offer rather than a tether. She could sense his calm, but it was not the serenity of ignorance—it was the resignation of someone who had long since stopped hoping for a different outcome.

Her voice cracked when she finally spoke. "It wasn't a vision of what could be. It was what will be."

Rhys didn't flinch. "I know."

She turned toward him, her eyes wide, lips parted with the beginnings of accusation—but she couldn't find the words. Not yet. The chamber around them pulsed faintly with shadowlight, as though the shrine were still watching, still listening, waiting for something more.

"You knew this," she said finally, the betrayal in her voice quiet but sharp. "You've always known."

Rhys's gaze dropped to the floor, his jaw tightening. "Not always. But long enough."

Eira pulled herself upright, not quite standing, her hands still trembling. "Then why bring me here? Why show me something you already believed to be inevitable?"

He looked up at her then, and there was no cruelty in his expression—just sorrow, so deep it seemed carved into the shape of him. "Because you needed to see it for yourself. Because what comes next doesn't depend on whether we know—it depends on whether we accept it."

Her magic recoiled at those words. "Accept it? That I become that thing? That I destroy everything, that you kneel before me like some... sacrifice?"

Rhys exhaled slowly, his eyes never leaving hers. "I brought you here because I thought I might change it. I thought if you saw it—really saw it—you'd fight harder against it than I ever could. That maybe, you'd find the path the rest of us couldn't."

Eira's hands clenched into fists. "But what if there is no other path?"

"Then we take this one," he said. "Together. Knowing exactly what it will cost."

The chamber seemed to press in on them then, the glowing runes dimming like a heartbeat slowing. The prophecy had spoken. It had shown them its shape. But the choices still lay ahead—bitter, brutal, and unkind.

Eira rose to her feet, unsteady but upright. Her magic swirled close to the surface, uneasy, crackling like a storm barely restrained. She looked at Rhys, not with fury, but with something deeper—a grief for the war that had already begun inside her.

"Then we move forward," she said, voice low. "But don't ask me to accept it yet. Not while there's still something left to break."

Rhys nodded once. "That's more than I hoped for."

And beneath their feet, the runes in the stone flared once—brief and bright, like the last flicker of light before a candle dies.

Eira moved through the low corridor of the shrine with her fingertips grazing the wall, her pace unhurried but taut with the weight of everything she now carried. The stone was cool beneath her touch, dusted with the fine grit of forgotten centuries, but beneath that—beneath the silence and shadow—there was a current. The magic here had recognized her. The prophecy had claimed her. And her magic... her magic had answered.

Shadowlight stirred beneath her skin in slow, deliberate waves. No longer the flickering, restless thing it had been in the beginning. It breathed with her now—deeper, steadier, darker. In this place, it had grown aware. It had begun to whisper, not in words but in sensation, in instinct. It no longer simply obeyed her call; it reached for things before she willed it to. It sought weakness in the walls, tested the boundaries of her control.

She paused at the mouth of the shrine, where the light outside painted the rock in long, pale lines. The forest beyond waited, vast and gnarled, but it no longer felt like the greatest danger ahead.

Rhys lingered a few paces behind her, letting her walk in silence, letting her breathe in what she had seen. He didn't press her. And that restraint—more than any cryptic truth or whispered prophecy—made her want to turn and speak.

"I can feel it watching me," she said finally, her voice quiet but unflinching. "Like it's no longer content to wait for me to use it. It's learning me. Adjusting."

Rhys approached, stepping beside her without breaking her gaze. "It will. It always does. Shadowlight doesn't simply inhabit—it integrates. It becomes part of who you are, even when you're not ready to claim it."

She folded her arms across her chest, the breeze teasing strands of hair from her braid. "So what happens when the part of me that is shadowlight stops asking and starts taking?"

Rhys didn't answer immediately. The wind brushed through the trees like a low breath, and the forest beyond the shrine rustled softly, as if echoing her unease. When he spoke, his voice was steady, but not cold. "Then you learn to bleed with it instead of against it. That's how you survive."

She turned to him, her eyes sharp. "That's how you survived. What makes you so sure I'll do the same?"

He studied her, and in that moment, she hated the softness in his gaze—the knowing. The reflection of what he saw in her, whether she accepted it or not. "Because you're still asking what happens if you lose yourself. That means you haven't. Not yet."

Her mouth tightened, but she didn't look away. Inside, her magic pressed against her ribcage like a heartbeat out of sync with her own. It wanted more. It wanted her to let go.

She exhaled slowly. "It won't make this easier."

"No," Rhys said quietly. "But it will make you powerful enough to face what comes next."

She nodded once, the motion small but final. They would walk forward from this place, but not as they had entered it. The prophecy had shifted her path, but it was the magic that would shape her choices. The part of her that feared it had not gone—but it no longer ruled her.

And as she stepped into the waiting light beyond the shrine, Eira carried that magic not as a weapon, not yet as a burden, but as a truth she could no longer ignore.

The light outside the shrine was thinner now, stretched across the sky in pale filaments that made the trees appear taller, sharper, more spectral than they had before. Eira walked ahead without speaking, her boots finding the path even as the undergrowth thickened with each step. The weight of the prophecy clung to her like a second cloak, but she did not stumble under it. Instead, it shaped her gait, straightened her spine, and filled the hollow behind her sternum where fear had lived just hours ago.

The trees around them grew closer, twisted trunks leaning inward as though eavesdropping on secrets whispered in the stillness. Leaves shimmered with an oily sheen when caught in the light, and small veins of luminescence pulsed beneath their surfaces. Somewhere in the distance, a bird called—low, broken, like a memory of song instead of the thing itself. It was the first sound of life they had heard since entering the shrine, and it felt out of place. Like the land was shifting in answer to what they now carried.

Rhys followed her without the air of a protector or a guide. He moved like a shadow just beside hers, never overtaking, never retreating. When they finally reached a place where the ground flattened and a break in the canopy revealed a crescent of slate sky, he stopped.

"This is where I leave you," he said.

Eira froze mid-step. She turned slowly, her brows pulling together. "What are you talking about?"

He stood with one hand resting lightly on the hilt of his blade, the other loose at his side. "You don't need me to find the next part. Your magic will lead you now."

She stepped toward him, eyes narrowed. "You think after everything—after the vision, after the shrine—I'm just supposed to let you vanish into the trees like some half-spoken myth?"

His expression didn't shift, but there was something brittle beneath his calm, something that vibrated too quietly to be heard. "You saw what I saw," he said. "What comes next... isn't about me."

Eira shook her head slowly, jaw tight. "No. What comes next is why I need you. That vision wasn't prophecy—it was a warning. And if we both saw it, it means you're still part of it."

Rhys was silent for a long moment. Then: "I'm not afraid of the end. I made peace with it a long time ago."

"That's not courage," she said quietly. "That's surrender."

His eyes met hers, and for once, she saw the truth he tried so hard to bury—the guilt, the sorrow, the exhaustion of being bound to something that had already claimed too much.

"I'm not ready to be alone in this," she said, her voice barely above a whisper. "And I don't think you are either."

The wind moved between them, lifting the edges of their cloaks, stirring the dust beneath their boots. Rhys didn't move. But he didn't leave.

After a moment, he nodded—small, careful. And he fell back into step beside her.

They stood in the clearing longer than either of them intended, the wind threading softly between them, tangled in the edges of silence. The trees no longer seemed to press inward with menace but instead held their breath, as if the forest, too, sensed the shift between them. Eira's shadowlight had quieted, settled into a low hum beneath her skin—not dormant, but observant. At peace. For now.

Rhys hadn't stepped back. That fact alone felt heavier than his earlier words. He remained beside her, his stance relaxed but not indifferent, and when their eyes met again in the hush of that moment, something passed between them that hadn't needed prophecy or pain to form. Something human. Fragile. And all the more dangerous for it.

"You didn't run," Eira said, her voice low, almost amused, but touched with wonder.

"No," Rhys answered, his lips twitching just slightly at the corners. "I usually do. But I'm starting to think you're worse to run from than the Shadowborn."

A soft breath escaped her—not quite a laugh, but close. She turned her gaze back to the open sky above them, where the clouds were slow-moving and silver-washed, like bruises just beginning to fade.

"It's strange," she said, quieter now, "how quickly everything inside me is changing. The magic. My choices. The way I think about what comes next." She hesitated, then added, "And you."

Rhys didn't respond immediately. But she felt him shift closer, just enough that his presence warmed the space between them. His voice, when it came, was softer than she'd ever heard it. "You terrify me," he said. "Not because of what you are—but because you still believe you're something more than what the world wants to make you."

She turned to him, slowly, her expression unreadable, and for the first time in days, there was no mask between them. No shadow of roles they'd once played. No guard. Just a man who'd nearly died for prophecy, and a woman carrying the weight of its next chapter.

Eira stepped forward. Just a breath's distance. Her hand lifted, almost uncertain, fingers brushing lightly against the sleeve of his cloak. "Do you think we get to choose what becomes of us?" she asked.

Rhys didn't pull away. He didn't speak right away either. Instead, he brought his hand up, carefully—so carefully—and rested it over hers. His thumb brushed the back of her knuckles with a reverence that made her breath catch.

"I think," he murmured, "if there's still a choice left, it begins here."

Neither of them moved.

And for a moment—a heartbeat suspended in a story written in shadows—they let themselves just exist. Not as prophecy's chosen. Not as haunted and hunter. But as Eira and Rhys.

Bound. Becoming.

The stillness shattered.

A low vibration rippled beneath their feet, subtle at first—like a tremor felt only in the bones, a warning whispered to the body before the mind caught up. Eira's hand jerked instinctively from Rhys's grasp as the earth gave a muted groan, like something ancient waking in the deep. The shadows cast by the trees no longer leaned like curious onlookers; they recoiled sharply, fleeing from a pulse of magic that hissed through the clearing like a blade drawn from a sheath.

Rhys's eyes snapped toward the treeline. "That wasn't you," he said, voice stripped of softness now. "Was it?"

"No." Eira's shadowlight surged before she called it, pulsing through her limbs like a heartbeat out of rhythm. "And it's close."

From the eastern rise came the sound of splitting bark and a shriek not born of any living throat—a sound like grief made flesh. The trees writhed at the edges of the clearing, their trunks twisting unnaturally, and something large crashed through them, dragging the stench of ancient rot and a chill that withered the breath in her lungs. Eira caught only a glimpse—a hulking form shrouded in a hide of ash, limbs too long, too many—but it was enough. This thing had followed them through the broken corridors of the shrine, waited in the bones of the city's collapse, and now it had chosen this moment—theirs—to strike.

"Run?" Rhys asked, already reaching for the curved blade at his back.

"Fight," Eira growled, the lines of her face hardening. Her hands lifted, veins illuminated by the growing pulse of her magic, shadowlight lashing to the surface like lightning trapped beneath skin. "I'm tired of running."

The creature lunged from the trees, and the sky darkened unnaturally as it roared, shaking the ground beneath them.

Side by side, they met it.

The clearing became a storm of motion and noise, the kind that blurred edges and frayed the seams of time. Eira's pulse beat in her throat like a war drum, each strike of her magic matching the rhythm of Rhys's blade as he moved with that predatory grace, all fury and calculation. The creature snarled, a sound torn from the jaws of forgotten nightmares, and lunged again—only to be met by the combined force of steel and shadowlight.

It wasn't clean. It wasn't easy. But the thing bled, if such a thing could, and the ground beneath it blackened where it fell. Still it rose, still it clawed, dragging broken trees in its wake as though it were feeding on the ruin itself.

The forest, already half-dead, recoiled from the battle, its branches like skeletal fingers grasping at nothing. And in the chaos, Eira saw Rhys falter—just a moment, a breath—but enough. Enough for her to step forward and cover him, magic roaring from her hands like a tidal wave of night. It struck true, driving the thing back with a shriek that split the sky, but not before it fixed its eyes—all of them—on her.

Then silence.

Not peace, but silence.

The thing vanished into the trees, not defeated, but retreating. Watching. Waiting.

Eira lowered her arms, the tremble in them betraying just how close it had been. Rhys stepped beside her, a smear of blood across his jaw—not his own—and said nothing for a long time.

When he finally spoke, it was quiet. Measured. "That wasn't just a creature."

"No," Eira whispered, still staring into the forest's blackened maw. "That was a warning."

Behind them, the shrine pulsed once—low and mournful—as if echoing a truth neither of them dared speak aloud.

Chapter Four

Ashes Beneath the Skin

The forest wore its wounds like old scars, the trees blackened and curled from the heat of old fire, their bark split and brittle where shadowlight had once licked up their trunks. Dawn seeped in through the crooked canopy in fractured rays, pale and cautious, as if the light itself feared to touch this place. Eira stepped lightly over the fractured remnants of stone statues whose features had long been eaten away by time and something darker. The shrine they left behind still pulsed faintly in the distance—like a dying heartbeat fading into the bones of the world.

They didn't speak for the first hour. Silence hung thick in the air between them, not from distance, but preservation. Words would make real the things they had seen—and felt—in that place. Eira kept her eyes trained ahead, but her thoughts were weighted by the vision that had gripped her: the face of the First Mage carved into smoke, her agony laced with prophecy, her voice carrying the weight of a choice still unmade. She didn't know what it meant—only that Rhys had known more than he'd said.

The ground sloped downward now, the forest giving way to gnarled hills threaded with veins of glassy stone that shimmered faintly underfoot. Rhys walked just ahead of her, his steps careful, but not hesitant. There was a tension in his shoulders, a new stiffness to his posture. He'd seen something too. She had watched it settle behind his eyes like stormclouds too heavy to hold. But when she'd tried to speak of it, his deflection had been quick and sharp, his voice colder than before. And yet, he stayed close.

"Are you going to keep looking at me like I've just gutted your favorite book," he muttered finally, not turning.

Eira arched a brow, surprised. "You assume I'd care enough about anything to call it a favorite."

His breath caught on a quiet laugh. "You're a liar, mage."

"And you're worse."

But there was something softer beneath the words. A careful tether that had begun, somehow, to thread between them—not trust, not yet—but recognition. That the path ahead might devour them both, and perhaps it would be better to face it tethered to something.

The air thickened as the terrain dropped further into a hollow wrapped in curling mists. Trees became stranger here—trunks spiraled unnaturally, as if trying to twist away from some unseen force beneath the soil. The canopy dimmed until the sky was little more than a shadowed whisper overhead. Eira's boots crunched over a thin carpet of brittle moss that gave off a faint scent of old iron and burnt herbs, a combination that made her skin crawl in recognition. It was the same scent that had clung to the shrine's stones, the same that wove through the robes of the Order when they cast their forbidden rites. This place had been touched by magic too ancient to name—and it remembered.

Rhys slowed without being told, his gaze flicking across the rising stones that framed the descent like the ribs of some buried giant. Sigils marred the rock—lines etched too deep, not with hands but by will alone. The language of shadowlight. It pulsed faintly as they passed, a soft shimmer just below the surface like firefly embers trapped under glass. Rhys didn't speak, but Eira saw how his fingers curled slightly at his sides, how his shoulders rolled back with the weight of recognition. He'd been here before. Or somewhere like it.

They reached the center of the hollow, where a stone disc lay half-buried in the earth, cracked through the center but still unyielding in presence. The carvings etched across its face spiraled outward like a star collapsing into itself, and at its heart—something shimmered. A glyph, simple and jagged, familiar in a way that made Eira's breath catch. It was the same mark from her vision. The First Mage had worn it on her skin, burned into her collarbone as though to remind her of what she carried.

"It's calling to you," Rhys said lowly, his voice rough from disuse or restraint, she couldn't tell. "This place. The mark. It knows."

Eira didn't ask how he knew that. She stepped forward and knelt before the disc, her hand trembling as it hovered above the central glyph. When her fingers touched stone, the world shifted.

Sound vanished. Color leeched from the world around her, replaced by a palette of silver and void. Her body stilled, frozen, while her mind was pulled into a current of memory not her own. She saw the First Mage again—standing on a battlefield of ash, her eyes glowing with shadowlight, hands dripping with power that warped the air. She was not alone. Around her stood twelve figures, all marked, all bearing different forms of the same burden. The prophecy wasn't about one mage. It never had been. It was about them all—threads woven together across generations, destined to unravel in unison.

One voice rose from the vision, deep and feminine, echoing through Eira's bones. "One will betray, one will awaken, one will fall, and one will rise from the ruin.

Only when all paths are broken shall the true shape of fate be seen."

Eira gasped as she snapped back into her body. Rhys caught her just before she collapsed, his arms steady, his expression unreadable—but his eyes burned with questions. She clutched at his tunic, breath ragged, mind reeling.

"There are others," she said hoarsely. "We're not the beginning. We're... somewhere in the middle."

And for the first time, Rhys looked afraid.

The forest had begun to thin into low, skeletal trees, their limbs twisted skyward like charred fingers clawing at a sky perpetually cloaked in bruised gray. The path ahead unraveled into shallow, winding ravines, the soil loose and slick with decay. Eira moved carefully, the hem of her cloak soaked through with cold dew and something darker—sap or blood, she couldn't tell. Rhys stayed just ahead of her, silent but tense, every movement measured as though listening with more than his ears. Something had changed in the air—an undercurrent of pressure that set her teeth on edge.

It was near dusk when they came upon the remnants of a barricade—fallen wood blackened by fire and age, lashed together with vine and sinew long since rotted.

Beyond it, the ground dipped into a shallow basin, and Eira felt her breath catch in her throat. Dozens of bones lay scattered across the depression—some small, animal-like, others unmistakably human. Not buried. Not burned. Left to bleach under the sickly light that filtered through the trees. She stepped closer, her magic rippling with the sensation of something coiled just beneath the surface, like nerves brushed by a phantom hand.

Rhys reached out, catching her wrist. "Don't," he said, his voice low. "This place—it's not a graveyard. It's a lure."

Even as he spoke, the shadows beneath the bones shifted. At first, she thought it was a trick of the light—a passing cloud—but then she saw it. Movement. Fluid and low. Something crawling through the ribcages, the hollow sockets, the broken spines. Not a single beast, but a collective. Small creatures fused by the same hunger, the same whispering pull of the dead. Shadowmire scavengers. Born of old magic and corpses unburied. Their chittering sounded like broken wind chimes, soft and sweet, utterly wrong.

They scattered as Rhys drew his blade, but did not flee. Instead, they began to circle, dozens becoming hundreds, slithering over one another with snapping jaws and bulbous eyes that reflected nothing. Eira summoned her shadowlight in a rush, the magic flooding her palms with violet flame, flickering like breathless candlelight. But the moment it flared, the scavengers hissed in unison—a sound too uniform to be natural—and reared back.

"Magic draws them," Rhys said grimly, stepping to her side. "But not just any magic. They were made to find shadowlight."

"They're hunting me."

"No," he said. "They're announcing your presence."

The realization struck with the force of a hammer. Whatever had made these things had not done so blindly. They were messengers—sentries, perhaps—for something older that had marked her. Eira pushed her power outward in a defensive ring, holding the creatures at bay, but they didn't press the attack. Instead, they stood just at the threshold of the ward, eyes locked on hers, waiting. As if they knew that eventually, her strength would waver.

Rhys raised his blade. "We need to go. Now."

They fled through the underbrush, the creatures chasing from a distance—not overtaking, but never falling far behind. Eira could feel them like a pressure at the base of her skull, a cold tether that bound them to her presence. Even when the trees began to thicken again, the sun fully setting behind them, she knew they were still there.

By the time they made camp hours later, the air was wrong again—too still. The fire crackled loud in the silence, and Rhys didn't sleep, only sat with his blade across his knees, eyes never drifting from the dark. Eira lay close by, magic curling restlessly under her skin. Her fingers itched with the memory of those eyes, the hive of minds behind them. Something ancient had noticed her. Not because she was a mage.

Because she was the mage

Sleep came for Eira slowly, like a tide dragging her under—not gentle, but suffocating in its persistence. Her body yielded to exhaustion, but her mind did not still. The moment her eyes closed, the firelight faded, and a chill took root in her bones, the world around her folding in on itself like a page turned backward through time. When she opened her eyes again, she was no longer in the forest. No longer in her body. She stood at the edge of a cliff overlooking a field scorched to ash, the sky above it red with the hue of a dying sun and swirling with plumes of smoke that moved like serpents.

Figures knelt in a wide circle below, robed and hooded, each of them bent in reverence—or penance—toward a single, towering effigy of wings spread wide. Not feathered. Not divine. These wings were skeletal, forged from carved bone and obsidian shards, black veins of magic pulsing from their tips into the ground like roots seeking blood. In the center stood a woman, face obscured by shadowlight coiling around her like flame made flesh. She held a dagger over her heart, and the magic pulsed in sync with her heartbeat—a heartbeat Eira felt within herself.

"This was the first pact," a voice whispered near her ear, though no one stood beside her. "A soul given to the wings of shadow to shelter a thousand others. She was the first. You may be the last."

Eira stepped forward, the ground beneath her feet littered with names burned into the soil—too many to count, too many to carry. The woman turned toward her as if sensing her presence, and though her face remained hidden, her voice reached across the divide of centuries. "You are not meant to survive this. None of us were. We chose power, and in doing so, we chose ruin. But one of us must carry it far enough to choose again."

The dagger plunged downward, a scream echoing through the field—not of pain, but of release. Shadowlight exploded from her chest in a wave that burned away the world. And in that moment, Eira knew the truth. This wasn't a memory of another. It was a memory she would create. A future sealed in blood and magic, already echoing backward through time.

She woke gasping, fingers curled into the earth, her palms glowing faintly with shadowlight that had not been summoned. Rhys was beside her in an instant, hand hovering near the hilt of his dagger, face tight with concern. "What did you see?"

Eira couldn't speak at first. The vision had carved itself into her like a brand, a mark that throbbed with each breath she drew. Finally, she met his gaze, the crackle of their fire no longer warm but warning. "The prophecy... it doesn't predict what will happen. It remembers what already did."

His eyes darkened. "Then we're not fighting to shape it. We're fighting to survive what's already been written."

Eira nodded, swallowing the dread that rose in her throat like bile. "And someone has to make the choice she couldn't. Or become what she did."

The fire had long since dwindled into embers, but neither Eira nor Rhys dared sleep again. Her vision lingered between them like a third presence, invisible yet suffocating. The forest around their hidden camp had fallen into an unnatural hush, the kind that crept under the skin with crawling silence. Even the wind seemed to avoid their clearing, as though the trees themselves had grown wary of the shadowlight pulsing faintly from Eira's palms. She extinguished the glow, but it was too late. The air had changed.

Rhys stood first, his hand brushing the hilt of his dagger. "Something's wrong," he muttered, voice barely audible over the crackling shift of leaves. "No insects. No birds. It's listening."

The forest answered with a snap of a branch far too thick to be mistaken for natural decay. Then another. Not close—not yet—but coming. Deliberate. Heavy. Eira moved beside him, eyes narrowing into the darkness, her hand hovering over the small pouch of powdered rune-dust she carried. The wards they'd set hours ago still held, faintly shimmering against the moss-covered stones, but magic was slippery when prophecy stirred. What had been written once could always be rewritten in blood.

A low hum rose from the earth—felt more than heard—a sound like breath exhaled through stone. Trees on the far side of the glade began to bend, not from wind, but from presence. A shape moved beyond them. Not animal. Not fully human. It was tall, robed in something that looked like tattered ritual cloths, its face hidden behind a helm of silver etched with weeping eyes. Its arms were too long, fingers ending in claw-like talons that pulsed with flickering runes. The being's chest glowed with the same hue as Eira's vision, a slow, steady pulse that matched her own heartbeat.

Rhys inhaled sharply. "A Watcher," he said. "I thought they were myths."

Eira felt her magic roil in her chest. "Not myths. Guardians of the old prophecy. If it's here..." she trailed off, gaze locked on the entity now standing just beyond the reach of the warding stones.

"It means we woke something," Rhys finished grimly.

The Watcher raised a hand, its fingers curling in a deliberate arc. The rune-ward shivered—then cracked, a single thread of blue light snapping like a frayed string.

"Run?" Eira asked, not moving.

Rhys grinned despite the danger. "Only if you're faster than me."

They didn't wait for the second ward to fall.

They ran, their steps breaking against the forest floor with a reckless urgency that swallowed silence. Eira's breath came hard and shallow, her heartbeat loud in her ears, but she dared not look back. The trees blurred in her periphery, their limbs reaching like skeletal arms, catching at her cloak, her hair, as if conspiring to keep her here. The air was thick with the stench of old magic, metallic and bitter, clinging to her skin like ash. Behind them, the Watcher glided rather than walked, its form cutting through the undergrowth as though the forest parted willingly before it.

Rhys led the way with sharp instincts born of too many hunts, ducking under low branches, pivoting around gnarled roots, always keeping Eira within reach. She clutched the rune-dust in one hand and pressed the other to her side where her magic pulsed, wild and volatile. The Watcher was not a beast she could strike down with brute force. It was born of something older than flesh. The very air trembled with its pursuit, every step closer like a stone dropped into her spine.

"Left!" Rhys called out, veering toward a narrow ravine. The path was steep, the rocks slick with moss, but it was the only break in the dense wood. Eira followed, slipping twice before she caught herself on a crooked root. Behind them, the ground cracked with unnatural sound as the Watcher descended after them—silent, but relentless.

They stumbled into a hollow, the trees bending in toward one another like the ribs of a great beast. The air changed again, charged and brittle, filled with the residue of old spells long spent. Eira skidded to a stop, her hands trembling, and cast a hasty circle with the rune-dust. The symbols flared with cold light—enough to stall pursuit, not enough to hold it forever.

Rhys collapsed beside her, his chest heaving. "It's still out there."

"It won't stop," Eira said quietly, voice raw. "Not until one of us is dead."

He glanced at her with something unreadable in his expression. "Then we should stop running."

Eira sat cross-legged within the faint, dying perimeter of the warding circle, her fingers curled into the dirt as if trying to anchor herself to something real. The silence that fell after the Watcher's retreat was not peace—it was too heavy, too anticipatory. Her breath still trembled as she exhaled, and her eyes refused to lift from the glowing runes as they slowly faded back into the earth. Each flicker felt like a thread unraveling inside her, a reminder of how close she'd come to breaking.

Rhys leaned against the thick trunk of a hollowed tree, one arm braced across his ribs, the other dangling uselessly at his side. Blood marked his sleeve but he hadn't mentioned it. His eyes never left her, not since the moment they'd stopped moving. "You're shaking."

She didn't answer at first. Her voice might have betrayed her. Instead, she clenched her jaw and forced herself to meet his gaze. "I shouldn't be. I've faced worse. We've both seen worse."

"That's not the point," he said, softer than she expected. "You're allowed to feel the weight of it. You don't have to pretend you're stone."

Eira looked away, throat tightening. "Pretending is the only thing that's kept me from falling apart since this all began."

He didn't argue. He just let the silence stretch, something complicated flickering behind his storm-worn eyes. Then, after a pause that settled between them like dusk, he asked, "Do you still think I'm your enemy?"

She studied him, not just his words but his posture—the slouch of exhaustion, the guarded tension, the faint pull of hope tucked in the line of his mouth. "I think," she began slowly, "that everything I've been taught tells me you should be. But…"

"But?" he prompted.

"But I don't want you to be," she whispered, voice splintering at the edge.

That broke something in his face. Not a smile, not relief, but a softening, like a storm losing momentum. He took a cautious step forward, lowering himself beside her within the faded circle. "Then we plan together. No more running. We strike before the Watcher finds us again."

Eira nodded, blinking the sting from her eyes. "The shrine's vision—there was more there. I didn't understand it before, but I think I'm starting to. This prophecy... it doesn't want us to survive it. But maybe if we break its pattern..."

Rhys's eyes narrowed thoughtfully. "Then we become what it didn't expect."

They leaned over the earth together, Eira drawing marks once more, not for defense this time—but for strategy.

The woods they stepped into next were not the ones they'd left behind. These trees bent at odd angles, their trunks hollowed and groaning with winds that didn't blow. The earth was damp and blackened as though fire had once scorched it but never fully cooled. Even the air was strange—charged, thick, and metallic on the tongue. Every step forward was muffled, sound absorbed by the forest itself, as if the very land resented their presence.

Eira walked ahead with her hand extended, fingers splayed, shadowlight licking up her palm in thin tendrils like mist obeying a forgotten wind. "We're getting close," she said, her voice low and flat. "Something old is buried here. Something powerful."

Rhys was silent behind her, eyes constantly scanning the warped tree line. He moved with the certainty of someone who had walked with monsters and still remembered their scent. He paused near the remains of a stone altar, its carvings long since worn to unreadable symbols. "This was a harvesting site," he muttered. "They used these ruins to extract raw ley energy—before they knew what it cost."

Eira knelt beside the altar, pressing her palm to the stone. The reaction was immediate. Shadowlight flared along the etchings, pulsing like a heartbeat. A low hum rumbled beneath the forest floor, deep and resonant. "There's enough power left here to fuel a strike," she whispered. "But if we draw on it—whatever still sleeps here will wake."

"Then we take what we need and run before it remembers how to bite," Rhys replied.

They set to work with brutal efficiency. Eira etched new runes into the altar stone, weaving her spell through the broken leyline, anchoring it with pieces of her own essence. Rhys laid glyph wards along their perimeter, each one a grim reminder of the darker rituals he had once mastered. They worked in silence save for the whispering wind that came from no direction and the crackling hiss of magic reigniting old scars in the earth.

It wasn't until the trees began to scream that they realized they'd overstayed.

The forest came alive—roots bursting from the ground like the limbs of drowned corpses, clawing toward them. Shadows thickened, not just from light's absence, but from something aware. Eira unleashed her magic in a broad arc, shadowlight turning silver with strain as it met the onslaught. Rhys darted through the chaos with a blade singing in his hand, cutting through twisted limbs as they closed in.

"We're not going to hold this place," Eira shouted, breathless.

"We don't need to hold it!" Rhys roared, already lighting the final rune. "Just light the fuse!"

With one final gesture, Eira drew her arm in a wide arc and flung the last of her magic into the spell lattice. The altar blazed like a second sun swallowed in shadow.

For a heartbeat, the world turned silent—then the clearing detonated in a shockwave of inverted light.

The force knocked them both to the ground as the forest imploded behind them.

They didn't stop running until the sky changed color.

The fire hadn't followed them, but its echo did. The forest miles behind was now a scar on the horizon, its twisted canopy illuminated by the dull throb of dying magic. They collapsed beneath the skeletal arch of a long-dead tree, their chests heaving, silence stretching between them like the pull of gravity. Rhys's blade was still slick with sap that bled black, and Eira's fingers trembled as she tried to extinguish the trailing wisps of shadowlight curling from her skin. The magic no longer obeyed her as it had before. It clung—feral, greedy, sentient.

She didn't speak at first. Neither did he. The quiet was too raw, their nerves too exposed. When she finally did, it was barely above a whisper. "That wasn't just a leyline strike. It... it recognized me. It called to me." Her eyes, usually so clear in their guarded defiance, were glazed now with something fragile—fear. "I don't know what I've become."

Rhys didn't look at her. He tilted his head back against the tree's crumbling bark, staring through the canopy at a moon that looked like it had been broken once and sewn back together. "You survived it," he said simply. "Whatever's growing inside you—wants to live. That counts for something."

"It's not just me," she snapped, sharper than intended. "You fed that power too. You lit those runes like you'd done it a hundred times."

His smile was humorless. "Because I have." He turned to her then, not with judgment or pride, but with weariness. "You don't walk through shadow and come out clean. You use it, or it uses you. There is no middle ground, Eira. Not for us."

Her mouth trembled. "Then what are we doing?"

He leaned in, slow and steady, his voice softer than she'd ever heard it. "Trying not to become the prophecy before we understand what part we play in it."

The space between them narrowed, not just in physical distance, but in the weight of unspoken truth. Neither trusted easily, and both had bled for secrets the other had barely begun to reveal. But there, in the hush between thunderclaps of fate, something shifted. A tether forming, not out of affection, but survival. Shared pain. Recognition.

She didn't pull away when he brushed the back of her hand with his. It was a fleeting touch, the gentlest contact between two people who had only known how to wound. But in that instant, it was a pact.

"We won't make it if we keep going like this," Eira murmured, more to herself than him. "We need more than strategy. We need to understand what this thing inside me is... what you really are."

Rhys stood, offering his hand. "Then we go where the lies began."

She took it.

And together, they turned from the ruined wood, their path leading deeper into the dark heart of Vaelwyth, where no sun had shone for generations.

They walked until the light no longer followed. The twisted branches overhead knitted themselves into a canopy so dense it choked the sky, and the silence of the woods deepened into something sentient. It was Rhys who noticed the shift first—a vibration in the soles of his boots that no wind could explain. Eira paused beside him, her palm rising slowly, attuned to the ripple in the air like a disturbance in water. Beneath the loam and moss, beneath the years of rot and creeping ivy, something ancient waited.

The ruin revealed itself not with grandeur but with a groan, a moaning sigh that echoed from the forest floor as the roots slithered back and the soil receded like breath being drawn. A staircase appeared, made of seamless obsidian, slick with time and shadowlight residue that glimmered faintly against the stone. The steps led down, disappearing into a pit of pure blackness where even magic dared not speak.

"This isn't just a shrine," Rhys murmured, his expression unreadable. "It's a womb."

Eira stared at the descent, pulse thunderous in her throat. "A womb?"

"Where the first Shadowborn were conceived. The place where shadowlight was bled into the world." He reached out, his fingers brushing the stone. "My ancestors brought sacrifices here. You don't create magic like this without tearing something open."

Eira's magic pulsed in her chest, a beat-for-beat echo of the ruin's hunger. She felt it now—deeper than fear or awe—something ancestral, something that whispered in a language older than her bloodline.

"This... this is part of me," she whispered. "Even if I never knew it. It knows me."

They descended together, each step drawing them deeper into memory that wasn't theirs. Murals flanked the passage, carved in deep relief, their edges worn smooth by centuries but still clear in their dreadful artistry. Serpent-winged mages with blindfolded eyes, hands raised to bleeding skies. A woman with a crown of flame, her mouth sewn shut. Children burned on altars of black stone, their screams etched in spiraling script.

Eira reached out to trace one symbol—an unbroken circle split down the center—and the wall recoiled, lighting up with shadowlight that bled into the air like spilled ink. The floor shook. A pulse of magic burst outward from the mural, slamming into her chest like a heartbeat made of flame and ice. Her knees buckled.

Rhys caught her before she hit the ground, kneeling with her as her magic roared to the surface, no longer a quiet whisper, but a scream. She gasped, clutching his coat as her vision swam, and in that moment, she saw—

A woman, cloaked in shadowlight, standing in this same ruin centuries ago, her face both foreign and familiar. Her hands bore the same split-circle mark, her eyes twin stars of white flame. She wept as she spoke a single word that echoed into Eira's bones.

"Betrayal."

The vision shattered.

Eira gasped back to reality, her breath ragged, sweat beading on her skin. "It's always been this," she said hoarsely. "This place... the power... the betrayal. It was never about kingdoms. It's about us. About what we become."

Rhys was quiet for a moment. Then, softly: "Now you understand."

They sat in the heart of the ruin, surrounded by the echoes of a past too broken to mend, too critical to ignore. And the ruin—alive in its decay—watched them, waited.

The silence within the ruin collapsed. It began with a low thrumming beneath their feet, subtle at first—like the hum of insects just beyond perception—but it deepened quickly into something more primal. The walls shuddered, not as stone disturbed by age, but as if the ruin itself had inhaled. A sickly light bled from the glyphs along the passage, crawling across the ceiling in jagged veins of violet and black. The temperature dropped instantly, sharp enough that Eira's breath misted in the air, her lungs burning with the frost that had no right existing underground.

Rhys surged to his feet, his hand at the hilt of his dagger, though they both knew no blade would save them from what now stirred. "You touched it," he muttered, though not with blame—more awe, or dread. "You woke it."

The ground beneath them cracked like splintering glass, fissures webbing outward from the mural Eira had touched. From its center, tendrils of shadowlight slithered free, slow and searching, almost sentient in the way they moved. They didn't lash out—they reached, curious, reverent, like the hands of children meeting a long-lost parent. But that reverence turned quickly. The tendrils stiffened, then struck.

Eira threw up a ward, her magic flaring brilliant with panic. The strands of shadowlight met it like fire meeting oil, exploding in a cascade of violet sparks that tore the air. She screamed as the backlash slammed into her chest, her body flung back into Rhys, who caught her and immediately dragged them both to the side as a pillar collapsed where she had stood seconds before. The ruin roared in fury.

"I didn't mean to!" she gasped, fighting to summon another ward.

"You're not the intruder!" Rhys shouted, eyes wide with something like recognition. "It's not attacking you—it's testing you. It wants to see if you'll yield!"

More tendrils erupted from the floor and walls, now less curious and more insistent, forming a cage of writhing light around them. Eira's hands shook as she reached for her magic again, but it stuttered under the weight of the ruin's demand. It wasn't just her power this place sought—it wanted her obedience. Her submission.

Rhys stepped in front of her, his body framed by the encroaching threads of shadowlight. "It's not going to stop," he said. "You have to command it, Eira. Make it remember that it belongs to you—not the other way around."

"I don't know how," she whispered, dread turning her limbs to ice.

"Yes, you do," he said, his voice low and urgent. "Feel it. Let it hurt. Let it in—but don't let it rule."

Eira inhaled sharply, shut her eyes—and reached.

She let the magic flood her, the shadowlight coursing through her veins with the bitter taste of memory and grief and all the pain she'd locked away. She didn't block it this time. She welcomed it, her body shuddering as it tore through her like molten iron. But she stood. She opened her eyes, now alight with the same fire as the mural's ancient sorceress, and raised her hand.

The ruin went still.

The tendrils froze, quivering as though caught between reverence and fear, and then—slowly—they bowed. The magic recoiled like a tide retreating from shore, slinking back into the walls, the stones, the waiting dark.

Rhys exhaled shakily. "Well. That's new."

Eira staggered, catching herself against the wall. "I didn't command it. I... became it."

He reached for her then, not to steady her but to look into her eyes, as if confirming something unspoken. "You're not just the wielder, Eira. You're its heir."

The ruin sighed once more, the echo of it folding into the quiet. Outside, the wind howled like a warning through the dead trees above, and far away, something stirred.

The ruin did not collapse, but it exhaled one last time—a breath that sounded too much like grief—and the oppressive magic that had filled its marrow withdrew with unnatural silence. The tendrils vanished like smoke, receding into the stone walls as if they had never been. Yet the memory of their touch remained, burned into Eira's skin and soul, a phantom weight that pressed against her ribs with every breath. She and Rhys stood for a long moment in the stillness, neither speaking, surrounded by broken pillars and flickering runes that now glowed with a soft, mournful light.

When they finally moved, it was not with haste, but with the reverence one offers sacred ground. Rhys guided her toward the exit, his hand lightly resting at the small of her back. Not controlling. Just... there. She didn't shake it off. Her limbs trembled as they ascended the uneven stone steps, and each step away from the heart of the ruin felt like leaving a piece of herself behind—one she hadn't realized she would miss.

Outside, the air was cooler than she remembered, touched by early mist. The forest surrounding the ruin held its breath as if listening. The trees leaned inward, their bark streaked with old blood, their branches gnarled into clawed silhouettes. Eira slumped to her knees at the edge of the glade, her hands sinking into the damp moss as she retched, not from sickness—but from the overwhelming pressure that had just released her. She felt hollowed out, scraped raw. A vessel that had been filled to the brim and poured out without consent.

Rhys crouched beside her, silent at first. When she finally sat back, wiping her mouth and dragging a shaky hand across her forehead, he offered her a water skin. "Drink. You're still here, which is more than I thought we could say five minutes ago."

She drank. The water tasted like ash.

"Is that what it always feels like?" she asked, her voice cracking. "When it answers?"

He shook his head slowly, eyes distant. "No. It never answered like that before. Not for me. Not for anyone."

"So why me?"

Rhys looked at her—not at her hands or her trembling shoulders, but into her. "Because you didn't just use the magic. You listened to it. And it listened back."

The firelight in her veins hadn't faded. Even now, under the greying morning sky, her fingers pulsed with shadowlight like a heartbeat. She clutched them close to her chest, unsure if it was fear or awe—or something more dangerous—that stirred behind her ribs. "What does it mean?"

"That the prophecy's wrong," Rhys murmured, his gaze unfocused as he stood and turned toward the tree line. "Or worse... it's right in a way we never understood."

Eira didn't move. Her body was still. Her mind, anything but.

Behind them, the ruin sat in silence once more. But something had shifted. The magic had not gone dormant—it had accepted her. Welcomed her. And what welcomed her would not forget her.

They didn't speak again until well past midday. The silence between them wasn't hollow—it was thick, weighty, like fog after a storm, hiding what hadn't yet surfaced. The forest grew darker with each step they took, not from the waning light but from the burden they carried, something the trees seemed to recognize. Their bark twisted in patterns reminiscent of ancient glyphs, and moss clung to them like old scars. Even the wind dared not stir here.

Eira moved slower than usual. Her steps faltered, her magic an undercurrent buzzing beneath her skin—dormant, but humming, like a beast dreaming with one eye open. Rhys kept pace, always within reach, but giving her space, as though even he feared she might unravel. He glanced at her occasionally, his jaw tight with things unsaid, but it was his silence that spoke most clearly. The ruin had changed something between them. The unspoken distance they'd held as a buffer now trembled like a glass edge teetering before the fall.

At last, Eira stopped beside a small ravine where a half-frozen stream trickled below, its surface reflecting the dull grey sky above. She crouched beside it, washing her hands, though the blood and ruin-dust had long since dried. She scrubbed until her skin turned raw. "We can't keep going blind," she said at last, breaking the silence like shattering glass. "Whatever's waiting ahead—whatever the prophecy wants—it's not just about fate anymore. It's about choice."

Rhys knelt beside her, scooping water into his cupped hands. His reflection in the water was distorted, his features a ripple of sharp lines and deep shadows. "Choice is a pretty illusion," he muttered. "It lets us pretend we're free."

"I don't want to pretend," she said, voice low but fierce. "I want to decide."

Rhys looked at her then—truly looked. The quiet thunder in his eyes softened, and for a moment he almost seemed to reach for her, but his fingers curled against his knee instead. "Then we need answers. Not from ruins or visions. From the ones who wrote the prophecy. From the source."

Eira nodded. "You said there were other sites. Places where shadowlight first bled into this world."

"There's one," Rhys said, standing slowly. "Farther north. A sanctuary that became a tomb. No one dares go there anymore. Too much death. Too much truth."

"Then that's where we go."

Their eyes met—hers steady, his uncertain—but in the space between them, something solidified. Not trust. Not yet. But understanding. The path they followed was etched in blood and ancient vows, but it was theirs now. And they would follow it to the edge.

They set out at dusk, when the sun had dipped low enough to paint the sky in bruised colors of violet and rust. The light clung stubbornly to the horizon, as though unwilling to surrender to the creeping night, and Eira felt the reflection of that resistance in herself. Her magic pulsed quietly in her veins, neither calm nor violent, but watchful—like it knew the sanctuary they sought would test its loyalty. Rhys walked slightly ahead, his cloak trailing along the uneven forest floor, and though his steps were confident, his shoulders bore a heaviness that had not been there before.

The land shifted as they left the ruined grove behind. The trees grew farther apart, their trunks pale and skeletal, their leaves like curled parchment. The wind carried a faint metallic tang, like the scent of rust and old blood, hinting at the violence that had been buried beneath these hills. They came upon a stretch of broken ground where stones jutted from the earth like fractured ribs. Rhys stopped here, kneeling to brush away the dirt clinging to one of the stones, revealing runes faintly etched beneath the layers of time.

"This was the outer boundary," he said quietly. "The first warning that the sanctuary is near. People would carve these symbols as a last prayer before stepping into its shadow." He glanced back at her, his dark hair falling across his brow. "Once we cross this point, we won't be able to turn back easily. The sanctuary... it doesn't let people leave without a cost."

Eira crouched beside him, her fingers tracing the cold, jagged lines of the runes. Her shadowlight stirred, reacting to the ancient magic buried here, and for a moment, the symbols flared faintly beneath her touch. She pulled her hand back, heart quickening. "It knows me," she murmured. "The same way the ruin did."

"Then maybe it will let us through," Rhys said, his tone rough but laced with something that felt like reluctant hope. "Or maybe it will devour us faster."

They pressed onward. The forest thickened again as they climbed a low ridge, the trees twisted into grotesque shapes by centuries of lingering magic. Eira felt eyes on her—though whether they belonged to living things or the land itself, she couldn't tell. At one point, a hollow tree split open with a groaning sigh, spilling a cascade of ash and brittle feathers at her feet. She shivered, instinctively stepping closer to Rhys, though neither of them mentioned the way their shoulders brushed as they moved through the gloom.

Night had fully fallen when they crested the ridge, and there—spread out below them—was the sanctuary.

It was not a temple, not in the way Eira expected. It was a labyrinth of stone pillars and broken arches, all of them half-submerged in a blackened swamp. The water was still, so still it reflected the faint stars above like a perfect, cold mirror. The very air around the place vibrated with magic, ancient and hungry. Even from this distance, Eira felt the pull of it against her heart, like a whisper threading through her veins.

Rhys exhaled slowly. "There it is," he said, his voice low and unreadable. "The place where shadowlight first chose its champions. The sanctuary of the Serpent Crown."

Eira's pulse quickened. "Then that's where we'll find the truth."

They stood at the ridge for a long while, neither speaking. The sanctuary sprawled below like a scar carved into the land, its ancient stones gleaming faintly beneath the pale light of a fractured moon. Eira could feel its presence tugging at her like unseen fingers hooked through her ribs, drawing her down, beckoning her into its dark heart. Beside her, Rhys was silent, his face cut sharp with both resolve and the unspoken memories this place stirred. The weight of what they were about to face loomed between them—inevitable, hungry.

Eira tore her gaze away from the swamp's mirrored surface and met his eyes. "We're going to find answers here," she said, more like a promise to herself than a declaration. "But I can't shake the feeling they won't come cheap."

"They never do," Rhys replied, his tone quiet but steady. "The sanctuary doesn't give without taking." He glanced once more at the labyrinth below, then back to her. "Stay close to me. Whatever happens, don't let it separate us."

Eira nodded, her fingers curling slightly as a faint shimmer of shadowlight traced her knuckles. Together, they started down the ridge, their footsteps crunching softly on the damp earth. The sanctuary awaited them, patient as the grave.

Chapter Five:

Into the Serpent's Crown

The air grew colder as they descended, the kind of cold that gnawed at the edges of the skin and seeped into the bones. The swamp was worse up close. It stretched out like a black mirror, reflecting the skeletal arches of the sanctuary as if there were two worlds—one above and one beneath—fighting for dominion. Strange lilies floated on the surface of the still water, their petals dark as ink but glowing faintly at the edges with a sickly white light.

Rhys tested the ground with his boot before stepping into the shallow edge of the water. "The path is submerged," he said, his voice echoing faintly against the stone pillars. "These stones lead through, but they'll shift. The sanctuary tests every step. It always has."

Eira followed him carefully, the swamp water cold enough to sting her ankles. Each stone she placed her foot upon vibrated faintly, as if the sanctuary itself was aware of her presence. She kept her shadowlight subdued, though every instinct screamed to call on it—something about this place felt like it would devour her power the moment she unleashed it.

The arches loomed taller the deeper they went, some half-broken, others twisted into impossible shapes, as if sculpted by unseen hands that worked in dreams rather than waking thought. Runes lined their bases, faint but glowing faintly now that they had drawn closer. Eira brushed her hand over one, and a ripple of energy shot through her fingertips, leaving behind a whisper that didn't belong to her.

"You feel it too?" she asked, glancing at Rhys.

"Always," he said, his tone grim. "The sanctuary remembers everyone who's ever stepped here. It knows who's worthy—and who's not."

A sudden rumble echoed through the water, deep and resonant. The stones beneath them shifted slightly, just enough to send a pulse of warning through Eira's body. The sanctuary had begun its test.

The tremor beneath their feet deepened, vibrating through the swamp like a living thing, and then it stilled. The silence that followed was not natural—it was thick and heavy, suffocating the breath in Eira's lungs. The arches ahead flared with light, not the pale glow of shadowlight but a piercing white that blinded her for a heartbeat. When her vision cleared, the swamp was gone.

She stood in a hallway of black marble, its walls veined with silver like lightning captured in stone. Torches burned with a cold blue flame, casting long, twisted shadows that writhed like living specters. The air was heavy with the scent of burnt incense and something coppery—blood, faint but unmistakable. Her heart hammered, not just because she didn't remember stepping forward but because she was alone.

"Rhys?" Her voice cracked, swallowed by the marble hall. No answer came.

A soft whisper brushed her ear, so close she spun to face it, but no one was there. The hallway stretched endlessly in both directions, each step she took making no sound. Panic tightened her chest as her own reflection appeared in the black marble walls—only it wasn't her. The woman who stared back had the same features, but her eyes were alight with pure shadowlight, her lips curved in a smile Eira would never wear.

"This is who you are," the reflection said, its voice a perfect echo of hers, but distorted—low and resonant, like the hum of distant thunder. "A vessel for ruin. Do you think you'll be the one to change the prophecy? They all thought that. And they all burned."

Eira clenched her fists, willing her magic to respond, but it resisted, coiling inward like a frightened animal. She slammed her palm against the wall, the reflection rippling as though she'd struck water. "No," she hissed. "I'm not you."

The reflection laughed—a sound that splintered down her spine. The marble floor beneath her feet cracked, and a memory flooded in unbidden. She was standing over a body—someone familiar, though she couldn't see their face. Blood pooled under her hands, and the shadowlight burned her palms as if punishing her for touching something pure. She stumbled back, gasping. "This isn't real. It's not—"

"Real?" the voice cut her off, now whispering directly behind her ear. "It's already written. You'll be the betrayer, Eira. The shadowlight chose you for that."

Across the sanctuary, Rhys fought his own ghosts. He was not in a hallway but a shattered battlefield, the same one he'd left behind years ago when he turned his back on the Shadowborn. Ash crunched underfoot, and the smell of charred flesh choked him as figures rose from the haze—faces he knew, faces he had killed. They looked at him with hollow eyes, mouths moving in silent condemnation.

He gritted his teeth, gripping his blade so tightly the knuckles of his hands whitened. "Not this again," he muttered. "I buried you. All of you."

One figure stepped forward—a man with Rhys's face, only colder, darker, draped in the robes of the zealot he'd once been. "No," his double said, its tone laced with venom. "You didn't bury me. You became me. You're still mine."

Rhys's breath caught. He swung his blade, but the shadow of himself caught it with ease, leaning close enough for Rhys to feel its breath. "You'll betray her. You'll kill her. You know you will. That's what we do."

The sanctuary's magic pulsed through both of them like a heartbeat, their trials linked though neither could see the other.

Eira's knees nearly buckled under the crushing weight of the illusion's voice, the words digging into her like knives forged from every fear she refused to name. The reflection smiled again, its mouth curling wider than humanly possible, and the marble around it began to melt like hot wax, dripping in streams of shadowlight that burned when they touched the floor. Her pulse raced. Every instinct told her to run, but the corridor had no end, no beginning, only this endless mirror and the hollow echo of her failures.

"No," she whispered, her voice cracking. Her hands shook, but she forced them together, weaving a crude sigil in the air—a symbol she'd learned in whispers and blood. The shadowlight within her surged, not as a beast this time, but as a pulse of raw clarity. "I am not you. I am the one who decides."

The mirror cracked. A hairline fracture split the image's twisted smile, and a hiss of fury poured from its lips. With a roar that wasn't her own, Eira slammed both hands into the wall. The shadowlight burst outward in a violent wave, splintering the marble, shattering her reflection into a storm of black shards that dissolved like ash. The corridor dissolved with it.

She fell forward, landing on damp stone. The oppressive illusion gave way to the sanctuary's true heart—an open chamber lined with jagged pillars, their surfaces alive with shifting runes. At its center stood Rhys, though he was not still. He swung his blade with savage precision, striking down spectral figures that rose from the floor like smoke. His breath came hard, his eyes dark with something primal.

"Rhys!" Her voice cut through the chaos, startling him for a moment.

The shadow-double he'd been fighting laughed, stepping from the smoke like a living wound. "Ah, she's here. Watch her, Rhys. Watch how easily she'll turn that magic on you."

"Enough!" Eira snarled, and her shadowlight flared. A lance of violet fire erupted from her hands, slicing through the double. It screamed, twisting into black threads that dissolved into the air like dust.

Rhys spun toward her, panting, his knuckles white around his blade. "You broke through."

"So did you," she countered, though her voice was softer, her gaze searching his. There was something raw in his expression—relief, yes, but also fear.

Before they could speak, the sanctuary itself reacted. The runes along the pillars blazed to life, shifting into new patterns that pulsed like a heartbeat. The ground beneath them trembled, cracking in places to reveal black water lapping hungrily below. From the farthest corner of the chamber, something began to rise—a mass of stone and shadow coalescing into a shape too large, too deliberate, to be natural.

"What now?" Rhys growled, pulling her toward him as the air grew heavy with magic.

Eira's eyes widened as the creature took form—a towering figure of fused stone and bone, its chest a hollow cage glowing with the same sickly light she'd seen in her vision. It had no face, only a jagged helm and a mouthless snarl of shadowlight. "The sanctuary's heart," she breathed. "It's not finished testing us."

he creature stepped forward, its weight sending tremors through the chamber. Each stride cracked the stone floor, and the black water below hissed as if the presence of this sentinel poisoned even the shadows. Its chest pulsed with a rhythm that felt almost alive—an imitation of a heartbeat, each throb radiating a wave of suffocating energy that pushed Eira and Rhys backward.

Rhys adjusted his stance, blade flashing in the flickering light of the runes. "We don't have time to think," he said, his tone low but charged with urgency. "Whatever that thing is, it's not going to let us leave alive."

Eira raised her hand, shadowlight spiraling along her fingers like living fire. "Then we don't run," she said, meeting his gaze. "We finish this together."

The sentinel lunged with terrifying speed, its arm—a pillar of jagged stone fused with sinewy shadow—sweeping across the chamber like a scythe. Rhys darted forward, grabbing Eira by the arm and pulling her into a tight roll just as the blow shattered a pillar behind them. The explosion of stone sent razor-sharp fragments into the air. One cut Rhys's cheek, a bright streak of blood contrasting the dark smear of ash and dust. He didn't flinch.

"Strike at its core!" he shouted, already moving again, his blade carving a deep slash across the sentinel's arm. The metal screeched like tortured steel.

Eira summoned her power, but the sentinel's presence fought her. Its energy tangled with hers, dragging her magic downward like heavy chains. It's part of me, she realized with a jolt. Or I'm part of it. The thought made her hesitate, but then Rhys's voice cut through the fog.

"Eira! Focus!"

Her shadowlight erupted like a dam breaking. With a scream, she flung a burst of violet energy at the sentinel's chest. The blow struck true, rippling across its body in waves of fire and darkness. The creature reeled, its form destabilizing for a breath before the glow in its chest flared brighter, angrier.

"It's regenerating," Rhys growled. "We need to strike at the same time!"

They circled the sentinel like predators, Eira's magic flickering at the edges of her control while Rhys moved with the precision of someone who had danced with death too many times to falter now. He feinted left, drawing the sentinel's attention, while Eira drew every last pulse of her shadowlight into her palms until it felt as if her veins were burning.

"Now!" Rhys bellowed.

He plunged his blade deep into the sentinel's knee joint, forcing it to stagger, while Eira slammed both hands forward. The shadowlight roared from her in a beam of blinding violet fire, striking the creature's glowing chest. For a heartbeat, the chamber held its breath—then the sentinel erupted in a cascade of shadow and shattered stone. The shockwave hurled them both backward, skidding across the rough floor.

Eira coughed, the acrid scent of burned magic clawing at her throat. She looked up just in time to see Rhys sprawled on the floor, breathing heavily, his blade still clutched tight in his hand. The sentinel was gone—nothing left but a crater and the trembling echo of its power.

Rhys dragged himself upright, his grin sharp despite the blood on his face. "You're terrifying," he said, voice hoarse but steady.

Eira wiped sweat and grime from her brow, a faint smirk ghosting her lips. "You didn't seem to mind."

The silence that followed the sentinel's destruction was deafening. The chamber, once trembling with the force of its presence, now lay still, as though the sanctuary itself had paused to take notice. Dust hung in the air like fog, catching the faint glow of the runes, and the smell of scorched stone and magic filled Eira's lungs with every breath. Her muscles trembled, both from the exertion of the fight and the oppressive weight of what they had unleashed.

Rhys limped toward the crater where the sentinel had stood, his boots crunching over shattered fragments of stone. "That thing wasn't guarding this place," he said, his voice low and thoughtful. "It was... waiting. Like a test we were meant to fail."

Eira joined him, her shadowlight flickering faintly as she extended her hand over the crater. The floor there was no longer solid. Instead, there was an opening—a spiral of carved steps leading down into a darkness deeper than the swamp itself. Faint runes glimmered along the edges of the passage, pulsing like a heartbeat, as if inviting them forward.

"This was beneath it all along," Eira murmured. Her fingertips grazed the topmost rune, and an electric pulse shot through her, sharp and knowing. Images flared behind her eyes—snatches of fire, serpents coiling around a crown of light, and a shadowed figure holding a blade forged from both light and dark. Her breath hitched, and she jerked her hand back.

Rhys noticed the look on her face. "What did you see?"

"A warning," she whispered. "Or a promise. I'm not sure which."

They descended cautiously, each step lit by the faint glow of the runes, which grew brighter as they went deeper. The air grew colder still, and Eira's breath misted in the dim light. At the base of the spiral, the tunnel opened into a wide, circular chamber. Unlike the rest of the sanctuary, this place was untouched by ruin. The walls were etched with symbols she recognized from the visions, their lines sharp and deliberate, as though freshly carved.

In the center stood an altar of black stone, its surface slick and reflective like a pool of ink. Upon it rested a single object: a shard of obsidian shaped like the jagged wing of a serpent, its surface humming with quiet power. Eira stepped closer, drawn to it by something she couldn't name, but Rhys's hand shot out to stop her.

"Don't touch it," he said, his tone harsher than usual. "I've seen artifacts like this. They're never what they seem. Sometimes they're not even alive until you make contact."

Eira hesitated, her gaze locked on the shard. "This is part of it. The prophecy. I can feel it. This... isn't just a relic—it's a piece of whatever started shadowlight in the first place."

Rhys's expression darkened. "Then we need to be careful. Because anything that started this kind of power won't give us answers without taking something from us in return."

Eira reached out, stopping just short of touching the shard. "Maybe that's the point. Maybe that's the choice the sanctuary was trying to show us."

The chamber seemed to breathe around them, the runes pulsing faster now, as if responding to her nearness. A deep rumble rolled through the floor.

Eira's hand hovered over the shard, her fingertips trembling with a mixture of fear and compulsion. The humming from the black stone grew louder, resonating with the pulse of her own heartbeat until it was impossible to tell where the shard's rhythm ended and her own began. Rhys's grip tightened on her wrist.

"Eira," he said, his voice firm but laced with an edge of something close to panic. "You don't know what it will show you—or what it will take. You've already bled enough for this prophecy."

She looked at him, her eyes dark but steady. "And you haven't?"

That silenced him. His jaw clenched, and for a moment, she saw the ghosts in his gaze—the battles, the betrayals, the lives lost. Slowly, she pulled her hand free. "We can't afford to be afraid of the truth anymore," she murmured, and before he could stop her, she pressed her fingers to the shard.

The world vanished.

A violent rush of shadowlight tore through her, dragging her consciousness into a maelstrom of visions. She stood in a battlefield drenched in black fire, the sky cracked open with veins of light and shadow twisting together like serpents. At the center of the chaos was herself—Eira—but not as she was now. This Eira was cloaked in black and silver armor, her eyes pure shadowlight, her hands dripping with blood that wasn't her own. A crown of serpents coiled above her head, hissing as they merged with the shadowlight pulsing from her skin.

And beside her—on his knees—was Rhys.

He was broken, his sword shattered at his feet. Blood ran from a wound across his chest, but his gaze was locked on her with something between horror and resignation. She felt his voice, rather than heard it: "You were meant to choose. And you chose this."

The scene shifted violently, pulling her deeper. She saw herself again, standing before a shattered altar, the shard now whole and forged into a weapon that pulsed like a living heart. The prophecy's words echoed in her mind: One must betray the other. One must fall for the other to rise. And in every version of the future that unfolded, Rhys was either the blade at her back or the one who bled for her.

"No," she gasped, shaking her head, but the vision clung like chains. She felt the prophecy like hands around her throat, a whisper curling in her ear: "You cannot save him. Not without destroying yourself."

She snapped back into the chamber with a cry, collapsing onto her hands and knees. The shard pulsed once beneath her fingers before going still. Rhys was immediately at her side, gripping her shoulders.

"What did you see?" he demanded. His voice was low, urgent, but there was fear behind it—a fear he didn't want her to recognize.

Eira's breath shuddered. She stared at him, the image of him broken and kneeling still burned into her mind. "Us," she said hoarsely. "The prophecy... it's not about kingdoms or battles. It's about us."

Rhys's jaw tightened. "And?"

"And one of us doesn't walk away from this," she whispered.

Rhys's expression darkened at her words, his eyes narrowing as if he could tear the truth from her lips by force of will alone. For a long moment, he didn't speak. His grip on her shoulders tightened, just enough to ground her, though there was a tremor in his hands that betrayed the tension coiling beneath his skin. Finally, his voice cut through the heavy silence, low and rough. "You saw me die, didn't you?"

Eira flinched. She hadn't meant to let that slip into her expression, but the answer lingered there anyway, unspoken and undeniable. "It wasn't... it wasn't just death," she said, her words stumbling over the memory. "It was more than that. It was... a choice. I saw a future where I could save you, but I—" She stopped, unable to force the words out.

"You chose something else," he finished for her, his tone as sharp as a blade. He turned away, raking a hand through his hair as his shadow stretched long against the glowing runes. "Of course. That's what prophecy does. It loves to show you how you'll fail."

"It wasn't like that," she argued, stepping toward him. "It's not about failure, Rhys. It's about the truth we don't want to see. About the parts of ourselves we've been denying."

He turned back to her, his jaw tight, his eyes cold but burning. "And what truth did you see about me, Eira? That I'll betray you? That I'll end up with my own blood on your hands? Because if that's the story, I'd rather not hear the ending."

Her breath hitched, his words cutting deeper than the vision had. "It doesn't have to be like that," she said, her voice low but fierce. "Prophecies are warnings, not prisons. We can choose differently."

Rhys laughed, but it was a hollow, bitter sound. "You sound just like I did once. You think you can outmaneuver fate. You can't. It doesn't matter how much you want to believe that."

Eira clenched her fists, shadowlight sparking faintly between her fingers. "I won't accept a future where I have to watch you die," she said, her voice trembling with anger—and something else, something fragile.

For a moment, his gaze softened. Just a flicker. Then he looked away, scanning the chamber as if searching for an excuse to end the conversation. "We should go," he said. "Before this place decides to test us again."

They gathered themselves in silence, the shard's presence looming in the center of the chamber like an accusation. Rhys avoided her eyes as they ascended the spiral staircase, his shoulders set in rigid determination. Eira followed, each step heavy with the knowledge that the vision had already carved a rift between them. They needed each other to survive, yet the prophecy had made them question if they could truly stand side by side without destroying one another.

The sanctuary seemed to sense their discord. The runes along the passage flickered as they climbed, their light dimming like a heartbeat fading to silence. By the time they emerged into the cold night air, the swamp around them was deathly still, the surface of the water reflecting not just their shapes but the weight of what now hung between them.

The swamp was too still. No wind stirred the skeletal reeds, no ripples disturbed the black surface of the water as Eira and Rhys stepped onto the broken path of submerged stones. The silence pressed against Eira's ears like a held breath, the kind of quiet that warned of danger long before it revealed its form. She glanced at Rhys, but his face was unreadable—focused, tense, as if every muscle in his body was coiled and waiting for the inevitable strike.

The first sign came from beneath the water. A single bubble rose to the surface, followed by another, then a slow hiss as if something massive exhaled in the depths. The water stirred, a soft ripple that spread outward until the swamp seemed to quiver around them. Eira stopped, her magic humming against her skin. "Something's awake," she whispered.

Rhys scanned the water, his grip tightening around the hilt of his blade. "It's this place," he muttered. "The sanctuary's not finished with us. It's trying to see how far we'll go."

The water erupted.

Something pale and serpentine lashed out of the swamp—a tendril, slick with black sludge, coiling around the nearest stone pillar and snapping it like brittle bone. Eira threw up a shield instinctively, her shadowlight sparking across the surface like violet lightning as another tendril swept toward them. Rhys grabbed her arm, pulling her backward onto a higher slab of stone just as the water surged beneath them.

"Keep moving!" he shouted, slashing at one of the tendrils as it coiled near their feet. The blade met resistance—it wasn't flesh, not entirely, but some kind of enchanted matter, half-stone and half-shadow. Sparks hissed where steel met magic.

Eira focused, her breath steadying as she sent a burst of shadowlight rippling across the swamp's surface. The light revealed a shape beneath the water—vast, almost serpentine, with a body that twisted like liquid shadow. Its many eyes, glowing faintly from the depths, turned toward her. She felt the weight of its gaze, like chains tightening around her lungs.

"It's not just a creature," she said, voice trembling. "It's part of the sanctuary—like a guardian born from the swamp itself."

"Then we cut through it before it drags us under," Rhys replied sharply.

Working together, they advanced along the submerged path. Rhys hacked at the tendrils that surged from the water, his movements swift and deliberate, while Eira directed focused blasts of shadowlight that burned through the serpentine coils like fire through parchment. Their movements began to fall into rhythm—each strike and counterstrike feeding into the other. For a brief, fierce moment, the tension between them didn't matter. There was only survival, and in that, they moved as one.

But the swamp wasn't done testing them. The creature beneath the water shifted, its massive form coiling directly beneath the stone they stood on. The slab buckled, tilting sharply. Eira stumbled, her balance faltering, but Rhys caught her arm, pulling her against him. Their eyes met, a breath of unspoken understanding passing between them.

"Jump!" he commanded, and together they leapt to the next slab of stone as the one behind them sank into the dark water with a deafening hiss.

The swamp roared as if it had a voice—an echoing, guttural rumble that sent shivers crawling down Eira's spine. The water surged violently, waves slamming against the stone path as the shadow-serpent rose, its body coiling and uncoiling like a whip beneath the surface. Another tendril lashed out, grazing Eira's shoulder. Pain burned where it touched her, not physical alone but something deeper, a coldness that sank into her bones as if the swamp's magic sought to claim her from the inside out.

"Eira!" Rhys's voice cut through the chaos, sharp and commanding. He struck at the tendril, his blade slicing through the slick shadowstuff, sending a spray of black ichor across the stones. He didn't wait for her to recover, grabbing her wrist and yanking her forward. "We can't fight this thing head-on—it's the swamp itself. We have to get to the edge before it swallows us whole."

Her heart pounded, every step a gamble as the stones beneath them shifted unpredictably, some sinking just as they leapt, forcing Rhys to catch her more than once. His grip was firm, grounding, and though his movements were fierce and efficient, she could feel the protective edge beneath his harshness. When another wave surged toward them, Eira didn't hesitate—she unleashed a blast of shadowlight so intense that it lit the swamp in searing violet hues, tearing through the tendrils and forcing the serpent below to recoil.

"Go, now!" she yelled, her voice ragged.

Rhys didn't argue. They moved together, slipping into a rhythm born of sheer survival. Every time her magic faltered, his blade cut the path clear. Every time his footing wavered on the slick stones, her shadowlight struck like a beacon to steady them both. It was messy and brutal and terrifying—but it was theirs, this dance between steel and shadow, and neither of them could deny that something in it felt... inevitable.

Finally, the path ahead narrowed, rising toward the edge of the swamp where broken arches and jagged earth offered a chance at escape. Eira's legs ached as she poured the last of her strength into a pulse of magic that split the water behind them, buying Rhys enough time to hoist her up onto the solid ground. He followed, landing hard on his knees, his chest heaving as the serpent roared below, thwarted but not destroyed.

For a long moment, they simply breathed. Eira lay on her back, staring at the fractured sky through the veil of swamp mist, her heartbeat pounding like war drums in her ears. Rhys sat beside her, leaning on his sword, his face streaked with blood and sweat but still sharp with focus.

"That thing..." Eira whispered, her voice hoarse. "It wasn't trying to kill us. Not exactly."

Rhys turned to her, brows furrowed. "What do you mean?"

"It was testing us," she said, sitting up slowly, her hands still trembling. "The ruin, the illusions, this swamp—it's all connected. It's like the prophecy is alive here, watching, waiting for us to prove something." Her gaze met his, shadowlight glimmering faintly in her eyes. "And it's not just about me. It's about us."

Rhys was silent, his jaw tight, but there was no denying the truth in her words. "Then we keep proving it," he said at last, his tone low, almost a growl. "We keep moving forward. Together. No matter what it throws at us."

For a heartbeat, Eira let herself believe him.

The swamp was a dark smear behind them, its stillness deceptive now that the serpent no longer thrashed beneath its surface. Rhys found a stretch of firm ground under a cluster of gnarled trees just far enough from the water's edge to make camp. They worked in silence at first—he built a small fire, its pale flames struggling against the damp, while Eira gathered what dry kindling she could find, her hands still trembling faintly from the fight.

When the fire finally caught, the thin warmth it offered felt almost foreign. Eira sat close to it, drawing her knees to her chest and watching the flames flicker. Her reflection in them was shadowed, her eyes glowing faintly with the remnants of her magic, and for a long while she said nothing. Rhys sat across from her, his blade resting at his side as he cleaned it with deliberate care, though his eyes kept drifting to her as if making sure she hadn't disappeared into her own thoughts.

"Back there," she said finally, her voice low, rough. "When the swamp tried to pull us under—I thought it was going to split us apart. It felt like it was searching for a weakness between us." She hesitated, her fingers tightening around her knees. "And I think it found something."

Rhys's hand stilled on his blade, his gaze lifting to meet hers. The firelight painted harsh shadows on his face, softening the lines of exhaustion but doing nothing to hide the tension in his jaw. "What weakness?"

She gave a humorless laugh. "Me. Or maybe us. I don't even know anymore." Her eyes shifted to the fire, reflecting its glow as though it had seeped into her soul. "The prophecy keeps forcing us into these trials, and every time we survive, I feel... closer to it. Closer to you. But that's the part that scares me most. Because if I care too much, I'll hesitate. And hesitation gets people killed."

Rhys leaned back, his expression unreadable, but his voice was softer than she expected when he replied. "Caring isn't weakness, Eira. It's what kept me alive long after I should have been gone. The people who taught me to fear it were wrong."

Her eyes flicked to him, startled by the honesty in his tone. "Do you care about me, Rhys?"

There was no hesitation in his answer. "More than I should."

The words hung in the cold night air, heavier than any prophecy. Eira's breath caught, and for a moment, all the battles, the visions, and the warnings felt like they had fallen silent, leaving only the two of them, raw and unshielded. She wanted to say something—anything—but her voice failed her. Instead, she reached across the small space between them, her fingers brushing his.

He didn't pull away. His hand closed over hers, rough and calloused, but steady and warm.

The warmth of his hand grounded her in a way nothing else had since this journey began. For a moment, neither of them spoke. The fire crackled softly, a fragile heartbeat in the darkness surrounding them, and the swamp hissed quietly in the distance as if whispering secrets they were not meant to hear.

Eira was the first to break the silence. "When I touched the shard in the sanctuary," she began, her voice barely above a whisper, "it showed me things. Not just pieces of the prophecy, but... possible endings. And in all of them, you were there. You were always there."

Rhys's grip tightened slightly, his gaze steady on hers. "I saw something too," he said, his tone low but sure. "When the illusions had me, it wasn't the battles or the blood that haunted me. It was you. It showed me what I'd become if I lost you—what I'd turn into if I let my fear eat away at me like it always has."

Her breath hitched, a swell of emotion breaking past the guarded walls she'd built around herself. "Do you believe the prophecy is absolute?" she asked. "Do you think we're trapped in it, doomed to follow the path it's already written for us?"

He leaned closer, the firelight tracing the sharp lines of his face, softening them just enough to make her heart ache. "Prophecies are like chains," he said. "They only hold if you let them. I've spent my whole life running from the Shadowborn because I thought fate had me in its grip. But standing here with you, I'm not sure I believe that anymore."

Eira swallowed, her throat tight. "I saw you kneeling before me, Rhys. Wounded. Dying. And I... I don't know if I have the strength to face that. To face losing you."

A faint, humorless smile tugged at his lips. "Then don't lose me," he said simply. "Whatever comes, we face it together. I'd rather burn beside you than live in the dark without you."

Her heart lurched at the raw honesty in his voice, and before she could stop herself, she leaned forward. For a fleeting moment, their foreheads touched, the warmth of his breath mingling with hers, both of them teetering on the edge of something deeper. He didn't kiss her, though the silence between them felt heavier than any touch. Instead, his hand brushed her cheek, his calloused thumb lingering there as if to memorize her.

Eira closed her eyes and exhaled, her magic stirring softly, not as a weapon but as something alive and vulnerable. "Then we keep moving," she murmured. "No matter what it takes."

Rhys released her hand only to rest his sword across his lap, a quiet vow in the gesture. "At first light," he said, his voice steady. "We'll leave this swamp behind. And whatever waits for us next, we'll face it on our own terms."

The fire burned low, casting long shadows over their resting forms. Eira lay with her back to the flames, staring into the canopy of twisted branches overhead, replaying his words in her mind. For the first time in what felt like forever, she allowed herself to feel something close to hope—a fragile, trembling thing, but hope nonetheless. The night pressed on, and as sleep finally claimed her, the whisper of the prophecy coiled softly in her mind, no longer a curse but a challenge.

Chapter Six:

The Weight of Dawn

The first light of dawn crept over the swamp like a reluctant promise, staining the mist with hues of pale gold and bruised violet. The water, now calm and deceptively serene, mirrored the glow as if nothing monstrous had risen from its depths the night before. Eira watched the sunrise through the tangle of twisted branches, her breath forming soft clouds in the cool air. There was a heaviness in her chest—not regret, but the quiet ache of something unspoken lingering between her and Rhys after the fire's confessions.

Rhys stood a few paces away, tightening the straps of his armor with a focus that seemed deliberate, as though each buckle he fastened was a shield not just against battle but against words neither of them were ready to revisit. His movements were sharp, efficient, but when his eyes met hers for a fleeting moment, the echo of what they'd shared flickered there, raw and unguarded.

"We should move," he said, his voice lower than usual, carrying the weight of determination. He glanced at the swamp one last time, as though daring it to stir again. "I don't trust this place to stay quiet now that we've survived its test."

Eira nodded, slinging her satchel over her shoulder. "The sanctuary isn't finished with us. Whatever that... thing was, it felt like a warning. Or maybe a reminder."

"Of what?" he asked, his tone edged but curious.

"That we're not just fighting what's outside of us," she replied, her shadowlight flickering faintly across her fingertips as though it agreed with her. "We're fighting what's inside. And I don't think either of us has seen the worst of that yet."

He didn't argue. He simply reached for his blade, its surface catching the light like a muted mirror, and gestured toward the rising sun. "Then we'd better start walking before we find out the hard way."

The swamp gave way to drier ground, the trees thinning into skeletal silhouettes as they left the dark water behind. Yet the air was no less oppressive; if anything, the silence ahead felt heavier, as though the world itself was bracing for what lay beyond the horizon. It wasn't long before Eira felt it—a shift, subtle but undeniable, in the currents of magic that threaded through the land. The shadowlight within her stirred uneasily, like a beast sniffing danger it couldn't yet see.

"Something's wrong," she murmured, stopping mid-step.

Rhys paused beside her, scanning the path ahead. A wind picked up, sudden and sharp, carrying with it the faint stench of ash and something sour, like rotting fruit.

His hand went to his weapon instinctively. "We're not alone, are we?"

"No," Eira said, her eyes narrowing as the horizon trembled with a faint shimmer. "And whatever it is—it's already watching us."

The shimmer ahead thickened, warping the air like heat rising from scorched earth. Eira's stomach tightened as her shadowlight pulsed in warning, prickling her skin with the sense of something unnatural. The wind stilled, too abruptly to be natural, and an eerie hush descended upon the clearing they'd just stepped into.

"Ambush," Rhys muttered, his hand tightening around the hilt of his blade. He stepped slightly in front of her, his posture taut and poised, every muscle ready to spring.

The first shape emerged from the wavering air—a figure cloaked in black, its edges blurred as though half-formed from smoke. Its face was hidden beneath a hood, but its presence radiated malice like heat from a forge. Then there were more. One by one, they stepped out from the shimmer—five, seven, ten of them—each carrying weapons wrought of dark metal that glimmered with a sickly green sheen.

"Shadowborn," Eira hissed, her heart pounding. These were not illusions; they were too solid, too heavy in the air. "How did they—?"

"Doesn't matter," Rhys cut her off, his voice steady but sharp. "They've tracked us since the sanctuary. They want you alive, but me? Not so much."

The Shadowborn moved with slow, deliberate steps, their formation tightening like a net. One of them, taller than the rest, raised its blade and pointed at Eira. The voice that came from beneath its hood was low and fractured, as though several voices spoke at once. "The vessel is ours. Step aside, zealot."

Rhys's jaw clenched, and he took a single step forward, the firelight from his eyes enough to challenge the shadows. "You'll have to carve me apart first," he growled.

The leader tilted its head. "Gladly."

The world exploded into motion.

Rhys moved like a storm, his blade catching the faint light as it sliced through the first attacker's arm. Eira barely had time to raise her hands before another Shadowborn lunged at her, its weapon aimed for her chest. She released a blast of shadowlight on instinct, the energy striking like lightning and hurling the figure backward with a guttural hiss. The air around them crackled, humming with the violence of clashing steel and magic.

"Eira!" Rhys's voice cut through the chaos. "Keep them back, I'll handle the front!"

She obeyed, her shadowlight forming a barrier around them, the violet glow arcing between the stones like living flame. Every time a Shadowborn touched it, the barrier snarled and burned their form into ash, but the strain of holding it up was immense. Sweat trickled down her spine, her hands trembling as the magic demanded more and more of her strength.

Rhys fought with brutal precision, each strike calculated but desperate. He was bleeding now—thin lines along his arm and shoulder—but he didn't falter. At one point, he caught Eira's gaze through the chaos, and for a moment, the world narrowed to just them.

"You're stronger than this," he called, his voice raw. "Stop doubting. Burn them."

Something inside her answered. Eira pushed harder, the shadowlight surging from her in a wave that turned the battlefield into a whirl of violet fire. The Shadowborn faltered, recoiling under the sheer force of her power, and Rhys seized the moment to cut through the remaining attackers with a final, savage strike.

When the last of them fell, the clearing was silent once more. Eira staggered, her breath ragged, and Rhys caught her before she could hit the ground. His hand was warm at her back, steadying her, his chest heaving against hers.

"You did it," he said softly, almost as if he couldn't quite believe it himself.

Eira's eyes lifted to his, her pulse still thrumming with the echo of her magic. "We did it," she corrected, though her voice was barely more than a whisper.

The clearing smelled of scorched earth and charred shadows, the remnants of the Shadowborn dissolving into black smoke that slithered into the ground as though returning to whatever abyss had spawned them. Eira sat on a flat stone at the edge of the clearing, her hands trembling as she tried to wipe the streaks of grime and blood from her palms. Every muscle in her body screamed with exhaustion, and her magic pulsed weakly under her skin, drained but restless.

Rhys crouched beside her, his movements sharp but deliberate as he checked a shallow gash along his forearm. The blood was already drying, a dark smear against his pale skin. "Hold still," she murmured, reaching for him before she could second-guess herself. Her fingers hovered just over the wound, shadowlight flickering faintly between them like fire catching its first spark.

"You don't have to—" he began, but stopped as her magic touched his skin. A shiver ran through him, though he tried to hide it beneath a quiet grunt. The shadowlight sank into the wound, knitting torn flesh with soft heat and the faintest hum of energy. When she withdrew her hand, the gash was gone, leaving only a thin scar where blood had been.

"Better?" she asked, her voice quiet.

Rhys flexed his arm, watching the new scar with a look of guarded gratitude. "Better," he said, then added after a pause, "but you shouldn't waste your strength on me. You're shaking."

"I'm fine," she lied, though the fatigue in her limbs betrayed her. She looked up at him, and for a moment, all the tension of the fight and the prophecy dissolved, leaving only the man before her—sharp-edged, scarred, and unflinchingly loyal in ways she didn't yet understand.

Rhys's gaze lingered on her face, his usual stoicism faltering as something softer flickered there. "You don't realize it, do you?" he said, his voice lower now. "You're... incredible when you fight. Terrifying, yes, but in a way that makes me want to believe in something again."

Eira blinked, caught off guard. "Rhys..."

He gave a crooked smile that didn't quite reach his eyes. "Don't look at me like that. I'm not good at this—talking, I mean. I've spent too many years trying not to feel anything. But today... you made me feel."

Her breath caught. The warmth of the fire they'd shared last night returned, curling low in her chest. "I'm not sure that's a good thing," she said softly, though the words lacked conviction.

"Maybe it's not," he admitted. "But I think I'd rather risk feeling something than go back to the emptiness I knew before I met you."

For a heartbeat, neither moved. Then Eira reached out, almost without thinking, brushing dirt and blood from his cheek with the tips of her fingers. His hand closed over hers, rough and warm, anchoring her in place. The moment stretched, heavy with unspoken words, and for once, neither of them tried to break it.

The silence between them felt almost sacred, as if the world itself held its breath. Eira's fingers lingered against Rhys's cheek, her thumb brushing the faint scar just beneath his jaw. The roughness of his skin was a strange comfort, grounding her even as her mind churned with what she had seen in the sanctuary. Finally, she let her hand fall, but the warmth of his touch lingered, an imprint she couldn't shake.

"It keeps coming back to us," she said quietly, her voice breaking the stillness like a ripple in water. "The prophecy... everything it's shown me—everything I've seen—it's like it's not just about the shadowlight or the Shadowborn. It's about you and me."

Rhys's eyes, dark and unflinching, held hers. "What exactly did it show you?"

She swallowed hard, her throat tight as she recalled the vision of him kneeling, broken and bleeding, beneath her hands. "A choice," she murmured. "A choice where I could save you or... become something I don't want to be. But in every ending I saw, you were always there. Always the one it came down to."

His expression darkened, not with anger but with something far heavier—a resignation she hated seeing in his eyes. "Maybe that's what it wants," he said. "To force us to care so much that when the time comes, it tears us apart. Prophecies love that kind of cruelty. They feed on it."

Eira shook her head, a flicker of defiance igniting in her chest. "No. I don't believe that. Prophecies aren't living things. They don't control us. They don't get to decide who we are."

"Don't they?" Rhys countered, leaning closer, his voice dropping to a harsh whisper. "Look at what's happened so far. Every step we take, it's as if the prophecy is waiting to test us. To break us. Do you think the Shadowborn attacked by chance today? Or do you think the prophecy made sure they found us, just to remind us how easily it could end?"

Eira stared at him, her jaw tightening, because part of her wanted to argue—but another part feared he was right. "Then we change the story," she said fiercely. "If our bond is what it's trying to use against us, then maybe it's the key to breaking it. Maybe caring is the only way we win."

Rhys studied her for a long moment, his gaze steady and searching, as if weighing the truth of her words against the shadows in his own mind. "And if you're wrong?" he asked softly. "If caring is the thing that kills us?"

Eira's breath trembled, but she didn't look away. "Then I'd rather die fighting for something I feel than live as nothing."

For a long, quiet moment, his expression softened, his guard lowering in a way she had never seen before. "You're going to be the end of me, Eira," he said, but there was no bitterness in his tone—only a strange, quiet admiration.

"Maybe," she whispered, "but I won't be the one to break first."

They found a patch of higher ground just beyond the gnarled edge of the swamp, a strip of earth nestled beneath a leaning arch of ancient stone. The fading sunlight washed the land in gold and rose, but the shadows here were deep and cold, clinging to the trees like a warning. Rhys set about gathering what dry wood he could find, his movements brisk and efficient, while Eira cleared a small space near the arch for the fire, her fingers brushing over the moss-streaked stone as though it carried a heartbeat of its own.

When the fire caught, it burned low and steady, the faint crackle of the flames the only sound between them. Eira sat close to the warmth, pulling her cloak tighter around her shoulders. Rhys lowered himself across from her, his knees bent, his forearms resting against them as he watched the flames. His face was half-lit, the rest shadowed, and for a moment Eira found it difficult to look away.

"You keep staring," he said finally, his tone light but carrying that sharp undercurrent that always seemed to mask something deeper. "Should I be flattered or worried?"

Eira huffed, though it was softer than a true laugh. "Maybe both."

His lips quirked into the faintest smile. "Not sure I like the sound of that."

For a moment, silence stretched between them again, but this time it was different—not heavy, but charged, like the stillness before a storm. She found herself studying the small scars along his jaw, the way the firelight softened the harsh lines of his face. "When you fought today," she said quietly, "you didn't hesitate. Even when it looked like they might overwhelm us. You—" She stopped, not entirely sure how to finish without revealing too much.

Rhys tilted his head, his eyes narrowing slightly as though he sensed the unspoken words. "I don't hesitate for you," he said simply. His voice was steady, matter-of-fact, but the honesty in it made her pulse stumble.

Eira looked down at her hands, her shadowlight humming faintly beneath the surface of her skin. "That's dangerous," she murmured. "For both of us."

"Maybe," he said. His voice softened, and when she looked up again, his gaze was on her—steady, unyielding, but with something warm smoldering there. "But I've made my peace with dangerous things."

Her breath caught, and she forced herself to look away, staring into the fire as if it could burn away the weight of his words. Yet she couldn't ignore the warmth that spread through her chest, or the way her hand itched to reach for his across the space between them. "Rhys," she said, her voice low, "if we let this... whatever this is between us... grow, I'm afraid it'll cost us more than we can pay."

He leaned slightly closer, just enough that she could see the glint of fire in his dark eyes. "Maybe it's worth the price."

The air between them seemed to crackle like her magic, full of unspoken longing and the sharp edge of fear. For a heartbeat, it felt as though either of them might close the distance—but neither did. Not yet.

The silence stretched, warm and volatile, as if the air itself held its breath between them. The fire had burned low, its flames shrinking to glowing embers that pulsed like the last heartbeat of the day. Eira sat with her knees drawn to her chest, trying to will away the memory of his voice, the way he had said Maybe it's worth the price. She stole a glance at him across the fire, only to find his gaze already on her, steady and unreadable.

For a long moment, neither spoke. Then Rhys shifted, leaning slightly closer, his hand resting against his knee as he said in a quiet voice, "You should sleep, Eira. You've carried more today than anyone should. The visions, the swamp, the fight... if you keep burning yourself this hard, you'll break before the prophecy ever has the chance."

Eira's lips curved into a faint, tired smile. "Since when do you care about me breaking?"

He smirked, but there was no cruelty in it—only something softer, like the ghost of a truth he'd never admit aloud. "Since I realized I'd rather see you fight me than fall apart." His eyes caught the glow of the firelight, reflecting a depth she hadn't noticed before. "You think you're alone in this, but you're not. Not anymore."

Her breath hitched, the words cutting through her walls with quiet precision. For a second, she wanted to say something—thank you, I'm scared, don't leave me—but none of the words felt right. Instead, she reached for his hand, her fingers brushing his. The contact was small, tentative, but he didn't pull away. Instead, his thumb traced a slow, deliberate line across her knuckles, as if memorizing the shape of her hand.

"Rhys..." she whispered, not entirely sure what she was asking.

"Sleep," he said again, softer now. "I'll keep watch."

She nodded, though her gaze lingered on him for another heartbeat before she lay down beside the fire, the warmth of his touch still tingling in her fingers. Rhys didn't move as she closed her eyes, his presence a steady weight on the other side of the flames, and for the first time in days, Eira felt safe enough to let sleep take her—though it came laced with dreams she couldn't quite name.

The night deepened around them, the stars barely visible through the tangle of branches overhead. The swamp was behind them now, but its presence still lingered—Eira could feel it in the weight of the air, in the way the ground seemed to breathe beneath the quiet hum of magic. She lay close to the fire, her eyes half-closed but restless, tracing the shapes of the glowing embers while Rhys sat across from her, sharpening his blade with slow, steady strokes.

"You don't have to sit up all night," she murmured, her voice carrying softly through the cool night air.

Rhys didn't look up. "Someone has to. You need the rest more than I do. That magic of yours burns you faster than you think."

"I'm fine," she said automatically, though the exhaustion pulling at her bones made the words sound hollow even to her. She turned slightly, propping herself on one elbow so she could see him better. "Why do you always do that? Put yourself between me and the fire, between me and every danger, like you're already prepared to bleed for me?"

He paused mid-stroke, the blade catching the faint firelight as he set it down. His gaze rose to meet hers, sharp and unflinching. "Because I've already bled for worse things. And because..." He hesitated, his expression shifting, softening in a way that seemed almost reluctant. "Because you're worth it, Eira."

The fire popped, breaking the silence, but the words lingered between them like heat. Eira's breath caught, her heart pounding in a way that had nothing to do with battle. "You don't even know me," she said softly, though her tone lacked conviction. "Not really."

Rhys leaned forward, elbows resting on his knees, his gaze never leaving hers. "I know enough. I know the way you don't let fear rule you, even when it should. I know you've got more strength in you than anyone I've ever met—and I've known people who would burn down kingdoms to survive." His voice dropped lower, almost a whisper. "And I know I'd rather stand beside you, even if it kills me, than watch you face this alone."

The admission left her breathless, her pulse thrumming in her ears. She wanted to argue, to remind him of the vision she'd seen—of him broken and bleeding, of the prophecy demanding his life—but the words tangled in her throat. Instead, she reached across the space between them, her fingers brushing the back of his hand.

His hand turned, rough fingers curling around hers with a gentleness that startled her. For a moment, it was enough to simply hold on, the firelight flickering over their joined hands like a quiet promise.

"You don't have to do this," she whispered. "You don't have to choose me."

His thumb brushed her knuckles, slow and deliberate. "You're right," he said, his voice steady but low. "I don't. But I will."

The night grew still around them, their unspoken feelings coiling tighter with every second. Eira's chest ached with a mix of fear and longing, and for a moment, she thought he might lean closer, might close that small, charged distance between them. But he didn't. Instead, he looked at her like she was something worth fighting for, something untouchable and fragile all at once.

The firelight danced across Rhys's face, softening the edges of his scars and turning his dark eyes into molten pools of amber. Eira couldn't look away. His hand around hers was warm, firm, and grounding, and yet the simple contact sent a rush of heat through her chest, a sensation both unsettling and intoxicating.

"Why do you look at me like that?" she asked quietly, her voice barely audible over the faint crackle of the fire.

"Like what?" His tone was calm, but there was something guarded in the way he asked, as if afraid of what she might see if he didn't hide it.

"Like you see through me. Like you know what I'm thinking before I do," she said, her words slipping out before she could stop them.

Rhys's lips curved into the faintest of smiles, though it held no mockery—only an ache that matched her own. "Maybe I do," he murmured. "Or maybe I just know what it's like to wear a mask until it feels like skin. You hide, Eira, but not from me."

Her breath caught, his words sinking into the spaces she'd tried to keep closed. "And what if I don't want you to see me?" she asked, though there was no strength in the challenge.

"Then I'll look anyway," he said simply, leaning just a fraction closer, his eyes catching the flicker of the flames. "Because the parts of you that scare you the most... those are the ones that make you stronger. They're the ones I—" He stopped himself, jaw tightening as if the next words threatened to reveal too much.

"You what?" she pressed, the whisper trembling from her lips before she realized she'd spoken.

Rhys's gaze locked on hers, steady and unflinching, and for a moment she thought he might close the distance between them. "They're the parts I can't seem to turn away from," he admitted, his voice quiet but raw.

Eira's heart hammered. Her instinct was to retreat, to guard herself, but instead, she found herself leaning ever so slightly toward him. The firelight painted gold across his features, his closeness both sharp and magnetic. "Rhys," she breathed, her voice carrying both fear and longing.

His hand shifted, fingers brushing her cheek with a tenderness that contrasted every brutal thing she'd seen him do. "Tell me to stop," he said, his tone barely above a whisper, "and I will."

But she didn't. She couldn't.

The silence between them stretched taut, and though he didn't kiss her, the weight of everything unspoken between them was enough to make her chest ache. His hand lingered against her cheek for another breath, then slid away slowly, reluctantly, as though tearing himself back from an edge neither of them was ready to fall over.

Eira stared at him, her breath unsteady, the warmth of his hand still lingering on her skin like the echo of a promise. The silence was heavy, intimate, and for a moment, she thought she might drown in it. Her fingers tightened slightly on his, as though letting go might break something fragile between them.

"I keep seeing it," she whispered, her voice trembling as if the words were fragile glass. "Your death. The prophecy doesn't just hint at it—it shows me. Again and again. It's like it wants me to believe that no matter what I do, I can't save you."

Rhys's expression shifted, a flicker of something softer crossing his features—pain, understanding, but also a strange calm. "Eira," he said quietly, leaning closer, "prophecies don't scare me. They've already taken everything they could from me once. If my death means you live—if it means you break this curse—then I'll accept it."

Her eyes widened, and a sharp, angry heat flooded her chest. "Don't say that. Don't you dare say that like your life doesn't matter. You think you're just some weapon, Rhys, but you're not. I can't—" She stopped, her voice catching on the raw emotion swelling in her throat.

"You can't what?" he asked, his voice softer now, urging her gently to speak the words she was too afraid to say.

Her gaze dropped to their joined hands, her fingers curling tighter around his. "I can't watch you die. Not for me. Not for any prophecy. I've already lost too much to this fight. If I lose you…" She trailed off, swallowing hard as the unspoken truth settled between them.

Rhys was quiet for a long moment, his dark eyes fixed on her face. Then he reached out, his fingers brushing a loose strand of hair from her cheek, the touch lingering longer than necessary. "You won't lose me," he said, his tone steady, almost fierce. "Not if I can help it. Whatever this prophecy says, whatever game it's playing with us—I'm not giving up on you. Or on us."

The word hung between them—us—heavier and more significant than either of them had intended. Eira's breath hitched, and for a heartbeat, she felt as though the entire world had narrowed to this single moment, this fragile connection forged in fire and fear.

"Rhys…" she whispered, his name both a question and a plea.

He smiled faintly, but it was tinged with something raw. "Sleep, Eira. You'll need your strength for whatever comes next. But know this—I'm not going anywhere."

She didn't let go of his hand as she lay back down beside the fire, their fingers still tangled together as if neither could quite bring themselves to break the contact. The firelight flickered between them, a warm bridge in the chill of the night.

Eira lay on her side, her back to the fire but her hand still clasped with Rhys's. The warmth of his palm seeped into her skin, steadying her in a way that felt as dangerous as it was comforting. She stared at the uneven canopy of branches above, their skeletal shapes silhouetted against the fading light of the stars. The world was quiet now, but it was the kind of quiet that hummed with the memory of what had just happened—the battle, the prophecy, his voice saying she was worth it.

Her thoughts moved in restless circles. She had seen his death in the vision, as vivid and cruel as any reality. It had burned into her mind, the image of him broken, kneeling, and still looking at her with that maddening mix of defiance and acceptance. The memory twisted something deep inside her chest, making her wonder if caring for him was the worst mistake she could make—or the one thing that might save them both.

The fire crackled softly behind her, a rhythmic reminder of his presence. She could feel him even without looking—his steady breathing, the faint shift of his weight when he adjusted his position, the quiet patience of someone keeping watch not just over the camp, but over her. The realization that he'd chosen to stay—for her—sent a warmth through her that frightened her more than any shadowborn could.

You're going to be the end of me, she thought, but there was no bitterness in the idea. Only a strange, reckless hope that perhaps the end wouldn't be as simple as death or prophecy. Perhaps, just perhaps, there was something beyond all of this darkness waiting for them both—if they survived.

Her eyes grew heavy, her last waking thought a quiet whisper in her mind: Don't let go, Rhys.

The fire dimmed to embers, casting a soft, trembling glow over their hands still clasped between them. Rhys didn't move, his steady presence a silent promise she hadn't asked for but desperately needed. Eira drifted into sleep with the memory of his voice lingering like an echo, warm and rough, a tether against the endless dark of her dreams. The prophecy loomed in the edges of her thoughts, whispering its cruel truths, but for the first time, it didn't feel unshakable. Not while his hand was holding hers.

The night wrapped around them like a fragile cocoon—half comfort, half threat—and in that dangerous stillness, hope began to take root. It was a fragile thing, perilous and sharp, but it burned brighter than fear.

Chapter Seven:

Shadows on the Horizon

Dawn broke reluctantly over the wilds, painting the land in shades of muted gold and gray. The swamp lay far behind them, yet its stench and memory lingered, a reminder of how close they had come to being swallowed whole. Eira stirred from sleep as the first pale rays of sunlight cut through the thinning mist. Her hand was still nestled in Rhys's, their fingers tangled as though neither had let go throughout the night. For a moment, she didn't move, simply watching the way the early light softened his usually harsh features. His breathing was steady, his head bowed slightly as he dozed in a sitting position, his sword resting across his lap.

Carefully, she withdrew her hand, though the loss of his warmth felt immediate and wrong. The moment her fingers slipped free, his eyes opened, sharp and alert. He didn't say anything at first, just studied her as if gauging whether she was ready to face the day—or whatever waited beyond it.

"You didn't sleep," she said softly, more a statement than a question.

"I slept enough," he replied, brushing a hand through his dark hair. He glanced at the horizon, where the sun's weak glow bled into the clouds like gold spilling into gray water. "It's too quiet. I don't like it."

Eira pushed herself to her feet, brushing dirt and moss from her cloak. "You never like quiet," she said with a faint, tired smile. "But you're right. Something's... off."

The air itself felt charged, as though the world was holding its breath. Even the usual rustle of the trees seemed muted, their blackened branches twisting as if reaching for something unseen. Her shadowlight stirred faintly in her chest, prickling against her skin. "It's like the land is watching us," she murmured.

"Then let it watch," Rhys said, rising fluidly to his feet. His tone was calm, but his grip on his sword was tight, his knuckles pale. "We've been tested enough to know when something is coming."

Before Eira could respond, the ground beneath them trembled. It wasn't strong, not yet, but it was enough to send loose stones rolling from the arch where they had camped. She froze, her eyes locking with Rhys's.

"That wasn't just a tremor, was it?" she asked, her voice barely above a whisper.

"No," he said flatly, his gaze sweeping the horizon. "It's something waking up."

The tremor deepened into a low, resonant hum that seemed to ripple through the ground, vibrating in Eira's bones. She stepped back instinctively, her fingers curling as her shadowlight flared faintly at her fingertips. The mist that clung to the horizon began to churn, twisting upward in thick, dark columns.

Rhys drew his sword, the steel catching the dim morning light. "That's no storm," he said grimly.

The mist coalesced into a shape—something vast, writhing, and grotesquely fluid, as if it were both shadow and flesh. A hollow, almost human face emerged from the swirling darkness, its mouth stretching into a soundless scream. The air thickened, heavy with a metallic scent like rain on blood.

Eira's breath quickened. "This isn't just a creature—it's a summoning. The prophecy is pulling the threads tighter."

"Then we cut through the threads," Rhys growled, stepping in front of her as the form lunged. Its limbs—long and spindly like skeletal branches—snapped forward, slamming against the ground with the force of a hammer. He intercepted the strike, his blade biting into the mist-flesh, sending ripples of sickly black energy scattering like shattered glass.

Eira moved beside him, her hands glowing with a surge of shadowlight that crackled in the air. She aimed a pulse of energy at the creature's core, the blast slicing through its chest and tearing a gaping hole in its form. But the thing didn't fall—it shifted, reforming with a shriek like tearing metal.

"Don't let it surround us," Rhys shouted, swinging his blade again, the arc of his strike cutting through the thickening mist. "Keep its focus on me."

Eira gritted her teeth. "You're going to get yourself killed if you keep baiting it!"

"Then make sure I don't," he shot back with a sharp grin, even as the creature lashed out again.

They moved together without thinking—her shadowlight weaving arcs of protective energy while his blade struck in precise, brutal cuts. It wasn't flawless, but it was enough to start forcing the creature back. Every time it shifted, Eira countered its form, and every time her strength faltered, Rhys was there, a shield of steel and relentless determination.

At one point, its spindly limb whipped toward her from behind, but Rhys was there in an instant, his arm bracing her waist as he spun them both out of the way. The moment was fleeting, but she felt the strength of his grip and the raw tension in his body—an unspoken promise that he'd keep her standing no matter what it cost.

"On my mark!" he barked, his voice cutting through the chaos.

Eira's pulse pounded in time with the creature's unnatural hum. "What are you thinking?"

"We break it—together." His eyes met hers briefly, and for a heartbeat, it was as if the rest of the world had gone silent.

Eira nodded, the weight of Rhys's gaze anchoring her. The creature loomed before them, its form pulsating like living shadow, tendrils curling and lashing as though sensing their intent. Her heart raced, her shadowlight thrumming beneath her skin, demanding release. She glanced at Rhys one last time, and in that silent exchange, a plan formed—simple, desperate, and dangerous.

"On your signal," she said, her voice firm despite the raw strain in her chest.

Rhys shifted his stance, gripping his sword with both hands. "Aim for its core. I'll open the path."

The creature lunged, its face distorting into a hollow scream. Rhys moved first, charging with the ruthless precision of someone who had survived far worse. His blade cut through the shifting limbs, each strike cleaving through shadow as if carving away pieces of night itself. The creature recoiled, screeching, but Eira was already moving.

Her shadowlight surged through her veins like wildfire. She raised both hands, pulling the energy tight until it burned at her fingertips, a storm of violet and silver crackling in the air. For a moment, time slowed—she felt the pulse of the land beneath her feet, the hum of Rhys's movements beside her, and the pull of the prophecy, heavy and unrelenting, as if it were watching to see if she would fail.

"Now, Eira!" Rhys shouted, his voice raw with effort. He plunged his sword deep into the creature's core, holding the writhing mass in place.

Eira unleashed everything.

The blast tore through the clearing like a bolt of living fire, wrapping around Rhys's blade and igniting the creature from the inside out. The thing convulsed, its scream shattering the air, its form unraveling into ribbons of shadow that burned away into nothingness. For an instant, the world was filled with a brilliant, violent light, then silence.

Eira stumbled forward, the energy ripping out of her so fiercely that she almost collapsed. Rhys caught her, his arm firm around her waist, his chest heaving with exhaustion. They stood together in the fading haze, both breathing hard, their bodies trembling from the intensity of the fight.

"It's gone," she murmured, leaning against him, her voice barely more than a breath.

"For now," Rhys said, though his tone carried more relief than warning. His hand lingered at her side, steadying her as though he wasn't ready to let go. "You nearly burned yourself out. Why didn't you hold back?"

She tilted her head slightly, her tired eyes meeting his. "Because you were counting on me."

The words hung between them, simple but heavy, and for a moment, neither of them moved. He was still close, his breath brushing her hair, his gaze locked on her face as if trying to memorize the way she looked in this moment—worn, fierce, and achingly real.

"You shouldn't do that," he said finally, though the softness in his tone betrayed him. "You shouldn't make me care this much."

Eira's lips parted, but no words came. Instead, she let herself rest against him for a heartbeat longer, knowing that for all the prophecy's cruelty, this connection—raw and fragile as it was—felt like the only thing keeping her grounded.

The clearing was eerily quiet, the last wisps of shadow from the creature dissolving into the morning mist. Rhys still hadn't let go of Eira, his arm steady around her waist as if he wasn't entirely convinced the ground beneath them wouldn't betray them next. When her strength returned enough for her to stand on her own, she stepped back, though she could feel the ghost of his hand lingering like warmth against her skin.

They moved cautiously, scanning the horizon for signs of more threats until Rhys spotted the jagged outline of a half-collapsed watchtower beyond the treeline. It rose out of the wilderness like a broken tooth, leaning but still standing—a relic of something ancient, long since abandoned. "There," he said, nodding toward it. "It'll do for now. Unless you're planning to fall over before we get there."

Eira shot him a look, though her lips curved into a faint smirk. "You nearly got torn apart twice today, and you're worrying about me?"

"I wasn't the one who nearly burned myself into a heap of ash," he countered, a spark of humor cutting through his gruff tone. "You need to stop throwing everything you have at whatever shadow monster comes crawling out of the dark."

"Would you rather I hold back and let you get skewered?" she asked, arching a brow.

He gave her a sideways glance as they walked. "I've been skewered before. I can handle it."

Eira snorted, shaking her head. "That's not something you brag about, Rhys."

The broken watchtower was more stable than it looked from afar. Its lower floor was mostly intact, and the remnants of a stone hearth still stood against one wall. Rhys kicked aside some fallen debris and set his pack down. "Not exactly a palace," he muttered, "but I've slept in worse."

"Your standards must be remarkable," Eira said, setting her own satchel down with a tired sigh. She knelt beside the hearth, brushing away dust as she coaxed her magic to spark a flame on the cold wood left behind by whoever had last taken shelter here.

Rhys sank onto a slab of stone, watching her as the fire flared to life. "I've noticed you're better at starting fires than putting them out," he remarked, his tone teasing but laced with an underlying seriousness that wasn't lost on her.

Eira glanced up, the flickering firelight catching in her eyes. "And I've noticed you're better at provoking me than shutting up."

He gave a short, amused laugh, the sound rare and disarming. "Touché."

For a few moments, they sat in silence, the firelight dancing across the ruins around them. The quiet wasn't uncomfortable, but it was charged, as if both were trying to find words they weren't ready to speak. Finally, Eira broke it.

"Back there," she began softly, "when we fought together... I felt something. It wasn't just the magic. It was like we moved as one. Like something... bigger was pulling us." She paused, glancing at him, searching his face for any sign of agreement—or denial.

Rhys didn't look away. "I felt it too," he admitted. "And I don't know if I trust it. Whatever this prophecy wants, it's twisting things. Maybe even us." He leaned back, his eyes narrowing slightly. "But I'll be damned if I let it decide how I feel—or what I'll fight for."

Her pulse quickened at the way he said it, the conviction in his voice hitting deeper than she wanted to admit. She managed a small smile, though her chest tightened. "You sound like you're trying to scare the prophecy into behaving."

"Maybe I am," he said with a half-smirk. "Wouldn't be the first thing I've stared down that thought it was in control."

The fire cast long shadows against the crumbling walls of the watchtower, its light wavering as if it sensed the weight of the words unsaid between them. Eira sat with her knees drawn close, her fingers absently tracing patterns in the dust while Rhys leaned against the cold stone wall opposite her, his sword laid within easy reach. For a moment, the silence was companionable, but beneath it was a current of something heavier—something neither of them had the courage to name.

"You know," Rhys said finally, his voice low and roughened by the day's battles, "I'm not sure which is worse—facing those things out there or wondering what the hell this prophecy plans to do to us next."

Eira looked up, her eyes reflecting the firelight like twin shards of amber. "What is it you fear, Rhys? Truly? Is it the prophecy, or is it... something else?"

He studied her for a long moment, his jaw tightening before he spoke. "I'm not afraid of dying. I've already come close enough times to know that's not what haunts me. What scares me—" He paused, exhaling slowly. "It's losing control. Of myself. Of what I feel. I've spent years trying to be nothing but a blade, because blades don't feel. Blades don't break. But with you..." He stopped, his gaze falling to the floor as though ashamed to finish. "You make me remember I'm still human. And that terrifies me more than any shadowborn monster."

Eira's breath hitched, the raw honesty of his words cutting deeper than any sword. She shifted closer to the fire, her own thoughts churning like a storm. "I don't know how to answer that," she admitted softly. "Because you scare me too. Not the way you fight, or the darkness you carry—but because I see pieces of myself in you. And if I lose you... I'm not sure there will be enough of me left to keep going."

Rhys lifted his head, his dark gaze locking with hers, unflinching and steady. "You won't lose me." The words were simple, but there was an intensity to them that made her pulse quicken.

She swallowed hard. "You can't promise that. The prophecy... it's not just pushing us. It's shaping us, twisting every moment to see which one of us will break first."

"Then let it try," he said with a quiet defiance. "Because if it comes down to breaking, it'll have to shatter both of us."

The fire popped, sending a brief shower of sparks into the air. Eira stared at him, the tension between them drawn tight like a bowstring. "You really mean that, don't you?" she asked, her voice trembling with something she wasn't sure she wanted to name.

Rhys gave a small, tired grin. "I've never been the kind of man to say something I don't mean. Not to you."

The vulnerability in his tone made something ache in her chest, and for a heartbeat, it felt as though the space between them had vanished, as if every breath they took was shared.

The air between them was thick with the weight of unspoken words, but the moment fractured when a faint sound broke through the quiet—a scraping noise, like something dragging across stone. Eira froze, her head snapping toward the doorway of the watchtower. Rhys was already moving, his hand closing around the hilt of his sword in one smooth motion.

"That wasn't the wind," she whispered, her pulse quickening.

"Stay behind me," Rhys said, his tone clipped but calm. His body shifted into that sharp, deadly focus she had seen in battle, the softness from their previous exchange gone like smoke.

The noise came again, closer this time—a soft, deliberate shuffle followed by the creak of something heavy pressing against the outer wall. Eira's shadowlight stirred in her veins, sparking faintly around her hands like violet fireflies. "There's more than one," she murmured, closing her eyes briefly to feel the threads of magic around them. "Three... maybe four. And they're circling."

Rhys glanced over his shoulder, his eyes dark but steady. "You still have strength left?"

"Enough," she replied, forcing a steadiness she wasn't sure she felt.

He gave a faint, crooked grin, a shard of sarcasm breaking the tension. "Good. Because I'm not much for gentle wake-up calls, and I'd rather you didn't pass out on me mid-fight."

Despite the danger, she snorted. "You'd deserve it for that comment alone."

The scraping stopped. For a moment, the world was utterly silent, as if whatever lurked outside the watchtower was waiting—listening. Rhys stepped closer to her, his free hand brushing hers just briefly. "We do this together," he said quietly, his voice like steel wrapped in warmth. "No hesitation. No doubts."

She met his gaze, her magic humming louder as if echoing the rhythm of his words. "Together," she agreed.

The wall shook suddenly, dust and loose stone falling from the cracks as something slammed against it. The first shadowed shape appeared in the doorway—hulking, distorted, its limbs too long, its head tilting unnaturally as though it could smell their fear.

Rhys raised his sword, the blade catching the glow of her shadowlight. "Ready?" he asked, his voice low but steady.

Eira nodded, her hands sparking with a violet pulse that lit the ruins like lightning. "Let's show them what happens when they pick the wrong tower."

The first creature lunged into the watchtower with a distorted hiss, its limbs scraping against the stone as if sharpened into crude blades. Rhys moved without hesitation, his sword arcing through the air in a perfect, brutal strike that severed one of its grotesque arms.

Black ichor splattered across the floor, sizzling where it touched the stone.

"Behind you!" Eira shouted, her shadowlight flaring as she sent a burst of violet energy at the second creature slithering through the broken window. The pulse struck with a crackling snap, throwing it backward, its body twisting and dissolving into smoke that shrieked as it scattered.

Rhys spared her only a glance, his eyes flickering with something almost like pride. "Good. Again!"

Eira gritted her teeth, raising her hands as the shadowlight built inside her, wild and searing. But the third creature was fast—it darted low, weaving through the flicker of her magic, its clawed hand reaching for her ankle. Rhys was there before she could even react, his sword thrusting clean through its chest.

"You're welcome," he muttered, pulling his blade free with a savage twist.

She shot him a look, sweat streaking her temple. "Try not to be so smug while I'm saving your ass."

"Noted," he said with a flash of a grin, just as the fourth creature emerged from the darkness beyond the doorway. It was larger than the others, its form rippling like liquid shadow, its hollow eyes burning with an unnatural light.

The tower shook as it slammed against the entrance, forcing its way inside. The air grew colder, the fire flickering violently as though being snuffed out by the sheer force of its presence. Eira's breath quickened; this was no mindless beast. It was something older, darker—a fragment of the magic that had birthed the prophecy itself.

Rhys stepped in front of her, his stance wide, blade gleaming. "Eira," he said, his voice steady but urgent, "you focus on its heart. I'll buy you the time you need."

She felt the truth of his words resonate through her, their unspoken trust binding them tighter than any promise. "Don't you dare let it kill you," she said, her voice low but trembling with something more than fear.

His lips twitched into the faintest smirk. "Wouldn't dream of it."

He launched himself forward, steel meeting shadow with a clash that sent sparks and black mist spiraling through the room. Eira's magic surged in response, the air around her alive with a fierce hum as she gathered the energy into her palms. She could feel it fighting her—wild, unrelenting—but she forced it into a sharp, focused point.

"Now, Rhys!" she called.

With a guttural shout, he slashed upward, exposing the core of the creature's chest. Eira released her magic, a blinding pulse of violet and white tearing through the watchtower like a living storm. The creature shrieked, its form fracturing and breaking apart in a swirl of ash and light.

When the silence finally fell, both of them stood breathless, the floor beneath them scarred and smoking from the intensity of the fight. Rhys's chest rose and fell heavily, his sword arm trembling from the effort. Eira leaned against the wall, her hands still faintly glowing, her face pale but fierce.

He crossed to her, his hand brushing her shoulder as if to ground them both. "You... were incredible," he said quietly, his voice roughened by exhaustion but softened with something more.

Eira met his gaze, her heart pounding not just from the battle but from the way his words burned into her. "So were you. You didn't hesitate—not once."

"Didn't need to," he replied, his hand lingering on her shoulder. "Not with you at my side."

The last echoes of the battle faded, leaving the watchtower draped in a silence that felt almost oppressive. Smoke curled from the blackened floor where Eira's magic had struck, its faint, acrid scent mingling with the cold morning air. Rhys leaned his sword against the wall and scanned the broken entryway, making sure no shadows lingered in the corners.

"Bar that door," he said, voice still raw from the clash. His movements were sharp but deliberate as he dragged a half-splintered beam across the entrance, wedging it against the crumbling stone. Eira added a pulse of shadowlight to the cracks, a shimmering barrier of violet that hummed like distant thunder. It wasn't permanent, but it would hold. For now.

Once the tower was as secure as it could be, Rhys sank onto the floor near the hearth, the fire casting a faint halo over his features. His chest still rose and fell heavily, each breath an audible reminder of how close the battle had come. Eira lowered herself beside him, her knees brushing his as she rested her head back against the wall.

For a long moment, neither of them spoke. The adrenaline was draining from her body, leaving her hands trembling slightly. She looked at him through the wavering firelight, noting the sweat clinging to his temples, the faint streak of blood along his jaw where one of the creatures had nearly caught him. "You almost didn't make it," she murmured, her voice quiet but heavy with emotion.

Rhys turned his head toward her, his dark eyes steady despite the exhaustion. "Neither did you." His tone wasn't sharp, but there was something fierce in the way he said it, as if the thought alone was unacceptable.

"I saw the way it grabbed you," Eira continued, her words spilling out before she could stop them. "For a second, I thought—" She broke off, her throat tightening, unable to finish.

Rhys's hand shifted, his fingers brushing hers where they rested on the stone floor. "But it didn't. Because you were there," he said softly. "You pulled me out of it. I... I don't think I've ever trusted someone like that before."

The admission hung between them, raw and unguarded. Eira's breath hitched slightly, her pulse quickening in a way that had nothing to do with the battle. She turned her hand over, letting their fingers intertwine, the simple contact grounding her. "You make it sound like I'm worth trusting," she said, her voice barely more than a whisper.

He gave a faint, tired grin, but his eyes didn't leave hers. "You are. Even when you're stubborn enough to scare me half to death."

Eira let out a soft laugh, though it was tinged with something fragile. "I don't scare you."

"You do," he said, his voice low and earnest. "Because I can't afford to lose you."

The words sent a tremor through her chest. She looked at him, really looked, and saw not just the hardened fighter, but the man beneath—the one who had fought tooth and nail to survive yet somehow still had the capacity to care. For her.

Without thinking, she leaned just slightly closer, her shoulder brushing his. "Then don't," she murmured, the words almost daring him to answer.

Rhys's gaze flickered to her lips, then back to her eyes, something unreadable passing over his face. He didn't speak, but his hand tightened around hers in silent agreement, the warmth of his touch a quiet promise neither of them could put into words.

The fire crackled softly, filling the silence between them with a gentle rhythm, as though the world itself was holding its breath. Rhys's thumb brushed over the back of Eira's hand in an unthinking motion, the gesture more intimate than any words they might have spoken. The tension between them was thick, not born of fear now, but of something far more fragile—something that trembled like glass on the edge of breaking.

Eira shifted slightly, turning just enough that the firelight caught her face. She could feel his gaze on her, unwavering, like he was memorizing every detail. "I don't understand you," she said softly, her voice barely above the hum of the flames.

"Not sure I understand myself," Rhys admitted with a faint, crooked smile, though there was no humor in his tone. "All I know is that you—" He stopped, his jaw tightening as though the words were too heavy to let fall.

Eira's pulse quickened, her chest tightening with the weight of everything unsaid. "You what, Rhys?"

His eyes met hers, unflinching. "You make me want to fight for something I don't think I deserve. Maybe that's dangerous, maybe it's the prophecy twisting my head, but I can't stop. Not when it's you."

Her breath caught. For a long moment, she couldn't speak—didn't dare to. The sincerity in his voice was raw, almost painful, and it resonated in a place she'd thought she had locked away. "Rhys," she whispered, "you don't get to say things like that unless you mean them."

"Do I look like I'm lying?" he asked, his voice low and steady.

She shook her head slowly, her eyes glistening with something unspoken. "No. And that's what terrifies me."

The silence stretched again, but this time it was charged, pulsing with a longing neither of them dared fully acknowledge. Rhys leaned closer, his hand rising to brush a stray lock of hair from her face, his knuckles grazing her cheek. The touch was feather-light, but it sent a shiver down her spine. For a heartbeat, it felt as though they might close the distance between them, that the fire and the ruins and the prophecy would fade into nothing but this moment.

But then the ground trembled, just faintly—enough to jar them both back to the reality they couldn't escape. Eira inhaled sharply, the warmth of the moment evaporating like mist in a cold wind.

Rhys pulled back slightly, though his hand lingered just a moment longer. His expression hardened, the softness retreating behind the sharp lines of his focus. "Something's coming," he said, his voice low, almost a growl.

Eira nodded, her magic sparking faintly at her fingertips as she rose to her feet. "Then let's face it. Together."

The tremor that interrupted their moment was subtle, but it carried a weight that set Rhys on edge. He rose fluidly, retrieving his sword and glancing at the crumbling doorway. The embers of the fire flickered violently, as though disturbed by an unseen presence. Eira's shadowlight stirred in response, glowing faintly beneath her skin like veins of living silver.

Then came the sound. A low, resonant clicking—measured, deliberate. It wasn't the mindless shuffle of the creatures they'd faced before. This was something calculated, something thinking. Eira stiffened, her senses brushing against the edges of its presence. It wasn't just alive—it was aware.

Rhys's grip tightened on his blade. "This isn't like the others," he muttered.

"No," Eira agreed, her voice low and steady though her pulse raced. "This one's hunting us."

A shadow shifted at the edge of the broken window. Not the amorphous, writhing darkness of the earlier monstrosities, but a humanoid silhouette, lean and almost graceful, its movements disturbingly precise. A glint of pale eyes flashed in the firelight, unblinking and far too intelligent.

"Get ready," Rhys murmured, his body lowering into a defensive stance.

The thing moved faster than Eira expected. It slipped through the narrow opening like liquid shadow, landing silently on the stone floor. The creature's features were wrong—too sharp, its limbs slightly too long, its movements eerily fluid. It tilted its head at them, almost studying them with something that might have been amusement.

Before Eira could react, it spoke—its voice a dry, rasping whisper. "The prophecy calls you forward… and yet you resist."

The sound of words coming from it sent a chill through her veins. "You understand us?" she asked, her magic sparking dangerously at her fingertips.

It tilted its head again, smiling with jagged teeth. "We do not need to understand you. We know you. You cannot outrun what has already been written."

"Then maybe I'll rewrite it," Rhys snarled, lunging forward.

The creature was faster. It dodged his strike with inhuman agility, its claws scraping across the wall as it tried to flank him. Eira unleashed a burst of shadowlight, forcing it back with a hiss. The blast scorched the stone, the air filling with the sharp tang of burned magic.

"Rhys, we can't stay here," she called, backing toward the exit. "If there's one, there might be more."

He slashed at the creature, driving it toward the broken doorway. "You think I want to stay?"

With a sharp, unspoken understanding, they moved together. Rhys struck again, his blade cutting a shallow line across the creature's chest. It shrieked, stumbling just enough for Eira to send a pulse of magic that blasted it into the outer wall, shattering part of the structure.

"Now!" Rhys grabbed her arm, pulling her through the opening before the creature could recover. The dawn was still pale and weak outside, the trees casting long shadows that made every movement feel like an ambush waiting to happen.

Eira glanced over her shoulder, her heart pounding. The creature had already risen, its jagged smile still curling as it stepped through the wreckage of the watchtower. "It's following us."

"Then we keep moving," Rhys said, his voice rough with urgency. "And we make sure it's the last thing that ever does."

The forest swallowed them in shadows as they fled the collapsing watchtower, the pale morning light struggling to pierce the thick canopy overhead. Every root and stone seemed poised to trip them, every gust of wind a whisper of pursuit. Eira's breath came fast, her heartbeat pounding like war drums as she ran, her shadowlight flaring faintly to light their path. Behind them, the creature's movements were silent but relentless, its presence a pulse of malice that crawled over her skin.

Rhys kept slightly ahead of her, his movements quick but calculated. "Stay close," he called over his shoulder, his voice low and firm. "It's fast, but it's not smarter than we are."

Eira nearly laughed—an incredulous, breathless sound—but bit it back. "Are you always this confident when something's trying to kill us?"

He glanced at her briefly, the faintest grin ghosting over his face. "Would you rather I panic?"

"Not exactly," she said, her tone strained as they vaulted over a fallen log. "But I'd prefer you don't tempt fate."

The ground sloped sharply, leading them into a dense thicket where the trees grew so close their branches wove together like skeletal fingers. Rhys slowed, motioning for her to do the same. He crouched low, his keen eyes scanning the dimly lit path. Eira followed his lead, her magic pulsing faintly, its vibrations warning her that the creature was near.

"Where?" she whispered.

Rhys tilted his head slightly, his brow furrowing. "It's circling us." He turned to her, his hand brushing hers as he whispered, "If it comes from behind, I'll take the hit. Focus on its core."

Her fingers tightened around his for the briefest moment. "I'm not letting you take anything alone, Rhys. Not anymore."

There was no time for him to respond. The air behind them shifted with a sudden rush, and the creature launched itself from the shadows. Rhys spun, his sword raised in a flash of silver, just as Eira's magic erupted from her hands in a blast of violet light. The combined strike slammed into the creature, but it twisted unnaturally, its body sliding like liquid around the attack.

"Go!" Rhys shouted, pushing her forward as he pivoted to block another swipe of its claws.

Eira hesitated for only a heartbeat, her instinct warring with reason. But then she turned, sending a wave of shadowlight up through the tangled branches. The trees answered her call, shuddering as their limbs cracked and shifted, collapsing behind them in a makeshift barrier.

They didn't stop running until they reached a narrow ravine, its shallow stream glinting with the weak light of dawn. Rhys bent over, catching his breath as he scanned their surroundings. "It'll break through eventually," he muttered, straightening.

Eira wiped sweat from her brow, her breath heavy. "Then we don't give it the chance. We keep moving."

Rhys looked at her then, really looked, and for a moment his sharp expression softened. "You're stronger than you know," he said quietly, almost like an afterthought.

Eira felt her chest tighten, the weight of his words pressing against something inside her she'd tried to keep locked away. "And you're better than you think," she replied.

His lips twitched into a faint smile, but he didn't answer. Instead, he reached out, his hand brushing her arm just long enough to steady her. "Ready?"

She nodded, though her gaze lingered on his for a beat longer than necessary.

The ravine narrowed as they pressed forward, its jagged walls looming like watchful sentinels. The shallow stream trickled at their feet, masking the sound of their steps but offering little comfort. Eira's shadowlight dimmed to a faint glow, just enough to illuminate the uneven rocks and twisted roots ahead. Every so often, Rhys would glance back at her, his gaze sharp and protective, scanning for the faintest hint of pursuit.

"Stay close to the wall," he murmured, his voice low and steady. "This place is a trap waiting to happen."

Eira adjusted her pace, brushing the cold, damp stone with her fingers as they moved. "Do you think it's still following us?"

Rhys gave a short, humorless laugh. "I don't think it's ever stopped." He tightened his grip on his sword, his knuckles white. "Something that smart doesn't give up. It learns."

The words sent a chill down her spine. She opened her mouth to respond when the ravine seemed to inhale—a sudden hush falling over the forest around them. The water stilled, the wind died, and an unnatural silence spread like a warning.

"Rhys," Eira whispered, her hand already sparking with shadowlight.

"Yeah," he said, his tone clipped as his eyes flicked toward the ridges above them. "I feel it too."

A flicker of movement darted across the ravine's lip, swift and predatory. Then another, on the opposite side. The creature—or perhaps more than one—was tracking them from above, its pale eyes glinting like shards of bone.

"Move," Rhys ordered, his hand brushing Eira's back as he guided her forward. "If we stay here, we're done."

They broke into a run, the narrow passage forcing them to stay close, almost shoulder to shoulder. Eira threw a pulse of shadowlight skyward, illuminating the jagged silhouette of the creature as it leapt between the walls, always just out of reach.

"Left!" Rhys shouted, pointing toward a jagged gap in the rock where the stream vanished. They ducked through just as the creature pounced, landing where they had stood seconds before, its claws raking the stone with a deafening screech.

They stumbled into a small cavern-like alcove, the air damp and heavy. Eira collapsed against the wall, her chest heaving, her hands still crackling with magic. Rhys crouched beside her, his sword resting across his knees as his gaze scanned the narrow entrance.

"That thing is playing with us," Eira said between breaths, her voice sharp with frustration.

"Let it try," Rhys muttered, his tone darker than before. "It'll regret underestimating us."

She turned her head to look at him, his face bathed in the pale glow of her magic. There was a rawness to his expression—exhaustion, determination, and something softer beneath the surface. "You always talk like you're invincible," she said, her voice quieter now, almost accusing.

Rhys tilted his head toward her, his lips curving in the faintest smile. "No. I just talk like I don't plan on leaving you to face this alone."

Her breath caught, the honesty in his words striking harder than any shadowborn threat. "Rhys…" She hesitated, her fingers brushing against his on the hilt of his sword. "I'm not sure I can do this without you. And I hate that I need you this much."

His hand shifted, turning to clasp hers. "Good," he said softly, his gaze holding hers with unflinching intensity. "Because I need you too. More than I'd like to admit."

The silence between them thickened, charged with everything they weren't yet brave enough to say. For a fleeting moment, it felt as though they were the only two people left in the world, their breath mingling, their hands lingering in a grip neither of them wanted to break.

The fragile quiet between them shattered with a guttural, scraping hiss that echoed through the alcove. Eira's pulse spiked. Rhys was already moving, his body tense as steel as he pulled her behind him. The shadow in the narrow entrance darkened, twisting into the jagged outline of the creature. Its pale eyes gleamed, glowing faintly in the dim light of her magic, and its unnerving grin stretched as though it knew exactly what it had trapped.

"Back-to-back," Rhys said sharply, his voice low but commanding. He positioned himself in the narrow center of the alcove, his sword raised, while Eira pressed close, her shoulder brushing his as her hands began to hum with shadowlight.

The creature lunged, its clawed limbs scraping across the walls, showering them with bits of rock. Rhys pivoted, his blade flashing in a tight arc that severed one of its hands. It shrieked, its cry bouncing painfully off the confined stone walls, but instead of retreating, it pressed forward with unnatural speed.

"Eira—now!"

She thrust her hands forward, a pulse of violet energy surging outward like a living wave. The blast hit the creature squarely, driving it back a step, but the confines of the space made it impossible for her to channel at full strength. It recovered too quickly, its liquid shadow form stretching unnaturally as it tried to slip around Rhys's defenses.

"Keep it off me!" he barked as he lunged, stabbing upward in a brutal thrust that pinned the creature's torso against the rock for a fleeting moment.

Eira gritted her teeth, her magic flaring brighter. She grabbed his shoulder for balance, pouring shadowlight down the blade like liquid fire. The sword ignited with her energy, the glow searing through the creature's form, which writhed and howled like mist caught in a storm.

Rhys didn't hesitate. With a fierce twist, he wrenched the blade free, their combined efforts tearing the creature apart in a burst of dark smoke and searing light. The sudden silence afterward was deafening, the air thick with heat and the metallic tang of magic.

Eira's knees buckled, the effort stealing her strength, but Rhys caught her instantly, his arm firm around her waist. For a moment, neither of them moved, both breathing heavily, their faces only inches apart.

"You all right?" he asked, his voice quieter now but rough with concern.

She swallowed hard, her fingers gripping the front of his shirt as she steadied herself. "I will be," she said softly, her gaze flicking up to meet his. "You didn't have to cover me like that. You could've been killed."

His lips curved into a small, tired smirk. "And leave you to deal with that thing alone? Not a chance." His tone softened, his eyes darkening as they held hers. "You should know by now—I'm not letting anything touch you if I can stop it."

Eira's breath caught, her chest tightening with a rush of emotion she couldn't name. The close press of his body, the heat of his hand at her back, the sheer intensity of his gaze—it all left her unsteady in a way no battle ever could.

The world narrowed to the faint echo of their breaths, the cooling glow of Eira's shadowlight, and the faint warmth of Rhys's hand where it rested against her back. Neither spoke at first; the silence was too thick, too raw. Eira's fingers were still curled into the fabric of his shirt, her pulse drumming beneath her skin.

"You keep doing that," she murmured, her voice low but edged with something vulnerable.

"Doing what?" Rhys asked, tilting his head slightly, though his grip on her remained firm.

"Throwing yourself between me and everything that wants to tear me apart," she replied. Her words trembled with a mix of frustration and gratitude. "You make it hard to remember that you're supposed to be impossible to trust."

His lips curved into the faintest smile, but his eyes were serious. "Maybe because I don't want to be impossible to trust. Not with you."

Her breath caught, and for a moment, she couldn't look away from him. The firelight in his gaze was sharper now, cutting through all the walls she'd tried to build. "You say things like that," she whispered, "and I don't know whether to be angry at you or—" She stopped, shaking her head, unable to find the right words.

"Or what?" His voice softened, almost teasing, but there was no mockery in it—only the quiet weight of a man who needed the answer.

"Or... trust you," she admitted finally, the word slipping past her lips like a confession she'd been holding for far too long. "And that terrifies me more than any creature we've faced."

Rhys's hand slid slightly from her back to her side, his touch steady but unhurried. "Good," he said, his voice low, his breath warm against her hair. "Because I feel the same. And I'm just reckless enough to think that maybe trusting you is the only thing keeping me alive right now."

The words settled between them, heavy and electric. For a heartbeat, Eira thought he might close the space between them, and she wasn't sure she would stop him if he did. But instead, he exhaled slowly and eased his hand away, the moment stretching into something unspoken but powerful.

"We should move," he said finally, his tone steady again, though his eyes betrayed the conflict lingering beneath. "That thing won't be the last."

Eira nodded, forcing herself to step back, though the loss of his warmth left her colder than she expected. "Then let's not give the next one the chance to corner us."

They stepped out of the alcove with cautious silence, the chill of the ravine clinging to their skin like a second shadow. The world outside was darker than it had any right to be, the dawn light swallowed by thick clouds that rolled low and heavy. Every sound seemed sharper—the crunch of loose gravel beneath their boots, the distant whisper of water flowing through the rocks, even the subtle cadence of each other's breath.

Rhys moved first, his gaze scanning the narrowing path ahead, his sword still in hand and his posture tense. Eira followed close behind, her fingers tingling with the echo of spent magic. Though they walked in silence, the words they hadn't spoken in the alcove seemed to hum between them, pulling tighter with every step. She caught herself studying the rigid line of his shoulders, wondering if the weight he carried was heavier because of her—or because of what he feared would come next.

The path twisted upward, forcing them to climb a jagged incline where black stone jutted from the earth like broken teeth. Moss coated the rocks in patches, slick and treacherous beneath their boots. A gust of cold wind swept through, carrying with it the scent of ash and damp earth—a reminder of the decay that lingered in this land.

Rhys offered his hand as they scaled a steep outcrop. For a moment, Eira hesitated, stubborn pride warring with practicality, but then she took it. His grip was strong, steady, and too warm for someone who lived so much of his life in the cold shadow of the past. When he pulled her up beside him, she didn't let go right away, and neither did he.

"Careful," he murmured, his eyes catching hers in a look that lingered just a heartbeat too long.

Eira exhaled softly. "You're starting to sound like you actually care if I fall."

"Starting to?" His tone carried a flicker of dry humor, but the way his thumb brushed against her palm betrayed more than he intended.

She gave him a sidelong glance, half-smiling despite the tension. "Don't get sentimental on me, Rhys. It doesn't suit you."

"Maybe it suits you enough for the both of us," he replied, the corner of his mouth twitching in a smirk as he finally released her hand.

The banter did little to ease the lingering weight pressing down on them. The air itself seemed to grow thicker the farther they climbed, the light dimming as if the world was holding its breath again. Eira's shadowlight stirred uneasily beneath her skin, warning her of something ahead.

"Do you feel that?" she asked quietly, her eyes narrowing as she scanned the horizon.

"Yeah," Rhys said, his tone hardening. "Something's waiting. And it's smart enough to let us come to it."

The ridge leveled out into a narrow plateau, the path widening just enough for them to walk side by side. But Eira's steps slowed as a strange pattern caught her eye—disturbed earth, claw marks etched deep into the stone, and blackened streaks of ichor that had not yet dried. The signs were fresh, too fresh. She crouched down, running her fingers lightly over one of the jagged grooves. The air here was wrong, heavier, as if the shadows themselves were leaning closer to listen.

"Rhys," she said, her voice barely above a whisper, "we're not alone."

He knelt beside her, his hand brushing over another gouge. His brow furrowed, and his jaw tightened. "No," he agreed, his voice low and grim. "These marks—they're from more than one creature. At least three, maybe four. Whatever's stalking us isn't just that thing from the watchtower." He straightened, his posture taut, every movement deliberate. "We're walking right into their nest."

Eira's chest tightened. "So what do we do? Keep climbing and hope they don't strike, or..."

"Or we stop pretending we're not being hunted," Rhys cut in, his tone sharp. He scanned the terrain—the twisted trees growing from cracks in the plateau, the jagged outcrops of rock that could offer either cover or a perfect vantage for an ambush. His hand rested on the hilt of his sword, but his other hand brushed hers in a fleeting, grounding touch. "If we keep running, they'll pick us off one by one. We choose the ground, not them."

The warmth of his fingers lingered on her skin, sending a wave of steadiness through her chest despite the creeping dread. "You sound like you've done this before," she said, forcing a breath she hadn't realized she was holding.

"Too many times," Rhys replied, his eyes hardening as he studied the path ahead. "The thing about predators—they get cocky when they think you're cornered. That's when they're weakest."

Eira rose, her shadowlight sparking faintly along her hands. "So we make them come to us."

His lips twitched into the ghost of a grin. "That's the spirit. Just try not to burn me when you're throwing that fire around."

Her brow arched. "Maybe if you stay out of my way."

The banter was thin armor, but it helped blunt the edge of fear. Together, they moved to a more defensible spot—a low cluster of rocks surrounded by the sparse remains of thorny shrubs. From there, they had a clear line of sight in three directions, though the fourth was blocked by a narrow canyon that seemed to breathe with its own chill.

Eira crouched low, her eyes scanning the horizon as she felt for the threads of magic winding through the landscape. "It's close," she murmured. "I can feel them watching."

Rhys crouched beside her, his shoulder brushing hers. "Then let them watch. We'll be ready when they strike." He turned to her, his gaze briefly softening despite the tension thrumming through the air. "I meant what I said, Eira. I'm not letting anything get to you—not while I'm breathing."

Her heart skipped, but she forced herself to hold his gaze. "Then you'd better keep breathing," she said quietly.

The first strike came like lightning. A dark shape leapt from the jagged rocks above, its clawed limbs catching the faint light as it plummeted toward them. Rhys reacted instantly, his sword flashing upward to deflect the creature's strike. The impact sent a jolt through his arm, but he pivoted with it, driving the blade deep into the thing's side. It shrieked, its form writhing like liquid shadow before crumbling into black mist.

"Two more," Eira hissed, her shadowlight already building around her hands. She could feel them closing in—one moving low through the thorns, the other circling high on the ridge behind them.

Rhys didn't need her warning. He lunged toward the thicket, cutting through the brush in a controlled arc, the edge of his blade catching the second creature as it tried to flank them. Eira raised her hand, sending a pulse of violet energy through the canyon wall behind him. The burst illuminated the third creature clinging there like a grotesque spider, its pale eyes fixed on her.

"Eira!" Rhys shouted, spinning just as the creature leapt.

She planted her feet, her power snapping through the air in a concentrated beam. The magic hit the creature mid-lunge, hurling it backward against the rock with a sound like shattering glass. But the force of the spell left her gasping, her vision swimming.

"Stay with me," Rhys growled, placing himself between her and the recovering shadow-creature. "On my mark, you burn it. I'll hold it still."

"Don't be reckless," she shot back, though her voice was thin, the echo of her magic vibrating in her bones.

"Reckless is what we do best," he said, his lips curling into a sharp grin before he charged.

The creature slashed at him, its limbs elongating unnaturally as if mocking the limits of flesh. Rhys ducked low, driving his shoulder into its core with brutal precision. He slammed it against the rock, pinning it there. "Now, Eira!"

Eira's magic flared, brighter and fiercer than before. She summoned every ounce of her strength, the shadowlight twisting around her like a storm as she hurled it forward. The blast struck true, her energy meeting the tip of Rhys's blade, amplifying its force. The creature let out a piercing wail, its body dissolving into a violent burst of black smoke and sparks of violet light.

The silence that followed was deafening. Rhys staggered back, his breath ragged, his sword still glowing faintly from the residue of her power. Eira's knees nearly buckled, but he caught her again, his arms steadying her before she could collapse.

"Are you hurt?" he asked, his voice low but urgent, his eyes scanning her as if searching for wounds.

"Only... exhausted," she admitted, leaning into him despite herself. "That was... close."

Rhys's hand tightened on her arm. "Too close. We need to move before more of them find us." His gaze softened as he added, almost reluctantly, "You saved my life. Again."

Eira's lips quirked into a faint smile, despite the ache in her body. "We saved each other."

The tension between them thickened once more, but this time it wasn't born from fear—it was the raw, unspoken bond forged by the chaos they'd just survived. Rhys didn't look away, his hand still lingering on her back, the warmth of his touch pulling her dangerously close to saying something she wasn't sure she could take back.

They moved cautiously through the aftermath of the ambush, each step deliberate as the adrenaline slowly bled from their veins. Rhys led them to a small clearing at the edge of the plateau, where a fallen tree provided a semblance of shelter. The air here was clearer, the wind cutting away the lingering stench of shadow and ichor. Eira collapsed against the trunk, her chest rising and falling with the rhythm of exhaustion.

Rhys dropped to a crouch beside her, his sword laid across his knees. He glanced over at her, his brow furrowed as he noted the tremor in her hands. "You're burning too fast," he said quietly, his tone carrying no judgment—only concern. "Every time you pour that much magic out, you're left shaking."

Eira exhaled, forcing her breathing to steady. "You think I don't notice? It's like the shadowlight wants to devour me from the inside. But if I hold back, we'd both be dead." She paused, her gaze flickering to meet his. "It's worth the risk."

His jaw tightened as he looked at her, something raw flashing behind his eyes. "It's not worth losing you. Not like that."

She froze, the words cutting through her like an arrow. The sincerity in his voice left no room for jest or sarcasm. "You don't get to say things like that unless you mean them," she murmured.

He leaned back slightly, his gaze steady on hers. "I don't say anything I don't mean."

The silence that followed was heavy, charged with all the emotions neither of them dared name. Eira looked away first, her hand brushing the ground as if to anchor herself. "I'm not used to this," she admitted, her voice softer now. "To trusting someone enough to fight like this. To... caring what happens to them."

Rhys's lips curved in the faintest smile, though it didn't reach his eyes. "You think I am? I've spent years making sure no one got close enough to matter. And now, here we are."

She turned to him again, searching his face. "So what are we, then? Allies? Or something else neither of us is ready to admit?"

For a moment, he didn't answer. Instead, he reached out, his fingers brushing hers lightly—a fleeting, hesitant touch, but it was enough to make her heart skip. "Whatever we are," he said, voice low, "it's the only thing that feels real in this nightmare."

Eira's breath caught, her chest tightening with something she couldn't name. She wanted to tell him how much she needed him—how much she feared losing him—but the words tangled on her tongue. Instead, she squeezed his hand briefly before letting go. "Then let's make sure we get out of this alive," she said, her tone steadier now.

Rhys smirked faintly. "Sounds like a plan."

Rhys rose to his feet, scanning the perimeter with sharp, calculating eyes. The forest beyond the clearing seemed to lean in on them, every shadow elongated, every whisper of wind a threat waiting to reveal itself. He tightened his grip on his sword before turning back to Eira. "We can't stay here. If those things regroup, we'll be boxed in before we know it."

Eira forced herself upright, the lingering ache from the battle making her movements slow but deliberate. "You're right. I can feel them," she said, her voice quiet but tense. "The shadowlight inside me—it's like it's pulling toward them. There are more out there. Watching." Her gaze flickered toward the treeline, her fingers twitching as faint sparks of violet light danced along her skin.

Rhys stepped closer, his presence grounding her. "Then we keep moving until we find somewhere they can't track us," he said. His tone was calm, but there was a quiet urgency behind his words. "I know a ridge about an hour from here. It's high ground, with caves that'll give us cover. We can hold out there."

She nodded, trusting him without question. The thought struck her then—how natural it felt to let him lead, how easily she'd begun to rely on his strength and instincts. It both comforted and unsettled her in equal measure.

The trek was silent, save for the rhythmic crunch of their boots against dirt and stone. The tension between them was palpable, a mix of exhaustion, unspoken words, and the shared awareness that danger stalked them with every step. Eira stayed close, not out of fear, but because she felt safer with the subtle brush of his presence beside her—safer with the way he would glance at her from the corner of his eye, as if to make sure she was still there.

When they finally reached the ridge, the caves appeared like dark mouths carved into the rock, half-concealed by trailing vines and jagged stone. Rhys checked the area meticulously, his every movement deliberate, before signaling for Eira to enter one of the larger caves. The interior was cool and dry, the stone walls etched with marks that might have been carved by centuries of wind or claw.

"We'll be safe here for the night," Rhys said, lighting a small fire from the kindling he'd gathered. Its glow softened the hard lines of his face, casting shadows that danced across the cavern walls. He set his sword within easy reach, then settled onto the ground beside her.

Eira stretched out slowly, her body aching as she sank into the rough but blessedly solid ground. For a while, the fire was their only companion, its crackle a fragile comfort against the silence. She turned her head to study Rhys, the exhaustion making her thoughts unguarded.

"You didn't have to keep pulling me out of danger today," she said, her voice low. "But you did. Every time."

He looked at her, his gaze steady. "Every time was worth it." His tone held no hesitation, no sarcasm—only a quiet truth that made her chest tighten.

Eira's breath caught. She wanted to say something—something about the way he made her feel stronger and more vulnerable all at once—but the words wouldn't come. Instead, she gave him a small, almost shy smile and whispered, "Try to get some rest. We'll need our strength tomorrow."

Rhys leaned back, stretching out beside her with just enough space between them to feel deliberate. But she could still sense the warmth of him, the steady rhythm of his breath mingling with hers. "I'll rest," he murmured, his tone softening. "But only because I know you're safe. At least for tonight."

The words lingered, warm and heavy, as they both lay in the dim firelight, neither truly sleeping but content to let the silence fill with unspoken understanding.

The firelight flickered softly, throwing wavering shadows across the walls of the cave. Eira lay on her side, her back half-turned to the flames, watching the dance of light and dark as though the movement might give her thoughts shape. Rhys sat with his back against the rough stone, his sword resting across his lap, though his grip on it had loosened now that they had a moment of peace.

"You don't have to stay awake all night," she said quietly, her voice carrying in the stillness.

Rhys glanced down at her, his expression softened by the warm glow. "And risk something creeping in while we're both dead to the world? Not likely." His tone was casual, but there was an undercurrent of protectiveness there—a weight that made Eira's chest tighten.

"You carry everything like it's your responsibility," she murmured, turning fully to face him. "Even me."

His lips curved slightly, but it wasn't a smile—it was something more guarded, more complicated. "Maybe because it is," he replied. "Maybe because... somewhere along the way, making sure you're safe became the only thing that feels like it matters."

The words hung in the air between them, heavier than any silence could be. Eira swallowed hard, her fingers curling in the thin blanket beneath her. "You shouldn't say things like that," she whispered, her voice trembling just slightly. "Not when we don't know what tomorrow will bring."

Rhys's gaze didn't waver. "Then let me say them while I still can." He leaned forward slightly, the firelight catching in his dark eyes, making them seem almost molten. "Eira, I'm not good with words. I've spent years being nothing but what I had to be—cold, sharp, untouchable. But with you, I..." He stopped, his jaw tightening. "You make me forget that I'm supposed to be unbreakable."

Her breath caught, her heart stuttering in her chest. She wanted to reach for him, to close the space between them, but something—fear, or perhaps the weight of what was coming—held her back. "Rhys…" she said softly, "you're not the only one who feels that way."

For a heartbeat, neither moved. The flicker of the fire painted the distance between them in gold and shadow, a fragile line neither dared cross. Then Rhys eased back, his gaze soft but lingering, as though he had made a silent promise to remember this moment, to hold onto it even when everything else turned to ash.

"Get some sleep," he said gently, his voice quieter now, almost tender. "I'll keep watch."

Eira closed her eyes, though not before she caught the faintest trace of something vulnerable in his expression. As she drifted into an uneasy rest, she thought of his words, of the warmth of his presence beside her, and the dangerous hope that curled inside her chest like a flame refusing to be smothered.

Rhys stayed awake long after her breathing evened, staring into the fire as though it held all the answers he would never have. And when he finally whispered, "I can't lose you," it was to no one but the shadows.

Chapter Eight:

The Forest That Remembers

Dawn broke with a cold hush, the kind that did not sing or stretch but crept. The first light touched the horizon like an uncertain hand, casting the ridge in muted golds and silvers, though it could not chase away the chill that settled deep into stone and bone. Mist clung to the treetops and pooled low over the ground like memory given form—unmoving, watchful, and dense enough to muffle even birdsong.

Eira stirred first. Her eyes opened to a pale ceiling of rock and trailing vines, her body still aching from the prior night's battle. She rolled onto her back, the faint scent of ash and steel lingering in her senses. Rhys sat near the cave mouth, just beyond the reach of the dying fire. He hadn't slept. She could see it in the quiet tension in his shoulders, in the stiffness of his posture that didn't ease even when the light touched him.

"You should've woken me," she murmured as she pushed herself upright, voice still thick with sleep.

Rhys didn't look at her immediately. "You needed the rest more than I did." His tone was gentle, but worn at the edges, like a blade that had seen too much grindstone.

She wrapped her cloak tighter around her, walking over to stand beside him at the cave's edge. From here, the wilds of Vaelwyth spread out below them like a fractured tapestry—trees like crooked spires, rivers that glinted like veins of mercury. The world looked wounded, as if the land itself remembered every battle fought across its soil.

"There's something in the air," Eira said, frowning. "The magic feels... unsettled."

Rhys finally turned to her, his eyes darker than before. "It's changing. I felt it all night—like it was watching us. And whatever attacked us yesterday wasn't acting alone."

Eira's fingers twitched. Her shadowlight sparked faintly, reacting to a presence just beyond perception. "We're being pulled deeper into this. The prophecy, the creatures, the land—it's all turning inward, like a snare tightening around our ankles."

He stood, shouldering his pack and tightening the strap of his scabbard. "Then we don't give it the chance to close. We stay ahead of it."

As they began their descent from the ridge, the mist seemed to follow them, trailing like smoke from the corners of their vision. The trees bent in ways that defied the wind. The path narrowed, the air thick with tension neither of them could dispel.

The trees closed in around them like a cage of blackened ribs, each one warped as though it had been bent mid-scream. Gnarled branches reached overhead, curling into one another so tightly they blotted out the morning light, casting the forest into a twilight gloom. A pale mist slithered between the trunks, coiling at their feet and soaking the path in a damp, unnatural silence. No wind. No birds. Only the sound of their breath and the slow crunch of boots against sodden earth.

Eira felt the pull first—soft, insidious, like a whisper brushing the edge of her mind. At first she thought it was memory. A flicker of her mother's voice, a cool hand on her brow, the scent of lavender and rain. She paused, blinking against the sensation, heart hitching in her chest. But when she looked up, the forest had shifted. Rhys was no longer at her side.

"Rhys?" Her voice was calm, measured—but it didn't carry. It seemed to vanish into the fog, like water poured into sand. She turned in a slow circle. Trees. Mist. Shadows layered so thick they distorted depth and distance.

Then a voice, just behind her. Her own voice.

"You never should've trusted him."

Eira spun, light flaring in her palm. Nothing. Only silence and the faint scent of moss and rot. Her pulse thudded painfully in her ears as the forest thickened around her. She could feel the shadowlight inside her twisting, reacting to the illusion. It fed off emotion. Fear. Doubt.

Elsewhere—nearby but unreachable—Rhys froze mid-step. One moment Eira had been beside him, the next, gone. He turned sharply, sword half-raised. "Eira?" No answer. The fog thickened. Something moved in the corner of his eye. A familiar silhouette.

It was her—Eira—standing in the mist, her expression unreadable. But something was wrong. Her shadowlight flickered erratically, and her eyes were too dark.

"You left me behind," the vision said, voice like cracking glass. "Again. Just like the others."

Rhys's grip tightened on his sword. "No. You're not her."

The illusion smiled. "Aren't I? You keep telling yourself you're protecting her—but you know you're going to destroy her."

He stepped forward, his voice low. "If you were real, you'd know I've already destroyed myself to keep her safe."

The figure dissolved into smoke. Behind him, another form moved. His younger brother, bloodied and pale, standing as he had the day Rhys failed him. "Stop," Rhys growled, shaking his head. "You don't belong here."

Meanwhile, Eira pushed through the warped trunks, her breathing ragged, her heart hammering. She whispered a grounding spell beneath her breath, light flaring along her collarbones. The illusions faltered slightly. A girl's face appeared in the mist—her younger self, wild-eyed and trembling.

"You've always been dangerous," the child-Eira said. "They were right to fear you."

Eira's voice broke. "That's not who I am anymore."

"You'll kill him too. Just like the rest."

"No."

She pressed her palm to a nearby tree, letting her magic surge. The bark split with a groan, and the mist recoiled. "You don't get to rewrite my truth," she said fiercely.

Through the veil of fog, a figure appeared—real this time. Rhys. Staggering forward, pale but solid. Their eyes met, and for a breathless moment, neither moved.

"Eira," he rasped.

She crossed the distance between them in three fast steps. Her hand closed around his arm, grounding them both. "It's trying to divide us," she said. "Feed off what we fear most."

Rhys nodded once, his voice ragged. "Then we don't give it the chance."

Their fingers twined without thinking, and together, they stepped into the heart of the forest.

The forest was not done with them.

As Eira and Rhys moved deeper into the gloom, their joined hands grew colder, as though the very air between them soured. The mist thickened into near-opacity, muffling every step, swallowing every breath. Light flickered and fractured, their surroundings shifting like the surface of disturbed water. The trees now leaned inward, their bark glistening like oil, branches creaking in a wind that didn't exist.

Then, without warning, their connection severed. Eira's fingers grasped only air.

"Rhys?" she called, spinning. No answer. Panic surged through her chest like a second heartbeat.

A shape stood before her.

It wasn't the forest. It was Rhys. Pale. Blood soaking his shirt. A blade in her hand—her blade—dripping shadowlight.

"You did this," the vision accused. His voice was hollow, more echo than sound. "You always would."

She staggered back, heart pounding, breath shallow. "No. That's not real. That's not you."

The vision stepped forward. "You think loving someone means you won't destroy them?"

The shadows curled tighter around her throat, feeding off guilt, her terror blooming into something close to despair.

Across the veil, Rhys fought his own specter.

A mirror of himself, smiling with cruel eyes, stepped from the trees. This version of Rhys moved with certainty, arrogance.

"You want her to trust you," it sneered. "You think your feelings make you strong. But you're the one who handed over the blade that killed her world."

Rhys gritted his teeth. "I didn't know. I couldn't have known."

"You think she'll forgive you when she learns what you were before?" The specter stepped closer. "You think she'll stay?"

His sword trembled in his grip.

Then, Eira's voice cut through the haze—soft but steady. "Rhys... I'm still here."

He turned, shoving through the fog, each step a struggle against the weight of dread.

And there she was, knees in the moss, breathing hard, her shadowlight flaring defensively.

He dropped beside her. "Eira. Look at me. That's not your truth."

She blinked, tears bright on her lashes, but her gaze locked to his. "Then tell me it's not yours, either."

"I'd rather die than lose you to it."

Their fingers found each other again, grounding. Shadowlight and steel—glow and grit.

The forest screamed. Not aloud, but within the marrow of their bones. A wrenching, bitter groan as the illusions began to peel away, stripped back by the raw light of unity the forest could not distort.

The mist thinned. The path opened.

Together, they stepped out into the dying light at the forest's edge, not untouched, but unbroken.

The trees behind them stood still, as if holding their breath. The twisted canopy gave way to a glade that opened beneath a silver-streaked sky, moonlight spilling across the clearing in quiet defiance of the darkness they had escaped. It wasn't warmth they stepped into—just space. Air that didn't cling. Light that didn't lie.

Eira moved first, her steps slow, unsure. Her hand was still locked in Rhys's, her palm damp with sweat, the memory of illusion not yet shaken from her skin. The glade had a stillness to it that didn't feel empty but reverent, like the land itself knew what they had just endured.

She knelt in the soft grass, her legs trembling, not from exhaustion but from the quiet ache of too many truths laid bare. Rhys stood beside her for a moment longer, watching the way her shoulders curled inward as though trying to protect something fragile in her chest. Then he sat down beside her, close enough that their knees brushed.

Neither spoke for a while.

The moonlight painted his face in ghostly silver, the dark circles under his eyes deeper now. He leaned back on his palms and stared upward, as if he could lose himself in the stars. "I saw things in there," he said finally, his voice low and rough. "Things I thought I'd buried so deep they couldn't find me anymore."

Eira didn't look at him. She traced idle patterns into the moss, her fingers glowing faintly with residual shadowlight. "The forest didn't show me anything new. It just made me believe it could be real." She paused. "It showed me you. Dead. By my hand."

He turned to her, his jaw tight. "And it showed me you... leaving. Not with your feet, but with your trust."

That made her look up. Their eyes met in the quiet, no illusion between them now, just the soft hush of wind in leaves and the ache of things neither had said until now.

"I don't want to be afraid of you," she whispered. "Of what I could do to you. Or what you could do to me."

Rhys's expression softened, and he leaned forward slightly, his hand brushing her cheek just enough to ground her. "Then don't be. Whatever the prophecy says, whatever the shadowlight becomes... I won't let it turn you into something you're not. And if it does—"

"No," she interrupted, catching his wrist. "You don't get to make that decision alone. Not anymore."

He held her gaze, and the tension that always lived between them now felt like something else. Something deeper. Their pain had been laid bare in the forest—and still, they were here.

Eira exhaled slowly and leaned her head against his shoulder. Not a surrender. A choice.

Rhys let her rest there, his eyes drifting to the stars again. For now, there were no monsters in the dark. No shadows creeping at the edge of their bond. Just silence, and breath, and the quiet promise that no illusion—no curse—would unravel what they were becoming.

Tomorrow, the world would claw at them again. But tonight, beneath the stars, they were whole.

The glade slept with them, or so it seemed—until it didn't.

Eira jolted awake first, her heart thudding in her throat, the shadowlight inside her reacting before her mind fully grasped the cause. Her palm lit with a soft violet pulse as her body snapped upright, breath catching in the back of her throat.

Rhys was already moving, rolling into a crouch with his blade half drawn. "What is it?" he asked, eyes sharp in the moonlight, scanning the dark.

They both turned toward the edge of the glade, where a rustling sound cut through the stillness—low and erratic, followed by a hollow snap of underbrush. Every muscle in Eira's body tensed. Rhys moved in front of her on instinct. The silence that followed stretched too long to be innocent.

Then came the answer—an animal. A deer, its antlers tipped with moss, eyes wide and white with fear. It burst from the thicket, paused as if realizing it wasn't alone, and bolted across the clearing with a flash of hooves and silence.

They both stood still for several breaths longer, muscles tight, until the realization sank in.

"Just a deer," Rhys muttered, sheathing his sword. He let out a sharp breath, the tension unraveling slowly.

Eira sat back down hard, rubbing her hands over her face. "I almost melted that poor creature's spine."

Rhys gave a low laugh, his voice gravel-thick from lingering adrenaline. "Would've made an excellent midnight snack."

She threw him a look, half a glare and half a smirk, and then lay back on the moss again, her shadowlight fading. "I'll never get used to this," she said softly. "Sleeping with one eye open. Waiting for everything we love or fear to leap from the trees."

He lowered himself beside her once more, lying on his side, facing her in the low firelight. "It's not just you anymore, Eira. I'm here too. That changes everything."

Her throat tightened, but she held his gaze. "That's what scares me."

"Why?" he asked gently. "Because you'll lose me? Or because you think you'll break me?"

She didn't answer immediately. The shadows stretched between them, the fire crackling low. "Because if I break you, I'll lose myself too."

Rhys reached for her hand in the dark, finding it easily. "Then we don't break," he said. "Or if we do, we put each other back together again."

Their fingers laced slowly, deliberately. The moment wasn't romantic—not in the storybook sense. It was raw. Honest. The kind of closeness that could only be forged by shared wounds and sleepless nights.

"You're not what I expected," she whispered, not pulling her hand away.

He tilted his head, a faint smile tugging at his lips. "And you're everything I didn't realize I needed."

They didn't say more. They didn't need to. As the fire dimmed and the forest kept its peace, they rested again—this time closer, not just by proximity, but by something harder won: trust.

The night held them in a cradle of silver and shadow, as if the forest itself had exhaled and, for once, chose not to haunt them. The fire dwindled to a low bed of embers, casting a flickering glow over the two figures lying close, the barest distance between their bodies hinting at something unspoken, delicate, and rising.

Above them, the sky had begun to shift, stars dimming as the earliest suggestion of dawn kissed the horizon—a hush of violet pressed gently into indigo. It was a fragile hour, a breath caught between darkness and day, and in it, they slept. Not with the restless edge of survival, but with the tentative peace of people who had endured something ancient together and come out not unscathed, but still whole.

Eira's fingers remained tangled with Rhys's, his presence no longer just protection but anchor. And for once, her dreams did not claw. They shimmered—half-formed visions of laughter never yet shared, of roads not yet taken, and of the dangerous, tender space between who they were and who they might become.

Outside the cave of sleep, the forest stilled. No whispers. No illusions. Only breath.

But far beyond the treeline, something stirred in the roots of the world—ancient, waiting.

And the dawn, when it came, would not come quietly.

Chapter Nine:

The Stone That Shouldn't Be

The glade was bathed in soft gold, a hush of light that filtered gently through the trees, painting the moss in molten tones. Dawn had come not with trumpets or wind, but like a held breath released slowly, reverently. The forest remained still, the mist burned off, the night's memories lingering only in the smell of extinguished embers and the quiet rhythm of two steady heartbeats.

Eira stirred first. Her lashes fluttered against her cheeks as the light warmed her face, and she blinked herself into waking. The world was quieter than it should have been. Even the birdsong seemed hesitant, as if nature itself waited for something else to rise. She turned her head, finding Rhys beside her, his arm just close enough to brush hers. He hadn't moved in the night.

She let her gaze wander—and that was when she saw it.

A glint beneath the ash of their campfire.

Eira sat up slowly, brushing her fingers through the remains of the coals. Her touch found something cold, something smooth where there should have only been dirt and stone. She dug gently, sweeping aside the blackened fragments until it revealed itself: a small, flat slab of polished stone. Oval-shaped. Unmarked by soot or time—except for a single carved sigil in its center.

Her breath caught.

The symbol pulsed faintly, no brighter than a heartbeat. A circle, half swallowed in shadow, intersected by a blade of light. She had never seen it before… and yet, she knew it.

Rhys stirred beside her. "What is it?" he asked groggily, pushing himself up to his elbows. But when he saw her face—tense, pale, transfixed—he moved quickly to her side.

She didn't answer, only pointed.

He crouched next to her, eyes narrowing as he traced the sigil with a single fingertip. The moment he touched it, the air in the glade shifted. Not wind—pressure. Like something unseen had turned to look at them.

"I've seen this before," he said quietly. "Not in books. Not in memory. In dreams."

Eira nodded slowly, her voice barely a whisper. "Me too."

They sat in silence, the stone between them, the sun rising like an eye above the forest. The glade that had offered refuge now felt different—charged, expectant.

Whatever lay ahead, the world had just drawn a new line in their path.

And neither of them would cross it unchanged.

Rhys turned the stone over in his palm, his thumb brushing over the carved sigil again and again, as if repetition might coax some hidden truth from its cold surface. Eira sat beside him in the fading shadow of the fire, her knees pulled close, gaze fixed on the way the morning light glanced off the stone's strange, polished sheen. Neither of them spoke for several breaths—there was a weight to the silence, one that clung like dew.

"It's not just shadowlight," she murmured finally. "Whatever this is… it's older. Deeper. Like the forest left us a message, but forgot how to speak."

Rhys nodded slowly. "Or maybe it never spoke in the first place. Maybe it only shows what we're already meant to find."

She frowned, reaching into the folds of her cloak to retrieve the worn leather notebook she kept pressed against her ribs. Flipping past pages of hastily scribbled runes and fragmented prophecy, she drew a clean one and sketched the symbol from memory. Then, beside it, she wrote: Watcher's Eye. Shadow divided. Blade of dawn. Blood path.

Rhys watched her, then nodded to the sketch. "You think it's a map?"

"I think it's a warning," she said, voice tight. "A choice. Or a threshold."

He stood, slipping the stone into his pack and offering her his hand. "Then whatever it is, we meet it head-on. Together."

Their packs were lighter than they should have been. Their legs heavier. But they stepped out of the glade with a sense of quiet resolve, the kind that came after truths were unearthed, after fears were shared. Yet as they walked down the familiar slope that had brought them to safety the night before, the world around them shifted.

The trees were not the same.

Branches leaned at angles that hadn't existed yesterday. Moss grew on the wrong side of trunks. The slope that should have curved east now dipped south. Even the sun felt misaligned, casting long shadows that pointed the wrong direction.

Eira paused, her boots sinking slightly into damp moss. "Rhys... this isn't the way we came."

"I know," he said, his jaw tight. "I've walked this terrain enough to know when it's lying to me."

The path narrowed to a corridor of crooked stone, the roots overhead woven like ribs, the way ahead swallowed in soft, humming fog.

Eira looked at him, her fingers brushing the side of his hand. "We keep going?"

His smile was thin, but steady. "We never stopped."

They walked forward, into a wilderness that was no longer just wild—but watching.

The forest ahead was quieter than silence itself. Even the wind dared not stir. As Eira and Rhys moved beneath the arching limbs of the new path, the air began to thicken—not with mist this time, but memory. It hung in the light like dust motes that never quite settled, glimmering faintly before vanishing the second either of them tried to focus.

Then the trees changed.

Not visibly at first—but subtly. Their bark lost its gnarled ridges and became smooth, pale, almost polished. The scent of soil and moss gave way to something drier. Ash and parchment. Candlewax and old ink.

Eira's pace slowed. Her breath caught.

A corridor opened before them—columns of tall, symmetrical trees that resembled the interior of the Sanctum where she had first trained in secret. She knew this place. Not as it had been in the world, but as it lived in her memory.

"I know this," she whispered. "This is the Echo Hall. My—my instructor brought me here after my first failed casting. She said... she said shadowlight doesn't answer fear. Only need."

Rhys said nothing, but his eyes flicked from the trunks to the shadows between them.

They kept walking, and the world kept shifting.

Now the trees bent into arches, stained by smoke and red-tinted light. The ground sloped, turning to gravel and scorched stone. Eira felt the heat before she saw the blackened doorway.

Rhys stopped cold. His shoulders stiffened, and a muscle in his jaw jumped.

"Rhys?"

He didn't answer.

A building rose from the trees—impossible in this wilderness, but there all the same. A fortress gate, half-cracked, iron and stone melted from within.

Eira looked between him and the illusion. "Where is this?"

He didn't move. "I watched it burn," he said, voice low and flat. "I set the fire. This was the Shadowborn archive."

She stepped closer. "You destroyed it?"

"I had to. They... they were performing something—something I wasn't supposed to see. Sacrifices. Of children. Half-trained initiates too weak to survive their trials. They said it was cleansing. I said it was slaughter."

The shadows shifted. Screams echoed faintly—not loud, but distant, like voices heard underwater.

Eira gripped his arm. "Rhys—this isn't real. It's memory."

"I know," he said, but his voice cracked. "But it still burns."

The ground beneath them trembled, not with an earthquake—but with the pulse of old grief refusing to stay buried. The shadowlight responded to it, feeding on it.

Eira stepped in front of him and reached for both his hands, forcing him to look at her. "You're not him anymore. Whatever you were then—whatever you did—you walked away from it. That matters."

He looked at her as though she were the first solid thing in a collapsing world. "And what about you?" he asked. "If it showed me this... what does it still want to show you?"

The answer came before she could.

A door opened behind them, grown into the side of a tree. A child's voice called out.

"Eira? Why did you leave me?"

She turned slowly.

And froze.

The voice was impossibly familiar.

High, small, and trembling with betrayal. Eira turned slowly toward the twisted archway that had grown out of the tree, the bark spiraling around it like ribs enclosing a wound. The shape beyond it shimmered—not fully formed, but solid enough to make her chest collapse inward.

A child stood there. Barefoot, hair tangled with leaves, eyes wide with hope. She couldn't have been more than eight years old.

And Eira knew her.

Not as a stranger, not as an echo. But as her sister.

"Lysa?" she whispered, the name breaking past her lips like a forgotten prayer. Her knees threatened to give out. "No, this—this isn't possible."

The little girl tilted her head, her voice laced with accusation wrapped in sorrow. "You said you'd come back. You promised."

Eira took a step forward, breath ragged. "You were already gone. I saw what the plague did. I saw what the priests left behind—"

"No," Lysa interrupted, the child's form flickering. "I called for you. I was still alive when the doors closed. I waited until I couldn't breathe. Until the shadows came. And you were learning magic while I died in the dark."

Eira staggered, reaching for the edge of a nearby tree to brace herself. Her hands burned with magic, but it had no shape, no purpose. Only pain.

"I was a child too," she said, the words trembling with weight. "I didn't know. I didn't understand what they were doing."

"You understand now," the illusion said softly.

Behind her, Rhys didn't move. He stood perfectly still, watching Eira as the specter of her past bled into her present.

He could stop it. He knew how. A pulse of shadowlight, a disruption of the illusion's tether—but at what cost?

She was facing something no spell could fix. Something that could harden or shatter the bond she was only just beginning to trust.

He took a breath, his fingers twitching. Then paused.

The decision hung between action and faith.

Rhys's breath caught in his throat as he watched her—shoulders squared but trembling, hands glowing with a storm that had no release. Eira stood like someone carved in defiance and regret, poised between two worlds: the woman she had become and the girl who'd once made a promise too heavy for her hands.

He didn't move. Didn't speak.

Instead, he let the moment hold.

He had seen what magic could do when stolen too soon. He'd seen what happened to people forced to face pain too deep, too young. But this—this was not his battle. This was hers.

Eira took a slow breath, drawing it through her nose until her lungs ached. The forest pulsed with expectation. Lysa's figure flickered in the threshold of the tree—less solid now, more like a memory begging to be rewritten.

"You weren't supposed to haunt me," Eira said, her voice low but sure, trembling at the edges. "You were supposed to be the reason I learned to heal, to fight, to protect. Not the guilt I never escaped."

The little girl's image stepped closer, expression unreadable. "Then why do I still hurt?"

Eira's shadowlight flared—not in violence, but in shape. It curved upward in a halo of violet and silver, folding over her like a cloak. She fell to her knees in the moss, eyes stinging with tears she hadn't let fall in years.

"Because I've never forgiven myself," she whispered. "Because even now, after everything, part of me still believes I could've changed it."

She reached forward—not to touch the illusion, but to release it. Her hand hovered in the air, fingers splayed as her magic flowed outward, not as a weapon, but as a truth made light.

"I love you," she said to the ghost. "And I let them take you. But you will not be my chain."

The little girl blinked, and for a fleeting second, her expression softened.

Then she faded—gently, as if melting into morning mist.

The tree behind her stilled, its bark smoothing, its breathless tension evaporating like steam.

Eira remained kneeling for a moment longer, her eyes closed, her hands limp. When she finally stood, Rhys stepped forward, not speaking—just offering his presence like a promise.

She looked at him, her voice hoarse. "You saw?"

"I did."

"And you didn't stop it."

"No."

Her gaze lingered on his, searching for something. She nodded once, slowly. "Good."

Rhys didn't smile, but there was something in his eyes—quiet and respectful—that flickered like a lantern lit anew.

Together, they turned from the dead tree, leaving behind what had once threatened to root them to the past. The path ahead curved again, but this time it no longer twisted.

The forest had taken its toll. But it had given them something too.

Not forgiveness.

But the chance to find it.

The forest, once snarled with shadow and memory, began to thin as they moved forward. The trees no longer whispered. The mist no longer clung. It was as if, in giving their pain voice, they had loosened the very grip the land had on them.

Eira's steps were steadier now, though her expression remained distant, as if the echo of her sister's voice still lingered in the back of her mind. Rhys walked beside her in silence, not because he lacked words, but because none would do justice to what she'd just endured.

They followed a narrow path that bent eastward, where the light came warmer through the leaves. The terrain dipped into a shallow ravine laced with vines and smooth stone, and as they descended, the trees opened into a clearing that was not wild, but carved.

Rhys slowed first. His eyes narrowed. "These aren't natural formations."

Eira moved ahead and crouched beside one of the stones—half-buried, weatherworn, and etched with symbols so old they had almost vanished. She brushed away the moss carefully. A familiar curve of shadowlight gleamed beneath the dirt.

"Rhys…" Her voice was breathless now. "This is a shrine."

Before them stood the remnants of a forgotten structure, ancient and hollowed by time. Stone columns, toppled but aligned with purpose. An archway intact enough to suggest reverence, if not ruin. Beneath the largest slab, a circular platform lay embedded in the earth, its center marked with the same sigil that had been on the stone from the glade.

"It's the same," Rhys muttered. "This place... it's connected to the first lightbearers. The ones who wielded shadowlight before the corruption. Before the war."

Eira stepped onto the platform, drawn as if by gravity itself. Her magic stirred, not violently, but with recognition.

Beneath her feet, the lines of the sigil glowed softly. The ancient stone warmed. Then a sound—a low hum like a breath held too long—rose from the ruin's core.

Words, carved in forgotten script, shimmered into view along the edge of the circle:

"In shadow's cradle, truth awakens. One must fall for light to rise."

Rhys read it aloud, the air growing colder with each syllable. "Another prophecy," he said grimly. "Or another piece of it."

Eira didn't answer right away. Her eyes were fixed on the circle, and her jaw had gone tight with dread. "It's not just prophecy," she said softly. "It's instruction."

Above them, a single beam of sunlight pierced the ruins' open roof, illuminating the center of the platform. A place where something—or someone—was meant to stand.

Rhys met her gaze, and neither had to say what they were both thinking.

This was not just a relic. This was a threshold. A test.

And one of them would not walk away unchanged.

The air within the ruin shifted again—still, but charged with an old breath, like something long buried had opened its eyes. Eira stepped cautiously off the glowing circle, her shadowlight still prickling along her fingertips. Rhys followed her without a word, his eyes scanning the low archways and fractured walls for any sign of traps, movement, or worse—presence.

They moved through a corridor of weathered stone, its ceiling mostly collapsed but lined with faint sigils that pulsed once in Eira's periphery before fading like dying stars. The further they went, the more the architecture whispered of intention: every slab cut too precisely, every fragment aligned to the next as if the entire place had once been a spell made solid.

At the far end of the ruin, nestled beneath the remnants of a roof laced with silver-veined vines, a half-shattered statue stood. It had once been tall—a robed figure whose face was eroded by time, one arm outstretched toward the center of the chamber. Its other hand rested on a stone basin, where runes curled in tight spirals around the rim.

Eira approached slowly. As she neared, the runes shimmered, and a faint blue light drifted up from the basin—like smoke, or thought.

Then a voice, not spoken but pressed into the air around them, whispered:

"Not all truth is meant to be survived."

Rhys reached instinctively for his sword, though the voice had no body. Eira lifted her hand, halting him. "It's a guardian," she said. "Bound to the basin. It's watching us... listening."

The mist rising from the basin began to swirl, shaping vaguely into the suggestion of a face. No features, only outline. It pulsed with each word as it continued:

"Two fates entwined by blood and silence. One must burn, that the other may bind."

Eira stepped forward. "What does that mean?"

The mist flared once, brighter. "You already know."

Rhys's voice was hard. "Tell us what happens if neither falls."

Silence. Then—

"Then all fall."

Eira's hands curled into fists. "Why does the prophecy demand sacrifice?"

The figure began to dissipate, its final words barely a breath:

"Because the shadowlight was never meant to choose. It was meant to cost."

The basin dimmed. The voice vanished. The ruin was silent again.

Eira turned to Rhys, her face pale but resolute. "They didn't build this place to preserve history," she said. "They built it to test what would survive it."

And somewhere deep beneath the stone, something ancient stirred.

Waiting.

The silence that followed was not empty. It was full—heavy with the aftertaste of words not wholly understood and truths that refused to soften.

The basin no longer glowed. The ancient statue loomed like a forgotten sentinel, faceless and still. Eira stepped back, the air cold against her skin, the echo of the spirit's voice still humming beneath her ribs like a held note that refused to die.

Rhys stood beside her, his arms folded tight across his chest, but his eyes betrayed him. They weren't angry. They were frightened—not of the ruin or the prophecy, but of what it might demand from them.

"They knew," he said after a long silence, his voice low and rough. "Whoever built this place... they knew what it would take."

Eira didn't respond right away. She stared at the basin, then back to the circle at the shrine's center, her pulse beating harder with every breath. "They didn't leave us a map," she whispered. "Just a cost."

They left the ruin in silence. The sky above had dimmed with the coming of evening, the clouds streaked in bruised colors—red, violet, indigo. No birds called. The trees that watched them no longer whispered. But they remembered.

And as Eira and Rhys stood at the edge of the clearing, looking back at the shrine swallowed slowly by dusk, they knew the path forward was no longer just theirs to walk.

It was a path already written—one forged in shadowlight and bound in blood.

And the forest was only the beginning.

Chapter Ten:

The Cost We Carry

They didn't speak until the fire was lit. Even then, the silence between them held its own voice—tension stretched thin as night spilled across the sky. The ruin behind them loomed like a broken memory, casting jagged shadows over the clearing. Its stone bones radiated a residual hum, soft and persistent, as if the ancient magic carved into its foundations was reluctant to sleep again.

Eira knelt beside the firepit, feeding small, dry branches to the flames with the mechanical rhythm of someone trying not to think too hard. The orange glow lit her face in flickers, casting warmth that never quite reached her eyes. Her hands moved steadily, but her thoughts were elsewhere—still circling the words from the guardian's voice like a predator that refused to close its jaws.

Rhys sat across from her, his back against a boulder, arms resting on his raised knees. His gaze flicked from her face to the fire and back again, but he hadn't spoken in nearly half an hour. The way he stared into the flames told her he wasn't seeing them—he was watching something deeper. Or darker.

Eventually, she broke the quiet. "We can't keep moving like this," she said, her voice roughened by fatigue and the weight of the day. "Every path is twisted. Every sign is a warning disguised as a direction. If the prophecy demands sacrifice, then we need to know... what it's willing to take."

Rhys didn't look up at first. When he did, his expression was unreadable. "It doesn't want something from us, Eira," he said. "It wants one of us. That ruin wasn't just a test. It was a promise. That only one of us gets to make it through."

The words settled heavy between them, like ash falling from the sky.

She drew her knees in closer to her chest. "So what? We just... choose who walks into the fire and who walks away?"

"No." Rhys's jaw tightened. "But we can't pretend we haven't both thought it. Who it should be."

Her shadowlight flickered to life for just a breath—subtle, like a pulse under her skin. "You're wrong," she said quietly. "I haven't thought about who it should be. I've only thought about how to make sure it isn't you."

That cracked the silence. He looked at her sharply, and for a heartbeat, neither of them blinked.

Then a rustle came from the trees.

Both of them moved instantly—Eira rising to her feet with a burst of shadowlight on her fingertips, Rhys unsheathing his blade in a smooth, practiced arc. The fire snapped louder, but the forest beyond it had grown unnaturally still.

The rustle came again. Deliberate. Watching.

Rhys stepped forward, his voice low. "It's not the wind."

Eira's magic brightened faintly in response. "Whatever's out there... it waited until now. Until we were talking about the prophecy."

Something shifted beyond the firelight, just out of sight. A silhouette moved behind the trees—tall, cloaked in darkness, and still as stone.

They were not alone.

The wind didn't move—but the trees did. Slowly. Almost imperceptibly, their limbs shifted as if drawn by breathless tides, not rustling but creaking, groaning in joints older than bark had any right to remember. The fire between Eira and Rhys flared once, high and wild, casting crooked shadows that danced along the stone ruin behind them and reached far too long into the trees.

Rhys took two silent steps toward the dark. His blade remained low, angled to catch the light, his free hand held back as a signal—don't follow, not yet. Eira didn't. Her pulse thundered beneath her ribs, shadowlight simmering just beneath her skin. Her fingers twitched with restraint, not fear.

The presence stalked just beyond the perimeter. It didn't move like an animal—no rustle of underbrush, no panic of clawed feet. It circled. With intention. As if the glade was prey and it the hunter... or worse, the judge. A shape flickered between two trees. Tall. Cloaked. Not entirely formed of flesh or shadow. Its silhouette flickered—each step a stitch unraveled and resewn from the fabric of the dark.

Rhys drew in a slow, steady breath. "It's not coming closer."

Eira shifted her stance, eyes narrowing. "Because it doesn't need to. It's waiting for us to decide who we are before it decides what it is."

The thing paused directly across the fire. Through the flickering flames, Eira could almost make out a face—or the idea of one. A hollow where eyes should be. Not empty, but vast. Its mouth did not move, but the fire shivered violently, and with it came sound—not spoken but shaped into thought.

"You carry the mark."

Rhys didn't flinch. He stepped forward, sword steady. "We carry nothing willingly."

The presence did not blink. If it even had eyes. Its form distorted the light, warping it like a smear of oil across still water. "One among you must fall. One must open. This is known."

Eira felt her spine tighten. The words weren't a threat. They were... inevitable. Cold prophecy folded into form.

She took a step closer, voice controlled but sharp. "We didn't come here to reenact someone else's fate. We came to break it."

The presence tilted, a sliver of mockery or curiosity twitching in the lines of its movement. "You do not break prophecy. You are shaped by it. And then, you shape others in your ruin."

Before either of them could respond, the figure stepped through the edge of the firelight.

It was not cloaked in cloth. It was wrapped in a living night—shadows sewn like muscle, edges trailing like mist. Its fingers were far too long. And where its chest would have been, a single glowing mark pulsed in the shape of the same sigil from the stone and the ruin.

Eira's magic surged at the sight of it. Her hand lit in a violet glow, her breath catching as her shadowlight flickered in resonance with the mark.

The creature's head turned slowly toward her. "You, child of echo. The Firstborn stirs in you. You are not ready."

Then to Rhys. "You, traitor of silence. Your death is written. But not yet inked."

The fire hissed violently, sparks clawing toward the canopy.

Rhys growled low, stepping closer. "What are you?"

The figure shifted—dissolving slightly at the edges, then reforming. It didn't move forward. It only tilted its head and said, almost softly:
"I am what waits. I am what watches. I am what chooses, when you will not."

The temperature plummeted. Eira's breath fogged in the air between them. Her skin prickled as though the shadows were reaching into her, not around her.

Then, just as suddenly as it appeared, the creature blinked out of existence. Not vanished—folded. As if it were merely a page turned. The woods behind it did not breathe. The night did not resume.

The silence that followed was deeper than before.

Rhys exhaled sharply, chest heaving. "So... it knows."

Eira didn't answer right away. Her gaze remained fixed on the spot where the presence had stood. Her hands slowly unclenched, shadowlight fading back into her veins.

"It knows more than we do," she said. "And it's waiting for us to fail."

The fire had nearly collapsed to coals, and yet neither of them moved to stoke it. Its warmth was no longer comfort—only reminder.

Rhys stood with his arms folded, his back half-turned to the now-empty space where the figure had stood. His jaw was tight, his shoulders stiff with something that wasn't just tension. It was calculation. A warrior's patience cracking against a wall of doubt.

Eira sat on the low flat stone where she'd knelt before. Her fingers, laced over her knees, had stopped glowing, but her magic hadn't settled. It curled in her veins like a second heartbeat, whispering possibilities she didn't want to name.

They'd both seen it. The shape. The mark. The words it had spoken. It had known them—not by name, but by weight. By truth.

"We can't go forward," Rhys said finally, breaking the long quiet. His voice was low, edged with iron. "Not like this. Not knowing what that thing was. Or what it still is."

Eira didn't look up. "And we can't go back. If it's waiting to choose, then every step we take is another game in its hand."

He turned to her, jaw clenched. "So you're saying we keep going? That we walk straight into the wilds it's already touched?"

Her head lifted slowly, eyes dark with defiance. "I'm saying it already has touched them. You saw the trees. They leaned toward it. They listened."

Rhys opened his mouth to reply—then stopped.

Because she was right.

The land had changed. The glade's edges no longer bowed with rest. They seemed... bent. As if the roots of the forest now followed some unseen pull. The air itself felt altered. Not foul or foul-scented, but expectant. Watching. Like the land remembered the presence and had not yet decided how to feel about its absence.

Rhys exhaled through his nose, then knelt across from her, forearms braced against his knees. "If we go east, we reach the Ember Chasm. The maps say the land there hasn't shifted as much. We'd lose time, but maybe avoid what's waiting."

Eira shook her head. "The prophecy didn't come to us by chance, Rhys. And that creature didn't reveal itself because it was curious. It's part of the path. Whether we want it to be or not."

He stared at her, searching her face. "And what if the next thing we find is worse?"

Eira's voice was quiet. "It will be."

They didn't speak for a long moment after that. The wind stirred faintly, brushing through the leaves like a sigh. A few embers snapped in the coals. Somewhere in the woods, a bird gave a single note—and then fell silent again.

Finally, Rhys stood. His silhouette caught the glow of the firelight, casting a long shadow across the circle of broken stones. "Then we move at first light. Into the wilds. Into whatever it's become."

Eira nodded. "Together."

He hesitated, then added, "And if it tries to choose between us again..."

"Then we don't let it," she said, rising to meet his gaze. "It doesn't get to decide who we are."

But neither of them could quite shake the feeling that it already had.

The fire had burned to ash by the time the first bruise-colored light bled across the horizon. Dawn arrived reluctantly, slipping through the trees in thin, gray strands. The forest around them remained unnervingly still, as if whatever soul it possessed now waited with bated breath. There was no birdsong. No rustle of breeze. Just silence—vast, and stretching.

Eira rolled her bedroll with methodical precision, her hands moving as if repetition could distract her from the weight in her chest. Her shadowlight pulsed faintly beneath her skin, muted now, but restless. Rhys strapped the last buckle of his pack, every movement sharp, controlled. He hadn't spoken since they'd doused the last ember. There was nothing left to say. Not yet.

They moved through the remnants of the ruined glade in silence, stepping over roots that had not been there the day before. Vines now curled across the stones in spirals, and the trees leaned closer, their limbs gnarled in ways that defied natural growth. It felt as though the forest was turning inward—gathering itself around a secret it hadn't decided to share.

As they walked, the path beneath their boots shifted subtly. What had once been moss gave way to a strange undergrowth of soft, velvet-like soil. It dampened sound. Even their footsteps felt like whispers swallowed before they could echo.

Then the land changed again.

The trees began to repeat.

Not identical, but familiar. A hollow trunk. A broken limb. A knot shaped like a closed eye. Eira paused mid-step, her brow furrowing. "We've passed this before."

Rhys glanced behind them, then forward. "We've been walking straight."

"No," she said, voice clipped. "We've been turned. The path's folding in on itself."

He drew his blade—not in threat, but in certainty. "Illusion?"

Eira reached out, touching one of the trees. Her magic flared, just for a breath. The bark rippled beneath her fingers—not as if enchanted, but responsive. It recognized her. Or remembered.

"It's not illusion," she murmured. "It's memory."

And suddenly, the forest moved.

Not physically—but atmospherically. The air grew heavy. Not dark, but emotionally oppressive. Rhys took a step forward—and the trees shifted in time with him, parting ever so slightly. Ahead, the path descended into a shallow vale where light pooled unnaturally bright, too golden, too perfect.

They crossed the threshold together.

And what greeted them was impossible.

A field opened before them, lush with tall grass and blooming flowers that hadn't existed anywhere else in this ruined land. Sunlight beamed down from a sky too clear to be real. In the center of the field stood a small cottage—its walls pale with ivy, smoke curling gently from the chimney.

Eira stopped. Her breath caught.

"I know this place," she whispered. "This... this was a dream I had when I was thirteen. The first time I lost control of my magic. The sanctum priest said it was my mind trying to protect me. This cottage—it's what I imagined peace would look like."

Rhys scanned the scene with narrowed eyes. "Then it's not a memory. It's a mirror. Of something inside you."

The air shifted again.

And a second path opened, veering to the left.

At the end of it, another structure stood. Towering. Dark stone. Gates of black iron twisted like spines. Smoke roiled from windows that weren't windows at all, but eyes. Rhys's entire posture stiffened.

"I... dreamed of that place too," he said quietly. "But it wasn't a dream. It was the temple where they made me kill my brother."

Their eyes met in the silence between the visions.

Eira's voice was barely audible. "It's not choosing for us this time. It's asking."

Two paths. Two trials.

And only one way forward.

They stood at the fork, suspended between two impossibilities—one dressed in gentleness, the other in shadowed ruin. Both too familiar. Too intimate. The field of Eira's imagined peace shimmered like a dream that refused to dissolve, the scent of lavender wafting through air that felt too warm, too kind. It called softly, the way one might call home.

But the other path bled a different song.

Rhys hadn't spoken since the black temple revealed itself. The color had drained slightly from his face, and though his hands were steady at his sides, his eyes had gone distant—like he was already standing at the threshold of that place again, its memory clawing at the walls he'd built to hold it back.

Eira shifted her gaze between them. "It's making us choose. One of us goes forward," she said. "One faces the other's truth."

Rhys didn't respond immediately. He looked between both visions, and his jaw clenched tighter. "It's not just a test," he murmured. "It's division. It wants to separate us. To see who fractures first."

Eira stepped forward, chin lifted in defiance. "Then we don't choose."

His eyes snapped to hers. "What?"

"We deny it," she said, fire rising behind her words. "Both visions come from within us, right? It's built to lure us, to corner us. But the prophecy wasn't written to reward obedience." She turned, sweeping her gaze over the glade. "It reacts to our will. To what we accept."

Rhys hesitated. "So you think if we refuse to walk either path…"

"…we force a third to reveal itself."

As if in answer, the earth beneath them rumbled—soft at first, then deep and resonant, like a distant drumbeat echoing through stone. The air grew thick. The golden sky above Eira's path dimmed. The smoke from Rhys's temple recoiled into itself.

A line of fire cracked through the ground between the two paths—thin, red, and glowing. It traced a new direction: forward, straight through the space that had moments ago been only empty glade. No road. No memory. Just raw, untouched terrain veiled in silver mist.

Eira's breath hitched. "It wasn't asking us to choose between each other. It was asking if we'd break apart."

Rhys stepped beside her, sword still in hand. "Then let's not give it what it wants."

Together, they stepped over the burning seam in the earth and followed the third path—the one not offered, but earned. As they walked, the mirages behind them withered. The field dissolved into dust, the temple into smoke. The world behind them had nothing left to test.

The path ahead was quiet. But it would not be kind.

The crystal hovered just beyond reach, swaying ever so slightly in the breathless stillness of the spiral altar. Its light was steady now—not pulsing, not flickering. Just waiting. Eira stood before it with her hand half-raised, Rhys just a step behind, his shadow falling across the black stone. Neither of them moved. Not yet.

The moment stretched between them like a blade held to still skin.

Rhys finally broke the silence, voice low. "What happens if we touch it together?"

Eira's gaze stayed on the crystal. "Maybe nothing. Maybe everything." A pause. "But I think... whatever this is, it was never meant for just one of us."

She turned her hand, palm up, offering it. Rhys didn't hesitate. His fingers laced with hers.

Together, they stepped forward. Together, they reached.

Their joined hands brushed the crystal.

It shattered soundlessly—into light, into memory, into motion.

The world dissolved.

Not in pain. Not even in disorientation. It simply folded away, like a curtain pulled back to reveal a stage that had been waiting for them all along.

They fell—not through space, but through meaning. Through everything they thought they knew.

When their feet found ground again, it was not earth beneath them.

It was water.

Still. Shallow. Reflective as glass.

They stood in a void of pale silver light, no sky above, no land in sight. Only water stretching endlessly in every direction—beneath their feet, not even a ripple. It reflected them perfectly. And yet... their reflections were wrong.

Rhys's image stared back at him, but his eyes were gone—hollowed by darkness, blood at the corners of his mouth. His hands trembled, but not with fear—with guilt.

Eira's reflection was worse.

Her shadowlight had consumed her—coiling up her arms, across her neck, threading into the whites of her eyes until nothing human remained. In the image, she smiled.

Faintly. And without mercy.

Rhys's hand tightened around hers. "This place…"

"It's a crucible," Eira whispered. "It shows us who we fear we might become."

Their reflections moved, even though they didn't. Eira's stepped forward, head tilted with a mimic's grace. Rhys's bled shadows from its mouth and laughed—no sound, only the shape of it.

Then both illusions spoke.

"One of you will betray the other. One of you will make the prophecy real."

Rhys flinched. "We already knew that."

The false Eira turned to the false Rhys. They held hands. They looked so much like them, and yet… older. Tired. Twisted.

"But do you believe it?" they asked in unison. "Or do you need to believe something else?"

The water trembled.

And then it cracked.

Lines spidered out beneath their feet—fractures racing across the mirrored surface until the ground shattered completely.

They fell again—this time into a cascade of memory, sensation, and emotion.

Eira landed alone. She stood in the sanctum, in her old chamber. Candles guttered. A voice whispered spells she hadn't learned yet, hadn't earned yet.

Rhys landed in the temple where his brother had died, the altar still wet with blood.

Each of them alone. Each of them surrounded by their deepest scars.

And the only way out was through the wound.

Eira

The sanctum was exactly as it had been the night she fled it—no older, no changed. The scent of beeswax and damp parchment clung to the air. The floor beneath her bare feet was ice-cold marble, veined with faint sigils that pulsed under her step like a heartbeat buried in stone. Candles lined the long chamber walls, dripping slowly but never reaching the floor, their flames strangely static. Frozen.

But the sound—oh, the sound. It echoed, low and rhythmic, like a woman whispering just behind her ear. Eira turned slowly.

And there she stood. Herself. Younger. Frail from weeks of overtraining. Eyes red from held-back tears. Hands trembling not from power but from fear. The moment before her first true failure. Before the accidental casting. Before the first time someone bled because she hadn't known how to stop it.

"Say something," the younger Eira begged, though her lips didn't move.

Present Eira took a step closer, breath ragged. "I didn't know how. I didn't know who I was."

"You could have walked away," the younger version whispered, shadowlight beginning to flicker in her veins. "You could've run and taken me with you."

"I didn't think I deserved peace," Eira said. "I thought I had to earn it by breaking."

The younger Eira reached for her, fingers glowing with that same early fire. "You still believe that."

The sanctum flared. Candles erupted. The shadows twisted into vines, creeping down the walls, reaching for her throat.

And then, Eira did something she had never done.

She stepped forward.

And embraced the girl.

The magic shuddered, surged, then shattered.

The chamber dissolved around her into white light.

Rhys

He stood in the temple again. The same altar. The same stink of blood and burned incense. The torchlight guttered on the high stone walls, casting grotesque shadows of the cloaked zealots standing silently in a semicircle.

And at the center, his brother. Bound to the altar, face bruised, lips cracked. But still—still—smiling at him.

"I told you not to come back here," the memory spoke, voice hoarse.

"I had no choice," Rhys answered, breath trembling.

"You did. You chose not to stop it. You chose to walk the path that gave you power." His brother coughed, blood blooming at the edge of his mouth. "You could've dragged me out of here. You were strong enough. But you didn't."

Rhys stepped forward, his blade at his side, as if the memory required him to finish what he started. "I thought I was saving something bigger than us."

"Did you?" the memory asked. "Or did you want the gods to owe you more than you owed me?"

Rhys's stomach turned. Every inch of him wanted to look away.

But instead, he fell to his knees.

"I didn't know how to be anything else," he whispered. "I've only ever been what they made me. And when I finally broke free, it was too late to save you."

The zealots faded. The walls cracked. His brother's image, smiling, reached out—not in forgiveness, but in release.

"Then stop being what they made you," the voice said. "And be what you choose."

The torchlight flared once more—and the temple collapsed into light.

They landed in the same breath.

Knees in shallow water once more. The sky above was not empty now, but streaked with color—gold and indigo. The liminal space that had once mirrored their fears now pulsed with possibility.

Eira turned toward him first. Her cheeks were damp, her eyes bright. Rhys looked stunned—exhausted—but a spark in him glimmered anew.

They reached for each other without words.

And between them, in the center of the mirrored water, the final line of the prophecy emerged, etched in light:

"Only through knowing the self shall the bond be unbroken. Only through truth shall the path to ending begin."

They had not been tested to fail.

They had been broken to see if they could still choose.

And they had.

The light receded like a tide, pulling away from their skin and breath and memory. The liminal world—a place stitched from time and self—faded into the hush of wind rustling trees. Grass replaced water beneath their feet. The sky above was no longer silvered void but a familiar gray-blue threaded with clouds bruised by late afternoon.

They stood again on the threshold of the ruins, not where they had fallen—but exactly where they had touched the crystal. No hours had passed, though their bones hummed as if they'd lived through years.

Rhys staggered a half step, catching himself with one hand against the altar's stone. His other hand never released hers.

Eira blinked once, then again, her eyes adjusting not just to light, but to gravity. Emotion clung to her ribs like smoke, like memory, like breath stolen and returned. "We came back," she said.

He turned toward her. "No," he said, voice quiet. "We never left. Not really."

And it was true. Something lingered in their veins—each still carrying echoes of the visions they'd endured. But something else now tethered them. Not shadowlight. Not prophecy. Trust. Forged not by obedience or obligation, but in that white-hot moment of being known and not forsaken.

The crystal was gone. In its place, a single silver line glowed across the altar's spiral. Another mark on the map neither of them yet understood.

Eira reached toward it—and the moment her fingers brushed the symbol, her magic pulsed, and the line shimmered into a shape: a mountain peak carved with stars. Beneath it, a name neither of them recognized was etched into the stone.

"Is that where we go next?" Rhys asked.

She nodded once, slowly. "It's where the next key to the prophecy lies. The mountain of the First Echo."

But before either could say more, the air split.

Not with wind. Not with thunder. But with a sound older than language—a groan of stone, of the world rending just slightly to make room for something wrong.

The forest trembled. A scream—inhuman, hollow, layered—ripped through the trees behind them. It came from no throat. It came from beneath.

Rhys stepped in front of Eira instinctively. "We're not alone."

And from the forest's edge emerged the creature.

It was taller now—twice as tall as before. Its limbs longer, cloaked in layers of shadow stitched together by threads of bone and glowing glyphs. Its chest bore the same sigil from the altar, only now it pulsed bright red instead of silver.

Eira's hand lit with shadowlight. Rhys raised his sword.

The creature didn't speak. It didn't need to.

Its presence alone told them what it meant.

They had passed the test.

Now came the punishment for surviving it.

The creature moved like unraveling smoke and shattering stone—its limbs folding and unfurling in sickening arcs as it surged forward, the red sigil on its chest pulsing in time with the low, thrumming quake of the ground beneath their feet. The forest behind it bent away, trees cracking and bowing as if unwilling to witness what came next.

Rhys stepped in front of Eira without hesitation, blade flashing in the fractured light, his eyes narrowed and calm in the way only warriors who'd already accepted death could be. But this time, he wasn't alone.

Eira stepped to his left, her magic already winding around her fingers like molten thread, a halo of violet shadow blooming in her eyes. She didn't ask if he was ready. She didn't need to. The bond between them no longer relied on words. It beat with a rhythm forged in fire and silence.

The creature struck first.

A limb—less an arm and more a writhing column of condensed darkness—lashed out. Rhys ducked low and swept upward, the edge of his blade catching and cutting through the shadows, cleaving a gash that bled flickers of light instead of blood. Eira surged forward with him, releasing a pulse of shadowlight that rippled through the creature's side like a second wound.

But it didn't fall.

It roared—not from pain, but from recognition.

The sigil on its chest ignited brighter, and a blast of red light erupted from its core. Rhys was thrown back against a half-shattered pillar, stone splintering under his weight. Eira barely shielded herself, her magic forming a barrier of mirrored light just in time to absorb the worst of it. Still, the impact knocked her to one knee.

She coughed once, blood in her mouth, but stood.

Rhys was already moving again, circling to flank. "It's bound to the sigil!" he shouted. "That's its anchor!"

Eira nodded, her jaw set. Her shadowlight curved into a lance in her palm. "Then let's cut the chain."

They moved in tandem.

Rhys darted in from the side, his blade whistling through the air with brutal precision, drawing the creature's focus. Eira dashed forward under its swing, using his distraction to get close. The creature raised a clawed limb to crush her—but too late.

She leapt.

And drove the lance of shadowlight straight into the glowing sigil.

The creature screamed.

Not in agony, but in defiance—as if trying to hold its shape against the truth pressing into it. Light burst from the wound like a thousand shattering mirrors. The sigil cracked. The creature convulsed, collapsing backward in a flurry of shadows unspooling into ash.

And then it was gone.

The forest stilled.

Silence fell like a closing door.

Eira stood panting, her knees shaking. Rhys approached slowly, a gash bleeding along his ribs, his breath ragged but his smile tired and real.

"Well," he muttered, "at least it didn't monologue."

She gave him a weak laugh and reached for him, their foreheads touching for just a breath as their pulses slowed in unison.

They had passed the test. Survived the punishment.

But the cost was far from paid.

The last remnants of the creature's body dissipated in a thin trail of red vapor, curling upward before vanishing completely into the branches above. The forest around them stood stunned—silent, reverent, as though it too recognized the finality of what had just unfolded. The ground beneath their boots no longer trembled, though the scent of scorched air lingered like a memory burned into the soil.

Eira lowered her hand, the last flicker of shadowlight fading from her fingertips. Her chest rose and fell with controlled breath, but exhaustion clung to her skin like damp cloth. Rhys stepped beside her, wiping the blood from the cut along his ribs with a torn strip of cloth, grimacing at the sting but making no complaint. The silence between them wasn't heavy—it was earned.

Ahead, the forest began to shift.

Not unnaturally this time—not the warped terrain of illusions or nightmares—but in gentle parting. The trees drew back, the underbrush thinning, as though the land itself acknowledged the change in them. The path that emerged was faint, but clear: a narrow trail of moss-covered stones ascending toward a distant silhouette in the clouds.

There—carved from storm-dark stone and crowned in mist—rose the mountain. Jagged, vast, and untouched by time.

The Mountain of the First Echo.

Rhys's eyes followed the line of the trail, his voice low. "It's farther than it looks."

"It always is," Eira replied. Her voice was quiet, but steadier now. "But we're not the same people who started this path."

He gave her a sidelong glance. "You still don't know how to take a compliment."

"And you still talk too much after being nearly eviscerated."

A smirk pulled at the edge of his mouth, even through the bruise forming along his jaw. "Fair."

They stepped forward together. No need to speak the choice aloud—it had already been made. The forest closed behind them without sound, sealing the trial in the shadows of the past. Ahead, wind whispered through unseen canyons high on the mountain, carrying with it a strange, melodic hum.

The next piece of the prophecy waited.

But for the first time, they would meet it not as two fractured survivors—

—but as one bond, forged beneath the wings of shadowlight.

The wind shifted around them as they climbed the first stretch of slope, brushing cool fingers through Eira's hair and tugging softly at Rhys's cloak. The air had thinned already—less heavy with magic now, but clearer in its purpose. Every breath seemed to cleanse what had lingered behind. There was no longer a whisper of test or trap in the land beneath their feet. This part of the world did not want to break them.

It simply waited to see who they would become.

The trees gradually gave way to sharp hills veined with silver rock, and the path ahead steepened into a series of narrow ridgelines that would guide them toward the Mountain of the First Echo. Jagged clouds clung to its summit like unraveling silk, and though they were still far from it, the enormity of its presence was already pressing down on them. Eira stared at it with quiet awe. It looked nothing like the dreams that had guided her, and yet she knew it just the same. Some part of her soul recognized the place where voices went to become truths.

They stopped near a break in the trail where a shelf of stone jutted out into open air, offering a view of the valley they had left behind. From here, the shattered trees and twisted glades looked distant, small. The ruin that had nearly claimed them shimmered as a pale smudge on the edge of the wood. Rhys leaned on his sword, not out of weariness, but for the steady rhythm it gave his stance.

"This next part," he said after a long pause, "we'll need more than strength to survive it."

Eira nodded, her voice calm. "And more than magic."

He looked at her then, and in that glance there was no armor. No shadows.

"Good thing we have each other," he said.

She reached out, fingers curling around his hand—no hesitation, no second-guessing. "Not just as allies," she murmured, the wind stealing half her breath, "but as something more."

He didn't need to answer. He only held her hand tighter.

The mountain loomed above them. The next challenge waited. But for now, there was no fear in their steps. Because what shadowlight had threatened to tear apart...

...they had chosen to forge together.

And that choice would carry them into whatever came next.

Chapter Eleven:

Echoes Above the Hollow Sky

The ascent began beneath a sky stained with pale gold, where light filtered through wisps of vapor like the last whispers of a dream that refused to end. The highlands welcomed no intruder kindly. Here, even the wind had teeth. It howled between the narrow switchbacks carved into the mountainside, dragging fingers of grit and ash across Eira's cheeks and whipping Rhys's cloak into a fluttering banner of worn black.

The terrain had changed. Gone were the trees, the muttering forest, the whispering roots and mirrored trials. Here, the earth had been stripped bare—carved down to the bone by old magic and older storms. The trail beneath their boots was brittle shale and fractured stone, cracking beneath weight like it resented being touched. Every step required intention, balance, and the kind of endurance born of pain remembered and not yet healed.

They didn't speak much.

The silence was not avoidance now, but purpose. Every breath they drew fed their resolve. Every glance they shared reaffirmed the bond that the liminal realm had sealed like flame to steel.

As the elevation climbed, the air turned colder—not merely in temperature, but in presence. Eira could feel it: the faint thread of shadowlight in her veins no longer shimmered freely but flickered with resistance. It was like trying to breathe magic through a curtain of ash.

She paused on a narrow ledge, bracing one hand against the cliff wall to steady herself. Her magic recoiled like it had touched something it feared to name.

Rhys stopped behind her. "What is it?"

"The mountain…" She swallowed, lips pale. "It doesn't want shadowlight."

He glanced around, eyes narrowing. "No. It wants truth." He looked at her, carefully, voice low. "It wants who you are when everything else is stripped away."

She nodded once, breath misting in the chilled air. "That's what it'll demand from both of us."

Far above, the wind shifted—and a sound, faint but piercing, echoed from the peaks.

Not an animal. Not weather.

A call.

Not meant to summon.

Meant to warn.

The path narrowed as the light faded, chiseled into the face of the mountain by hands long turned to dust. Jagged outcroppings leaned overhead like crumbling sentinels, their shadows cast long and skeletal across the trail. Snow drifted in thin ribbons along the wind's breathless edge—not falling, but hanging, as if even time moved more cautiously this high above the world.

Eira felt it before she saw it.

A shift in the pressure of the air, a subtle drop in sound—like the moment before a blade fell. Her skin prickled, shadowlight flaring to her fingertips unbidden, despite the mountain's resistance. It did not rage against her now. It watched. As if the land itself was weighing her presence against some unspoken measure.

Rhys was ahead, just around the curve of the path where the cliff arched outward into a shallow bowl carved by ancient rains. He stopped suddenly, one boot scuffing stone. Eira came to his side, and together they stared.

A single archway stood before them.

Not stone, not wood—but forged from interwoven light and bone-pale metal. It shimmered faintly in the gloom, the lines of its construction impossible—curved in ways that defied geometry, pulsing softly like something alive. Beneath it, the path split into two distinct trails: one leading up into a sheer climb toward the ridgeline, the other winding into a chasm, where light vanished completely.

Etched into the face of the arch in ancient script was a phrase that shifted each time Eira blinked—until it finally stilled:

"Only one may bear the weight. Only one may pass."

Rhys's breath hissed between his teeth. "Another test."

Eira stared at the inscription, reading it again, silently mouthing the words. Her fingers tightened at her sides. "No. This one's worse." She stepped forward, palm brushing the arch's frame. Magic pulsed through her like cold lightning. The metal glowed brighter, and a shape began to form behind the veil of the arch.

A scale.

Balanced. Empty.

And a single blade hovering above it.

Rhys joined her, jaw set. "It's a trial of balance," he said. "It's asking for a sacrifice."

She nodded slowly, eyes never leaving the scale. "One of us takes the harder path. The climb. The cold. The exposed ledge. The other walks through darkness alone." Her throat tightened. "It wants to know if we trust each other enough to choose, not by logic—but by heart."

He turned toward her then, and the wind tossed his hair across his brow, his eyes shadowed but steady. "Then I'll go down," he said without hesitation. "You take the climb. You've always seen clearer in the light."

But Eira caught his hand before he could step forward.

"No," she whispered. "You always bear the worst of it. Every time. You fight first. You bleed first." Her voice trembled. "Let me take the chasm this time."

He looked at her, his expression unreadable.

"What if we both fail our paths?" he asked. "What if the trial's about whether we can succeed apart?"

She held his gaze. "Then we make that choice together. And we meet on the other side."

He hesitated—then nodded once.

A decision made.

He stepped toward the climb. She descended toward the dark.

Behind them, the archway glowed once.

And the blade above the scale slowly began to fall.

The descent began without warning.

One step beyond the shimmer of the archway and the earth simply dropped. Eira stumbled forward into a cold so absolute it seemed to dampen not only warmth, but thought. The narrow ledge spiraled downward in a tight corkscrew, carved not by tool or time, but by some ancient act of will. Walls of slick obsidian loomed close to either side, and above her, the last sliver of sky folded shut like a final breath drawn and held.

The light disappeared completely after only a few turns.

She summoned a flicker of shadowlight, but it sparked violently—then hissed out. Whatever dwelled in the heart of this chasm did not want magic. Not yet. Not hers. She was to walk this path unequipped, unlit.

So she walked.

One hand on the cold wall. One foot carefully placed after the other. Her breath slow. Her senses drawn inward.

That was when the whispering began.

At first it was faint—no louder than the hush of silk against stone. Then words began to take shape, wrapping around her ears like fingers curling softly over skin. They didn't come from ahead or behind. They came from within.

"You were never meant to be more than a weapon."

She stopped.

The voice was hers—but older. Hardened. Twisted slightly with disappointment.

"You clung to Rhys because you needed a reason not to lose yourself."

The tunnel trembled. Eira pressed her hand against the wall, closing her eyes. "This is the trial," she whispered. "It's not physical. It's memory twisted to mirror fear."

The whisper laughed.

And suddenly, the wall wasn't there. The floor beneath her vanished.

She stood in the sanctum again—but not the one she remembered. This one was drowned in shadowlight, the sigils on the floor weeping black fire, the robes of the mages slashed and abandoned. At the center stood her—another version—radiant and monstrous.

This Eira turned slowly, smile sharp, power coiled around her arms like living flame.

"You could become this."

Her voice echoed from every wall.

"If you only let go of everything you still think makes you good."

Eira's heart pounded against her ribs like a war drum.

"I'm not afraid of power," she said, voice steady. "I'm afraid of losing the reason to use it."

The other Eira stepped forward. "Then prove it."

The shadows surged—rushing her like a tide.

Eira dropped to her knees, hands outstretched—not to defend. Not to attack. But to accept.

"I don't have to fight you," she whispered. "Because you are me."

The shadows halted.

And in the silence that followed, the darkness folded inward. The echo dissolved.

And light—real, soft, golden—poured in from above.

She was at the bottom of the chasm.

And the path forward opened beneath her feet.

The wind was not wind.

Rhys realized this as he gripped the ledge above his head and hauled himself upward into the freezing currents that howled along the exposed ridge. What tore at him now wasn't merely air—it was memory wearing the skin of storm. The moment he'd passed beneath the archway, the trail had twisted into sheer incline, the path turning cruel beneath his boots. Every foothold crumbled under his weight, every gust of wind felt designed to steal his balance.

Above, the sky darkened into bruised indigo, roiling with clouds that pulsed faintly from within—like a thunderstorm too exhausted to strike but too vengeful to pass. Snow flurried sideways across the stone, not settling but slicing, each flake a sliver of ice and time. Rhys pressed forward, muscles aching, breath rising in short, pained clouds. His blade clanged lightly against his hip with each climb, a steady reminder of his weight, of his purpose, of who he had chosen to become. Below, the world dropped away into mist, too far gone to offer comfort even in retreat.

At the summit of a narrow spire, he found it waiting.

Not a creature. Not a structure.

But a memory.

The cliff flattened briefly into a plateau, and on it sat a single stone slab carved with the image of two boys—arms locked, smiling wide, unburdened. His brother. And him. Before the gods. Before the blades. Before everything burned.

Rhys staggered closer, hands trembling—not from cold, but from the tremor in his chest. The image was exact, etched with such precision that even the scar beneath his brother's eye was perfectly rendered. Snow gathered at the edges of the stone, but not on the faces. They remained untouched. Sacred. Or cruelly preserved.

Behind him, the storm began to whisper.

It didn't carry words.

It carried the moment of the altar.

The scent of blood and incense. The weight of the blade in his hand. The sound—his brother's breath escaping in a final, fragile hitch. The knowledge that no redemption would come for this. Only prophecy. Only use.

Rhys dropped to his knees before the stone. His palms pressed flat to its frozen surface. "I would change it," he said aloud, his voice ripped raw by wind. "If I could. I would bear the chains in your place."

The storm pulsed above him. A flash of light ignited in the clouds—not lightning, but memory.

And then the second figure appeared.

His brother. Real. Or the memory made flesh. Eyes dark, but no longer accusing. Just tired.

"You were never meant to save me," the memory said. "Only to remember."

Rhys bowed his head. The wind stilled. The cold remained—but it was no longer sharp.

And then the path forward revealed itself—not carved into stone, but opening through it, as though the mountain had finally accepted him.

He stood.

And began to walk toward where he hoped Eira would be waiting.

The mist peeled away slowly, revealing a curve of ancient stone that wound from both the dark beneath and the heights above. The two paths—chasm and cliff—twisted inward like twin threads pulled tight, converging at a wide ledge carved into the side of the mountain. The space felt untouched by the wind, though it loomed on every side. Above, a ring of jagged peaks rose like the ribs of a sleeping giant. The air here held no storm, no shadow—only stillness, and a hush so deep it pressed against the skin.

Eira stepped onto the ledge first, her boots grinding softly on the frost-laced stone. Her cloak was damp, her hair tangled with ash and memory. But her eyes—her eyes were sharp. Clear. The storm within her had passed, though its mark still pulsed faintly beneath her skin.

From the opposite edge of the trail, Rhys emerged. His steps were slow, weighted. His shoulders carried a new gravity, as though something old had finally settled across them. His face bore a fresh cut along the cheekbone, but his expression was steady—still Rhys, but more whole somehow, as if the mountain had scraped away the final layers of guilt he no longer needed to carry.

When he saw her, he paused. Not from disbelief—but reverence.

Eira managed a breathless laugh. "You're late."

Rhys gave a dry smile, crossing the final distance. "I had to climb through my worst mistake. You?"

"Had to embrace mine." She stepped toward him, stopping when their hands nearly touched. "We made it."

"Almost," he said softly. "Look."

At the center of the ledge, nestled within a ring of stone etched in ancient glyphs, stood a monolith. Tall, black, cracked by time—but unmistakably alive. Its surface pulsed faintly, as though reacting to their presence. Carved into its base, a final inscription began to reveal itself—not in language, but in light.

Together, they stepped toward it.

And the voice of the mountain—deep, thunderous, yet gentle as falling snow—spoke into their minds.

"You have walked your shadows. You have held the blade of memory without flinching. Now choose."

The stone shimmered.

Before them, the monolith began to split—down the center, forming a narrow passage leading deeper into the mountain's heart. A stairway of light unfolded, descending into shadow shot through with stars.

Rhys's hand found Eira's.

"Are we ready?" he asked.

She squeezed his fingers. "We're no longer meant to be."

And together, they stepped through the stone.

The path through the monolith spiraled downward, narrowing into a corridor carved not by mortal hands, but by time and purpose. The air grew colder, the walls darker—not simply in color, but in intention. They no longer felt like stone. They felt like memory. Every breath Eira took was thick with echoes, every step Rhys made stirred some dormant awareness in the quiet around them. Their hands remained linked, not out of fear, but necessity. Together, they had chosen to face this, and the mountain intended to test the strength of that bond one final time.

The descent ended in a vast hollow chamber, perfectly circular, its edges lost to a haze of silver mist. The walls were faceted, mirror-like, but showed not their reflections—instead, flickers of their pasts played

in erratic glimmers. Moments not forgotten but buried:
the look on Rhys's face the night he left the Shadowborn
temple for good; the moment Eira first lost control of
her shadowlight and scorched the sanctum stones.
These visions didn't accuse. They simply were, as if the
mountain wanted only to remind.

At the center of the room hovered a shard of
obsidian, flawless and gently rotating above a cradle of
ancient stone. Light poured from its edges in delicate
filaments, like strands of memory drawn taut. Beneath
it, two stone pedestals rose, each bearing a single
unsheathed blade—one carved from bone-pale metal,
the other dark as midnight glass. Between them, an
inscription glowed faintly on the floor:

"Only one may bear the memory. Only one may carry
the truth. The other must be forgotten, until fate calls
again."

Eira stopped cold, her breath catching in her throat.
"This isn't a test of strength."

"No," Rhys said softly beside her. "It's the prophecy
choosing its vessel."

The realization settled over them like snowfall. The
shard's knowledge—whatever truth it held—was too
dangerous to exist in both of them. One would

remember everything. The other... would walk blind, until the time came to awaken that memory again. Not death. Not abandonment. But sacrifice.

Eira's eyes filled with heat, shadowlight flickering in her palm. "You can't ask me to forget you."

Rhys gave a small, tired smile. "I'm not asking. I'm offering."

"No," she said, fiercely. "We've come too far. We've earned this—together."

He stepped toward one of the blades—the dark one. She moved to intercept.

And suddenly the chamber reacted.

The obsidian shard pulsed with light, a low hum vibrating through the soles of their boots. Glyphs spiraled out from the pedestals, forming a circle of binding—closing the space, demanding resolution. The mountain no longer waited. It asked for a choice.

Rhys looked at her, pain written across every line of his face. "One of us must carry the truth forward."

Eira's voice was barely a whisper. "And the other must let go."

They reached for the blades together.

And as their fingers closed around the hilts, the world was swallowed in light.

The light did not explode. It bloomed.

A slow, all-consuming radiance poured from the shard and the blades, wrapping Eira and Rhys in a cocoon of warmth and soundless vibration, like standing inside a heartbeat made of starlight. Their hands remained locked around the hilts, though the weapons themselves had vanished—absorbed into the choice, into the ancient contract neither had truly understood until now. The glyphs on the floor pulsed once more, a ring of soft silver fire sealing the chamber in its breathless stillness.

Then—quiet.

And then—separation.

Eira gasped and stumbled forward, the world tilting beneath her feet as if she'd surfaced from deep water. Her head throbbed, not from pain but from weight. Words not hers pressed against the edges of her thoughts. Names she'd never heard formed behind her eyes like constellations rearranging. She tasted metal and starlight. Shadowlight pulsed at her fingertips, no longer wild, no longer seething—it was refined now, shaped by something vast and terrible and true.

She blinked hard and turned.

Rhys stood across the circle, his back half-turned, eyes distant, breathing slow. There was no recognition in his gaze—not lost or confused, but quiet. At peace in the way only someone who had just given something away could be.

"Rhys..." her voice broke as she said it, but he didn't flinch.

He looked at her. Smiled faintly. "You're alright?"

Her heart cracked.

He didn't remember. Not all of it. Maybe not any of it.

"Yes," she lied, softly. "I am."

The shard hovered above them, now dim and cracked down the center, its purpose fulfilled. It pulsed once—like a farewell—before fading into dust, scattering like ash on a current neither of them could see.

Eira crossed the circle. She didn't speak again. She simply touched his arm, gently, anchoring herself to the warmth of him, to the echo of what they had shared. There was still something in his eyes—an instinct, perhaps, or the smallest ember of memory untouched by the sacrifice. A hesitation when he looked at her too long. A question in the curve of his fingers as they brushed against hers.

The mountain had taken what it needed.

And left them with the bond only one of them could fully remember.

They turned toward the path that opened ahead—descending from the chamber into a tunnel bathed in gold, leading toward the next piece of the prophecy.

Eira whispered, not for him but for herself, "I will carry it. For both of us."

And Rhys, without knowing why, nodded.

They descended in silence.

The tunnel stretched long and winding, sloping downward into a world that no longer felt like the one they had left behind. Gone was the silver mist and the cold judgment of stone. In its place, a strange and reverent quiet had settled over the passage, as if the mountain itself were releasing them—not triumphant, not forgiving, merely finished. The walls gleamed faintly with veins of gold and shadowlight interwoven, pulsing not with magic, but memory. And though Eira walked beside Rhys, her thoughts drifted a half-step ahead, already pulled toward the burden now embedded within her bones.

The knowledge pressed against her ribs with every breath, humming behind her eyes like a second heartbeat. It wasn't language. It wasn't vision. It was awareness—a map etched into the marrow of her body. She knew the name of the city that must fall. She knew the place where the final gate would open. And she knew, more painfully than all else, that Rhys was meant to die again, though how and when remained veiled by the prophecy's cruel hand.

She glanced at him once—his silhouette bathed in the warm glow of the passage, his expression calm. He had lost something he didn't even know was missing, and still he walked beside her, instinctively aligned to her pace, her breath. There was an ache in her chest that had no name. No magic could soothe it. The bond remained, but now it pulled only in one direction.

When the tunnel opened at last, they stepped into a high vale nestled between cliffs, lit by a sun lower in the sky than they remembered. Hours had passed. Or days. Time here meant little. Below them, a winding path led into pine-thick forest. Beyond that, far on the horizon, the edge of a war waited—smoke rising in thin threads over a broken kingdom. Iridale, fractured. Fading.

Rhys drew a breath. "We'll need to move quickly."

"Yes," Eira said, voice steady. "There's a path east, through the Vale of Cinders. It will lead us to what comes next."

He looked at her then, curious. "You sound sure."

"I am." She smiled faintly. "I've... remembered something."

He didn't press her.

They walked again—toward the trees, toward the road, toward the storm still gathering beyond the veil of the world.

The mountain had given its truth.

The prophecy had chosen its vessel.

And the final war had begun to stir.

The mountain faded behind them like a dream remembered too clearly—one that left its weight even in waking. Below, the world had shifted. Kingdoms still burned. Shadows still hunted. But the bond forged in the hollow sky and the choice sealed in silence now moved forward in every step they took.

Only one of them carried the truth.

Only one of them remembered.

But both would shape what came next.

Chapter Twelve:

Ash Beneath Our Feet

The Vale of Cinders welcomed no traveler kindly.

Its threshold began not with a gate or wall, but with silence. A silence so thick it swallowed birdsong, wind, and breath alike. The trees, once pine and evergreen, stood petrified and skeletal—branches stripped bare, bark charred into patterns of blistered runes. Ash coated everything. The ground. The trunks. The air. It drifted in slow spirals, stirred only by their movement, as though time here had held its breath and forgotten how to exhale.

Eira stepped lightly, the crunch of burned soil under her boots too loud in the hush. Her eyes flicked to Rhys, who scanned the surroundings with practiced caution, his expression unreadable. The Vale had been a place of pilgrimage once, a cradle of ancient magic and forgotten kings. But no pilgrims walked here now. Only those drawn by shadow. Or prophecy.

They crossed the first threshold—a stone bridge crumbling into a dry riverbed—and the air changed. Not colder. Not darker. But charged. Eira felt the shimmer in her veins immediately. The shadowlight recoiled, then flared. It did not want to be here. Or perhaps it did. The prophecy had long since stopped distinguishing between fear and desire.

Rhys stopped beside a fallen marker stone, crouching low to brush away the ash. Beneath, old glyphs gleamed faintly with silver light. He touched them without knowing why, and they pulsed under his palm. His brow furrowed.

"What is it?" Eira asked.

He stared at the stone. "I don't know. But it feels familiar."

Her stomach tightened.

The magic buried in this land was waking. Not because they had arrived—but because it had known they would. The mountain had released its trial into the world, and now the world was beginning to answer.

High above, a single raven screamed into the haze.

And in the distance, something began to move.

Not footsteps.

Not wind.

Whispers.

The ash thickened the deeper they went—falling in slow, weightless flurries that did not melt on the skin, did not burn, but lingered like memory. It clung to Eira's cloak and hair, turned the edges of Rhys's worn armor dull and ghostly. The trees around them had long since died, their blackened trunks twisted into agonized shapes, frozen mid-reach toward a sun that hadn't touched this vale in generations.

This was the Veil of Ash.

Not a place, but a grave. A rift where the last of the failed Shadowborn rituals had been cast into the earth and left to rot. Eira could feel it in her bones—magic warped beyond recognition, the sick pulse of power that was no longer alive but refused to die.

Rhys walked ahead, his steps sure, his gaze forward. He hadn't spoken since they passed the ridge that marked the edge of the living world. Eira didn't push. She felt it too—the tension in the air, the weight of eyes that had no bodies, watching. The Veil was sentient in a way few things were. It remembered.

Shadowlight hummed faintly beneath her skin, more alert than afraid. But that only made her more cautious. Magic that wasn't afraid was magic that didn't think it could die.

"Rhys," she finally said, her voice low, almost reverent, "this place... it was built to contain something."

He didn't turn, but his voice reached her, muted by the thick air. "Not contain. Bury."

She stepped over a jagged root that looked like a spine. "Did it work?"

He paused. When he looked back, the ash framed his face like a funeral veil. "Do you think it did?"

Eira didn't answer. She didn't need to. The ground beneath their feet was soft, but not soil—burned fabric, bones ground into dust, memory thick enough to choke on. Nothing stayed buried here. It only waited.

A sound rose in the distance. Not a voice, not quite—but a sob. Staggered and sharp, rising in waves like someone crying behind a closed door.

Eira's hand went to her blade.

Rhys didn't move. "Don't listen."

She narrowed her eyes. "It's someone—"

"It's not." His voice was harder now, edged with something bitter. "The Veil echoes. It uses memory. Your memory. It will show you whatever you're most afraid of seeing."

Eira's breath caught, but she kept moving. The sobbing continued, then twisted—into laughter. Then screams. Her pulse quickened.

Up ahead, the ground split—not wide, but precise. A narrow canyon, like a knife had sliced open the earth. Ash drifted upward from the crack instead of falling in. Rhys stepped to the edge and knelt.

"There's movement," he said. "Something's waking."

Eira joined him, shadowlight pulsing along her fingers. "You mean the rituals?"

"No," he whispered. "The remnants."

A sudden rush of wind burst from the canyon—wind that carried no scent, only cold. And in it, Eira heard her own voice.

"You were supposed to save him."

She reeled back.

Rhys grabbed her arm, grounding her. "It's not real."

But it felt real.

The voice had been hers—but fractured, hollow, like it had traveled through centuries to reach her. And the image that followed it, flickering at the edge of the ash-clouds, showed her Rhys on his knees, bleeding. Her hand glowing. His name on her lips, right before she struck.

She turned away from it. Bit down the rising bile.

"Why is it showing me this?" she demanded.

Rhys didn't let go. His grip was strong, not unkind. "Because the Veil doesn't lie. It doesn't create illusions—it shows you the truth you've tried to bury."

"I haven't—"

"You have." His eyes were sad. "We both have."

A shudder ran through the canyon. The air snapped with sudden heat. From below, something stirred—a shape too large, too undefined. Not a creature. Not a person.

A shadow.

A shadow born from shadowlight itself.

Rhys stepped back. "It's found us."

Eira stood beside him, pulse steadying, magic igniting.

They would not run this time.

Whatever lived beneath the Veil was not a memory.

It was a consequence.

And it had been waiting for her.

The basin narrowed into a ravine, its walls bleeding down in slick sheets of blackened stone veined with molten silver. As Eira descended, her boots sank with each step, not into earth, but into a dense mulch of ash and rot—generations of failure compressed into a single, breathless descent. Above, the bruised sky glared with a cold twilight that refused to end, casting every edge in hues of violet and charcoal.

Rhys walked beside her, quiet but not still. There was a tenseness in him now, a draw of breath before each step, like he expected the ground to shift or vanish entirely beneath their feet. And perhaps he wasn't wrong.

The path did not lead them forward. It bent—downward, inward, as though the land itself funneled them toward something buried too long, something that had grown restless in its sleep. The deeper they went, the louder the silence became. Not just the absence of sound, but a hunger that gnawed at the edges of Eira's mind, whispering half-formed memories she'd never lived. A city swallowed by flame.

A child with eyes like broken starlight. A blade she had never touched—but whose weight she remembered all the same.

At a bend in the path, a structure emerged—not built, but grown from the stone, a jagged spire curled in on itself like a claw piercing its own heart. Veins of shadowlight pulsed faintly along its surface, beating like a dying heart.

Eira's breath hitched. "This is a sanctum," she whispered. "One of the old ones."

Rhys only nodded. "And it still breathes."

They approached, and the ash shifted underfoot—not randomly, not with the wind. But with intention. Like breath. Like warning. Glyphs emerged as the soot parted beneath their steps, curling in labyrinthine loops. Some she recognized from the Arcanum's oldest scrolls. Others were wrong—bent, malformed, corrupted by time or something worse.

A gust of wind howled through the spire's archway, and the world seemed to tilt. Eira stumbled forward, catching herself on the stone just as it flared beneath her palm. The glyph lit up, searing hot and ice-cold all at once.

Rhys caught her elbow, steadying her. "What did it show you?"

She didn't answer. She couldn't. The vision had been brief but blinding—a mirror image of herself, cloaked in light and shadow, standing atop a tower of bones, her eyes alight with fury not her own. And behind her... Rhys. Not kneeling. Not dying.

Gone.

She pulled her hand back, gasping. "It's changing."

He frowned. "The prophecy?"

She shook her head. "No. Me."

Their eyes met, and in that moment, something passed between them—something wordless but clear.

The prophecy had not predicted the shape of this moment.

It had reacted to it.

The sanctum breathed.

Eira felt it in her lungs, tight and sharp, a rhythm not her own. The air tasted of scorched metal and distant thunder, and each inhale drew something ancient into her chest. The glyphs that lined the inner walls pulsed softly now, a cadence that matched neither her heartbeat nor Rhys's, but something deeper—older. The rhythm of a curse kept alive by memory.

Inside, the walls were curved, not with architecture but with growth. It felt as though they had stepped into the hollow bones of some buried leviathan, its marrow hollowed by time, its ribs lined with ink that shimmered in languages she didn't know—and somehow understood. As they moved, the walls whispered. Not with voices, but with knowledge, pressing thoughts against her mind like cold fingers against fogged glass.

She tried to ignore them, but the words slithered in regardless.

The broken will rise. The whole will burn. The serpent remembers.

Rhys said nothing, but Eira could see the flicker of recognition in his eyes. He walked with purpose, but not confidence. As though he, too, feared what they might find—not because of its power, but because of its truth.

They reached the inner chamber slowly, the spire tightening into a chamber shaped like an eye—one single, massive iris of stone, cracked through the center, bleeding a faint trickle of shadowlight that pooled in a shallow basin.

Eira's breath caught again. She knew this place.

She'd never stood in it before.

But her dreams had.

"This is where the first vessel was made," Rhys said, voice barely above the hush of memory. "Where the prophecy was first spoken in full. The others think it was carved into scrolls. But it was breathed here—into bone, into blood."

She stepped forward. The pool at the center shimmered with an inner glow, a slow undulation of light and dark chasing itself in endless spirals. Her reflection wavered on the surface, but it wasn't alone.

Rhys stood behind her in the vision—not as he was now, but cloaked in black and gold, his face marked with sigils that pulsed with living ink. His eyes—still golden—burned from within, as though something had taken root behind them.

And her reflection—gods. Her reflection smiled.

Not with joy. Not with peace.

But with knowing. With power.

"I don't want this," she whispered.

Rhys said nothing for a long moment. Then, quietly: "Neither did I. But here we are."

She turned to him, the edges of her voice frayed. "Do you believe it still ends the way they said? That you die, and I... become this?"

He studied her. And for the first time, he looked unsure.

"I believe," he said slowly, "that we've already broken parts of it. Just by walking in step. Just by not turning on each other yet. But prophecy is like the tide. You can wade against it for a while. In the end... you drown. Or you change the shore."

Eira stepped closer to the basin. The liquid shadowlight pulsed again, rising and swirling until the vision deepened. A battlefield unfurled—Vaelwyth shattered, the sky burning violet, the mountains split like cracked teeth. Figures clashed in the distance, faceless, nameless.

But in the center... Eira stood.

Alone.

Crowned in flame and shadow.

Her hands were covered in blood.

One word echoed through the chamber, spoken by no mouth—just carved into the air with the weight of inevitability:

Choose.

The word did not fade—it echoed, folding back on itself in a thousand whispered tongues. It rang in the stone, in the marrow, in the hollows behind Eira's eyes. She flinched, but not from pain. From recognition. Somewhere, in some corner of herself untouched by memory, she had heard this word before.

Rhys stood motionless beside her, jaw tight, gaze fixed not on the basin, but on the jagged glyphs etched into the sanctum walls. His eyes weren't golden anymore. They were lit—brimming with shadowlight barely restrained.

"Don't look at it again," he said, voice low and strained. "It'll keep asking."

Eira straightened. "What does it want me to choose?"

He didn't answer right away. A flicker of something crossed his face—an emotion she hadn't seen from him before. Not rage. Not sorrow.

Fear.

"Tell me," she pressed. "You've been here before. You've heard it."

"Yes," he said softly. "And I chose wrong."

The words landed like a blade point-down. She watched him closely now, not as a reluctant ally, but as someone unraveling before her eyes. His posture remained composed, but his voice… his voice was the sound of a dam cracking beneath too much weight.

"I didn't come here alone," he said, his gaze never leaving the wall. "Years ago. When I still believed in what the Shadowborn promised. We came seeking answers. There were three of us—only I walked back out."

Eira felt the weight of that truth settle like fog across her shoulders. "Did you kill them?"

"No." His breath hitched. "I let them make the choice. And I stood by while the sanctum took their answer as law."

He finally turned to her, and the pain in his face was not that of guilt alone. It was of complicity. Of survival bought with someone else's ruin.

"I chose to be the vessel," he whispered. "And I watched the prophecy etch itself into my skin while the sanctum consumed them—body, soul, name. As if they had never existed. As if they were nothing but fuel for the truth it wanted."

Eira's mouth was dry. "And now it's asking me."

He nodded once. "Because you're the next key."

She glanced back at the basin, now still, but somehow more alive than it had been moments ago. The shadowlight within had dimmed, not in surrender, but in patience—waiting for her to ask again. Waiting for her to be desperate enough to choose.

"I don't understand," she said. "What am I choosing? Between lives? Between fates?"

"You're choosing how it ends," Rhys said. "Who breaks. Who burns. And who remembers."

A heavy silence swelled between them, made worse by the pulse of the walls—a faint, rhythmic pressure that mimicked a heartbeat not their own. Eira turned away from the basin, from the visions, from the watching stone. Her voice was low, uneven.

"You said we might be able to break the prophecy."

Rhys exhaled. "Maybe. But not without cost."

Her eyes met his. "Yours?"

He didn't flinch. "If I must."

The shadowlight beneath her skin surged at that—reactive, warning, mourning. It did not want that answer. Neither did she.

"Don't be so willing to die," she said, each word a lash. "If fate demands a life, why does it always have to be yours?"

Rhys gave a bitter, tired smile. "Because I've already lived through the end once. I won't ask someone else to carry it again."

Something in her twisted—something too vulnerable, too human to be shadowlight. "I never asked for this."

"I know."

And then, after a beat that stretched like breath held too long, he added—

"But you might be the only one who survives it."

The sanctum did not release them.

It exhaled them—slowly, deliberately, as if reluctant to relinquish the weight of their choices. The curved walls pulsed one last time, each glyph dimming in tandem with their retreat, the heartbeat of the structure fading until it became nothing more than stone again. But even in silence, it watched. Eira could feel it in the hollow of her back, like a second spine pressing against her own.

The ascent was steep, the ash deeper than before. It clung to them in wreaths, forming ghostly cloaks of memory that drifted behind with each step. Rhys was quiet. His earlier confession had peeled something raw and red from behind his eyes. He no longer moved like a man resigned to prophecy—but like one searching the edges of it, trying to find the seams.

They climbed until the spire's crown fell behind the crag, swallowed by mist and altitude. A narrow ridge extended west, where the cliffside broke open like a scar, revealing a series of tiered ledges that spiraled downward into a depression between two crumbling hills. Eira paused, squinting through the swirling light.

Below, barely visible beneath overgrowth and time, lay the shattered bones of a ruin—an atrium built of glass-veined stone and bone-white marble, overrun with vines that shimmered faintly in response to the magic in her blood. The structure was elegant in a way the sanctum was not—less a prison, more a shrine.

Rhys stood at her side. "I've never seen this."

Eira's breath left her in a hush. "I think... I have."

She didn't wait. Her feet carried her down the narrow path, over ledges carved by hands long forgotten, until they reached the broken mouth of the atrium. The doors—if they had ever been doors—were splintered, their hinges rusted to whispers. She stepped through the threshold, shadowlight blooming across her skin like an awakening.

Inside, the chamber stretched open like the inside of a dome, its ceiling collapsed, its floor fractured by time. In the center, a dais stood untouched by age—smooth, polished, pristine. Around it, a mural curled across the curved wall, faded but intact. As Eira approached, the stone lit softly beneath her boots, revealing a circular sigil at the heart of the dais.

Rhys remained at the edge of the room, gaze scanning the carvings. "This wasn't Shadowborn."

"No," Eira whispered. "This was hers."

She moved closer to the mural, brushing away dust and moss with gentle fingers. The images came alive beneath her touch—no magic, just memory hidden in stone.

A woman stood at the center. Her face was obscured, but her hands glowed with opposing lights—one dark as pitch, the other gleaming like moonlight over deep water. Around her, a storm of runes coiled, spiraling outward into an army of faceless shapes.

Beneath the carving, words had been etched in long, elegant lines. Not in the language of kings or scholars, but the tongue of magic—fluid and instinctive, readable only by those born to it.

Eira's eyes traced each one.

I burned for the truth.
I broke the chains they gave me.
I drank from the well of shadowlight and was remade.
Not light. Not dark.
But the wound between.
You who come after—do not fear the cost.
Fear the silence that follows.

A shiver ran down her spine.

"She was the first," Eira said, voice small. "The first wielder of shadowlight. She wrote this not for the world. But for me."

Rhys approached slowly, reverence in his every movement. "This is older than anything I've seen. Older than the war. Older than prophecy."

Eira nodded. "Because she was the prophecy. The beginning of it. Maybe not by name, but by consequence."

She touched the sigil at the center of the dais, and her magic surged—not out, but inward, pulling toward something sealed in the stone.

A tremor passed through the ruin. Not violent. Not unnatural. Like breath drawn in before a name is spoken.

The sigil cracked.

And a hidden panel opened beneath her hand, revealing a shard of stone—smooth, obsidian, humming with restrained magic. She lifted it, her fingers trembling.

Carved into its surface was a single line:

The prophecy does not end. It returns. Always. With a new name.

Rhys's breath caught. "She knew."

"She was me," Eira said. "Or I'm her. A continuation. A variation. The shadowlight chooses vessels. Again. And again. And again."

Rhys looked down at the fragment in her hands. "And what happens when one refuses?"

Eira met his gaze, her voice low, certain.

"Then we find out what prophecy fears."

They emerged from the atrium beneath a sky the color of bruised glass.

The wind had changed. It no longer moved with the languid hush of a place long forgotten. It cut—sharp as fractured bone, laden with the scent of burning stone and something fouler. Eira paused at the threshold, the shard of prophecy still clenched in her hand. It vibrated faintly, warning pulsing from its edges like a heartbeat that did not belong to her.

Rhys stepped past her, hand on the hilt of his blade, eyes scanning the gorge beyond. The mists that had thinned near the sanctum now returned in coils—thicker, faster, unnatural.

"Something's wrong," he murmured.

Eira followed his gaze. The ridge they'd descended was gone—swallowed by fog so dense it seemed solid. The trees at the edge of the Vale no longer bent with age, but stood rigid, as though listening. Waiting.

And then she saw it.

A shape—at first motionless, then shifting, impossibly slow. It stood halfway between smoke and substance, limbs jointed in the wrong places, its form half-formed by ash and memory. Where a face should have been, there was only a hollow curve, mirroring Eira's own reflection in the sanctum's basin. A not-being. A mimicry.

It moved without sound.

Her magic ignited in response, roaring up her spine and spilling through her veins like molten ink. Rhys drew his blade.

But neither of them struck.

The creature tilted its head—impossibly smooth, impossibly familiar—and from the depth of its faceless mask came a sound not meant for ears.

"You chose."

Not spoken aloud. Breathed into the marrow. Both of them staggered.

Eira recovered first, heart hammering. "What are you?"

It didn't answer. Instead, it moved—not with footsteps, but as though the air bent around it. When it reappeared ten feet closer, the sigils across its body flickered—copies of hers. Twisted. Mocked.

Rhys stepped between them.

"You saw the sanctum," he said. "You understood it."

The creature twitched again. "We were one. Now you fracture it."

It raised a hand, and the earth cracked—ash lifting, curving into a blade made of sorrow and prophecy, black as night and whispering in tongues. Rhys didn't hesitate. He lunged.

Their blades met with a sound like shattering glass.

The force of it knocked them both apart—Rhys crashing into the stone wall behind, his armor splitting along the seam at his shoulder. Eira's scream caught in her throat as the creature turned its hollow gaze to her again.

It didn't attack.

It watched.

As if it was waiting for something she hadn't done yet.

She raised her palm. Shadowlight exploded from her skin, a storm of violet flame that scorched the stone and seared through the creature's chest.

It staggered.

Then... laughed.

Not with a voice, but with the echo of her dreams. Her nightmares. Her fate.

"You can't be real," she whispered.

The thing moved again—this time toward Rhys, who had just begun to rise.

Eira didn't think.

She moved.

Her magic flared like a second sun. The ground beneath her feet split as she hurled it forward—raw, untempered. Not a weapon.

A refusal.

The blast struck the creature square in the back, and for the first time, it recoiled—not with pain, but with confusion.

"You are not she," it hissed. "You are not ready."

Eira stood over Rhys now, her cloak torn, her eyes glowing. "Then let me be wrong."

She raised her hands again, not to strike—but to unbind.

The spell she cast was not in any book. Not from the Arcanum. It came from the first mage's inscription, from the shard still clutched in her other hand. Words born not of prophecy—but of defiance.

Light and shadow erupted around her in spirals, merging, resisting, dancing.

The creature screamed—not in pain. In rage. In fear.

Because it knew what she was becoming.

Rhys, coughing, pulled himself upright, eyes wide with something close to awe.

"You've changed it," he whispered.

Eira didn't look back. "No. I'm just not what it expected."

The creature began to unravel—its form fracturing, breaking apart into strands of prophecy denied. It did not die. It fled, screaming into the fog.

As it vanished, the mists parted.

And ahead, the first glimpse of the outside world returned—burning gold against the distant ridges, a sunset she hadn't seen in days.

They stood in silence for a long while.

Then Rhys turned to her, blood at his temple, eyes unreadable.

"You were meant to be the end," he said softly. "But now..."

"Now I might be the one rewriting it," she finished.

He didn't smile. Not quite.

But he didn't look like a man waiting to die, either.

They crossed the final ridge in silence.

The forest that greeted them was not the one they had entered. It bore the same trees—gnarled and silver-veined—but they stood taller now, straighter, as if watching them with a warier kind of reverence. The mist had thinned to a silver breath on the wind, no longer suffocating, but echoing behind them like a reluctant goodbye.

Eira felt the shift in her magic the moment they stepped beyond the shadow of the Vale. It was not relief. Not even peace.

It was awareness.

The kind that made her skin prickle and her spine straighten, like the air had learned to listen. Her shadowlight burned lower now, but heavier, as though infused with something weightier than power—presence.

Rhys limped slightly, but didn't speak. He had been quiet since the creature fled. Not withdrawn. Just... changed. There was something less brittle about him now. His silence no longer felt like armor. It felt like reckoning.

They reached a stream veined through a copse of pale birch, their bark like parchment and branches fluttering with the sound of wind-chimes. Rhys stopped there, cupping water into his palms, then letting it fall through his fingers as though unsure it was real.

Eira stood apart, fingers tracing the edge of the shard she still carried, its surface warm against her skin. The glyphs had dimmed since the atrium, but the weight of it remained—a relic of another life, another voice. Another version of herself she hadn't yet met.

She didn't realize she'd closed her eyes until the voice spoke—not from behind her.

But within.

"You felt it too."

Her eyes snapped open.

Rhys still stood by the water, unmoving.

But the voice had been his.

Clear.

Unmistakable.

And inside her head.

She staggered back a step, hand clutching at her chest. Her magic flared instinctively, defensive, confused.

"Rhys?" she whispered aloud.

He turned. His expression unreadable. "What is it?"

"I... I thought you—" She broke off, breath shallow. "I heard you. In my mind."

His brow furrowed, then slowly smoothed. "What did I say?"

Her voice barely passed her lips. "You said, 'You felt it too.'"

He inhaled sharply.

Then nodded.

"Then it's started," he murmured.

Eira's stomach turned. "What has?"

He stepped toward her, his golden eyes no longer hard—but unbearably knowing. "When I died before," he said softly, "when the prophecy marked me, I came back with voices in my blood. Not whispers. Not madness. Echoes. The memories of every vessel before me... lingering."

He hesitated.

"And now, I think... I've become one of yours."

The words hit her like a blow to the chest.

She shook her head. "That's not possible. You're alive."

"For now," he said gently. "But the bond has already formed. Whatever that creature was, whatever it awakened in the sanctum—it forged something between us. I don't know what it means. I just know this: when the time comes, you may carry more than just your power."

Eira didn't respond. Couldn't.

Because in that moment, deep in her core, her magic shifted.

It wasn't Rhys's voice this time. Not truly. It was something else—half-felt, half-formed. A flicker of him, curled between her bones like a coil of memory, waiting.

Not haunting.

Protecting.

She looked at him—really looked—and the sorrow in his eyes told her he had known. Long before the atrium. Long before the Vale.

"You think this is how it ends," she said.

He met her gaze.

"I think this is how it continues."

And with that, the sun broke through the canopy.

A shaft of gold pierced the shadowed glade, falling across them both, illuminating the jagged edges of their armor, the soot on their faces, the blood beneath their fingernails.

Neither of them moved.

Because ahead, down the ridge and past the thinning trees, the world waited.

Not with welcome.

But with warning.

The war had changed shape.

And somewhere beyond the horizon, it had already begun again.

They made camp that evening in a clearing surrounded by birch trees so pale they looked ghost-kissed, their bark peeling in long scrolls that whispered in the wind. The air here was lighter—thinner than the vale, but fragrant with moss and late-blooming elderleaf. A thin stream murmured nearby, winding like silver thread between knotted roots, its banks dotted with foxglove and sleeping violet clover.

Eira exhaled slowly as she set her pack down, the weight of the last few days sinking fully into her bones now that her mind had quieted. The tension hadn't left her shoulders entirely—magic still hovered beneath her skin, alert and restless—but it was the first moment since the sanctum that her hands weren't curled into fists.

Rhys crouched a few feet away, coaxing flame from flint with a precision that spoke of old habits. His sleeves were rolled up to his elbows, revealing scars crosshatched like faded runes across his forearms. Eira watched him in the glow of sunset, a slow wash of gold slipping across his jaw, turning the soot in his hair to bronze.

"How many camps like this have you made?" she asked, voice low, just enough to drift toward him with the smoke.

He didn't look up immediately. "Too many. Not enough." Then, after a beat: "The quiet ones stay longer in my memory."

Eira knelt beside him and held out a hand. A curl of her magic flared between her fingers, catching the fire alight with a sigh of embers. The flames rose, soft and blue-tinged, casting long shadows across the clearing.

Rhys gave her a look. "Show-off."

"You're welcome," she replied, smirking.

They sat near the fire as dusk folded into night. The warmth crept into their clothes, into their chests. Beyond the birches, stars began to reveal themselves—brighter than in Vaelwyth, clearer. Unburdened.

"So," she said, picking a stalk of clover and twirling it absently, "what now? We keep walking until the world decides to fall apart again?"

"We walk until it doesn't," Rhys said simply. "Until we find what's left to fight for."

She tilted her head. "And if we don't?"

"Then we keep going. That's always been the truth beneath the prophecy, hasn't it? It doesn't end. It just... changes its name."

His voice was steady, but not without fatigue. Eira recognized it—the particular weariness of someone who had survived so many losses that hope no longer sounded heroic, but foolish. And yet, he was here. Alive. Speaking of futures.

"I used to think if I survived long enough, the answers would come," she murmured. "That if I read the right book, mastered the right spell, I'd be safe from the choices."

Rhys didn't laugh. He leaned forward, elbows on knees. "And now?"

"I think the choices are the answers. And the punishment."

The fire cracked softly between them.

A breeze moved through the clearing, lifting strands of her hair, brushing against her cheek like memory. Her magic hummed—quiet, listening—and she realized it wasn't just listening to her. It pulsed gently in the direction of Rhys, the tether between them now no longer sharp or invasive, but rooted. Like something that had decided to stay.

Rhys shifted, and his hand brushed hers as he reached to stoke the fire.

She didn't move away.

He didn't either.

For a long moment, they sat like that—hands not clasped, not held, but aware.

Eira spoke again, her voice quieter now. "Do you ever wonder what we would've been... without the prophecy?"

Rhys turned his face toward her. The firelight caught the edge of his expression, softening the lines, gentling the shadows.

"No," he said. "Because I think we would've found each other anyway."

The words slipped between them like warmth, settling somewhere deep, beneath armor and magic, beneath all the scars prophecy hadn't claimed.

And as the fire burned low and the night thickened, they didn't speak again. They simply stayed. Side by side. Choosing not to run.

The fire burned low, shrinking into a bed of slow-breathing coals, and the night settled over the clearing with a hush that was almost reverent. Above, the birch canopy swayed gently, their leaves catching starlight like the reflections of a shattered sky. The sound of the stream hummed behind them, the constancy of it grounding in a way that few things had been since Vaelwyth fell behind them.

Eira remained still.

Still beside him. Still within herself.

Her body ached from days without real rest, but it was a softened ache, the kind that invited sleep rather than resisted it. The firelight flickered across her skin, playing along the curves of the shard at her hip—the same shard that had once burned with prophecy, now merely warm.

Or maybe not.

A slow pulse throbbed in it now. Subtle. Synced.

She glanced at Rhys, whose eyes were open, staring into the fire as if it held truths he hadn't yet gathered the courage to name.

"Sleep," she said quietly. "I'll keep watch."

He didn't move. "I don't think I could, even if I wanted to."

"You're exhausted."

He finally looked at her. Not just turned his head—looked at her. And there was something in his gaze that unsettled her more than shadowlight ever had.

Not pain. Not pity.

Reverence.

"You healed more than my wound back there," he said. "You didn't just give me your magic, Eira. You gave me... room. To be something other than what I was."

The words struck something in her, a place so deeply buried beneath discipline and sorrow she hadn't realized it could still respond.

"You make it sound like I saved you."

"You did," he said. "In that sanctum, in that moment... you chose me. You chose. And that matters more than you know."

Her throat felt too tight. "I didn't want to lose you."

"I didn't want to be worth keeping."

Silence bloomed between them.

Not awkward.

Not unfinished.

Just heavy with what wasn't said. What couldn't be, yet.

Rhys shifted beside her, laying back slowly on the bed of pine needles and soft ash that made their camp. He exhaled with a long, steady breath, one hand resting across his chest, fingers splayed slightly open as if ready to catch a dream.

"You should rest too," he said. "The bond will keep us safe. If something comes close... we'll feel it."

Eira hesitated. The tension still lived in her spine, the old habit of sleeping with one eye open and a dagger beneath her ribs. But here—beneath these trees, beside him, with the tether like a second heartbeat—there was a strange sense of stillness.

Not safety.

But something nearer to it than she'd felt in years.

She curled on her side, her cloak drawn close, facing him.

In the fire's last glow, his features softened. Not the hardened zealot. Not the doomed companion. Just Rhys. A man made of contradictions and consequence, caught in a fate he never asked for, choosing—again and again—not to run from her.

She let her eyes fall closed.

Sleep didn't come gently.

But it came.

And when it did, she dreamed not of prophecy, but of hands outstretched in water. Not pulling her down. But holding her above the surface.

Dawn came slowly—pulling itself across the treetops in long fingers of peach and pale gold. The birch canopy stirred above them with a restless rustle, the leaves now dry and brittle beneath the wind's caress, as if they too were bracing for something unseen. Eira stirred beneath her cloak before opening her eyes, but even in sleep, she had felt it.

The magic in the earth had shifted.

It wasn't loud—not yet—but it was undeniable. The deep, humming pulse she'd come to know like her own breath had grown faintly discordant, a thread of dissonance fraying beneath the surface.

She sat up slowly, brushing needles from her sleeve. Rhys was already awake. He stood just beyond the remains of the firepit, silhouetted by the soft blaze of dawn. His posture was tense—not with threat, but listening.

He didn't turn when he spoke. "The birds aren't singing."

She froze.

It was such a simple thing. So obvious, once named. But the absence felt like a hollow drumbeat. No morning calls. No rustling of wings. Only the distant sound of the stream, thinner now, as though the water itself were retreating.

Eira stood and stepped to his side. The air had grown colder, drier. Even the light, soft as it was, felt distant—like it had to cross too far to reach them.

"What is it?" she asked quietly.

He shook his head. "I don't know. But it started before the sun touched the horizon."

She let her senses stretch, her magic unfurling like mist into the ground. It reached through soil and stone, brushing against roots and the breath of buried memory.

And then—
A snap.
A fracture.

Something in the distance cracked. Not wood. Not rock. Something older.

Eira staggered back, hand to her chest.

Rhys caught her by the elbow, steadying her.

"What did you see?"

She blinked. "Not see. Feel. A… break. Something ancient. Like a door coming unhinged beneath the world."

He frowned. "You think it's the veil itself?"

"I think the veil's already thinning. This—this was different. Like a barrier meant to hold something back. And now it's not."

A long silence stretched between them.

And then Rhys murmured, "The Shadowborn didn't leave the world. They were pushed out. Locked away. If that lock is breaking…"

Eira looked out across the clearing, toward the hills beyond.

The landscape seemed unchanged at first glance. But the longer she stared, the more she noticed the tilt of it. The unnatural bend of a tree's trunk. The way the sunlight didn't quite touch the valley below. Like the world had turned slightly wrong in its sleep.

"We need to move," she said. "This place isn't safe anymore."

They packed in silence, the quiet between them no longer wary, but sharpened with purpose. The bond between them stirred again—stronger now, more than magic. A resonance that flared when one moved, and was answered by the other. Not control. Not imbalance. Just response.

As they made their way along the narrowing path beyond the clearing, Rhys slowed to walk beside her.

"You slept well," he said, a hint of warmth in his voice. "First time I've seen you rest without waking up armed."

She gave him a sidelong glance. "You were watching me?"

He didn't look ashamed. "I wasn't sure if the bond would—if it might... take more than it should."

"And did it?"

"No." He smiled faintly. "But you murmured something."

Eira raised an eyebrow. "Oh?"

He nodded, smirk tugging at his lips now. "'If you die, I'll kill you.' Very poetic."

Despite the heavy air, she laughed. A short, sharp sound. "Sounds like me."

But then, softly: "And I meant it."

He didn't reply.

He didn't need to.

The trail ahead twisted through a narrowing gorge, the earth cracked with signs of something moving beneath—hairline fractures that pulsed faintly when her shadowlight brushed them. The roots of the land were trembling. And the world was changing shape around them, readying itself for something that had not yet arrived.

Eira stopped once at the crest of a ridge and looked back at the fading birchwood.

"I think that was the last place we'll ever find peace," she said.

Rhys stepped up beside her, shoulder just brushing hers.

"Then let's make sure it wasn't wasted."

They walked for hours beneath a sky that didn't seem to shift, though the sun climbed. The light remained pale and diffused, a watercolor morning stretched too thin. The trail twisted along the northern ridge, and the valley below looked wrong from above—trees leaning toward a single unseen point, mist gathering even as the day wore on.

The wind changed, too.

No longer cool or dry, but thick with the metallic tang of something distant—like ozone before lightning, or blood on old steel. Rhys tasted it on the air, his jaw tightening. Eira didn't speak, but her grip on her staff had shifted subtly—more weight in her fingers, the magic in her blood alert.

They came to a break in the trail by midday, where the ridge gave way to a collapsed slope, the earth sheared clean like a sword had taken the mountainside in one cut. The trees below had been burned—not in fire, but in pattern, their bark flayed in spirals, their roots exposed and curling away from the soil like they'd tried to flee.

Eira crouched near the edge, her eyes narrowing. "This wasn't a natural collapse."

"No," Rhys agreed, crouching beside her. "It's a mark. A boundary."

She looked at him.

"Someone—or something—wants to remind us we're crossing into the threshold."

She brushed her fingers against the cracked earth and hissed as her magic recoiled.

It wasn't rejection. It was recognition.

"It knows me," she said, her voice low. "Whatever did this... it knows what I am."

Rhys didn't move. "Then it knows what I am too."

They stood in silence, wind curling past them with a whispering hiss.

And then—
The earth beneath them pulsed.

A single, deep thump, like a heartbeat echoed through stone.

They staggered. The slope below shifted, just barely—enough for dust to slither between the crevices, for the cracked roots to twitch and twist.

Eira's magic surged. Not in panic—but in response.

The shard at her hip flared softly, warmth crawling up her side like it was whispering through her bones. A rhythm not her own. A pull.

She staggered back from the edge, breathing fast.

Rhys steadied her again. His hands on her shoulders were familiar now, not invasive. Just there.

"I'm fine," she said, though she wasn't sure it was true. "It's just—my magic. It's starting to act before I do. It's learning him."

She didn't need to explain who "him" was.

Rhys's expression darkened, not with fear, but gravity. "That thing in the sanctum—if it marked you…"

She shook her head. "No. Not a mark. A memory. A piece of something trying to wake up inside me."

"Are you afraid?"

She looked at him then. Really looked.

And whispered, "I don't know if I'm afraid of it—or of what happens if I stop letting it in."

He was quiet, then said, "Let me carry some of it. Whatever's coming… we face it together."

She gave a small nod, then, and though the magic still stirred in her chest, it didn't claw.

It rested.

They continued on, finding a narrow path that skirted the edge of the drop, barely wide enough for one at a time. The world beyond was silent, save for the quiet churn of leaves caught in forgotten corners, and the occasional groan of trees shifting against the unnatural pull of something on the horizon.

When they finally stopped to rest, it was in the hollow of a dead tree, the trunk so wide that both of them could sit beneath its curled ribs. The bark had gone black from within, veins of silver laced through its wood like frost, humming faintly when Eira touched it.

"It's responding to me," she murmured.

Rhys crouched beside her. "Your magic's bleeding into the land."

"No," she corrected. "The land is welcoming it."

The implications of that weren't lost on either of them.

She reached for her waterskin and took a long drink, passing it to Rhys. Their fingers brushed. Her magic flickered.

But not in warning.

In recognition.

The tether between them sang, low and quiet—something warmer now, something alive. Not prophecy. Not threat.

Choice.

"Every step we take," she said, "it's like the world is watching."

Rhys looked up at the dead branches above, the way they curled inward like fingers.

"It's not watching," he said. "It's waiting."

Eira turned to him. "For what?"

He didn't answer right away. His golden eyes were fixed on her—not with fear, but something sharper.

"Not what," he finally said. "Who."

The silence that followed was not heavy. It was sacred.

Because in that moment, beneath the curled heart of a dying tree, they understood that the coming war would not begin with armies.

It would begin with them.

They reached the old watchpost by late afternoon, just as the wind began to shift again—picking up speed, curling through the trees like a breath drawn too deep. The structure appeared first as a silhouette: a jagged, leaning tower rising from a ridge of broken stone, half-swallowed by thorns and time. Vines coiled up its legs like old wounds, and moss clung to the fractured archways where banners had once flown.

The trail leading to it was uneven, cracked, as though the land itself had recoiled from its presence.

Eira felt her magic stir the moment they approached. Not a threat—but a pull.

"Someone lived here," she said under her breath. "Recently."

Rhys looked at the trampled brush, the stones half-cleared near the entrance, the faint remnants of old wards carved into the wood. "More than lived. They stayed."

Inside, the air was musty with rot and dust, but laced with something brighter. Like sage burned in quiet prayer. The upper levels had collapsed, but the main chamber remained intact—a domed interior of stone, lit by a skylight cracked but still open to the bruised sky. There were signs of habitation: a cold hearth, a pile of bones carefully buried beneath woven cloth, a journal wrapped in oilskin resting on a stone table blackened by flame.

Eira approached the table cautiously. Her magic fluttered across the surface like breath on glass.

When her fingers touched the journal, the tether between her and Rhys flared.

He stepped forward immediately, drawing closer without touching her. "What is it?"

She didn't answer at first. She unwrapped the journal and opened it.

The ink was old, faded, but still legible. Not Shadowborn. Not Arcanum. Something else.

Something older.

She flipped through the pages, skimming fragments:

The veil cracks further each night.
 I see her in my dreams now—eyes like mine, but changed. She's coming.
 The tether must be formed before the fourth gate. If not, she will walk alone into the dark.
 If you find this, Eira, know that I failed—but you don't have to.

She stopped breathing.

Rhys stepped beside her, reading over her shoulder. "They named you."

Her voice barely passed her lips. "This journal is... a message. From someone like me."

She turned the page. A sketch stared back—a crude drawing of a woman cloaked in shadowlight, a shard at her side, her hand extended toward a silhouette. The figure beside her bore Rhys's unmistakable profile.

It was them.

But the next line chilled her:

The tether binds more than magic. It binds endings to beginnings. If she kills him too soon, she becomes the gate. If she waits... she becomes the key.

Eira stumbled back.

Rhys caught her. His hands at her elbows, grounding.

"I don't understand," she whispered.

He looked down at the page. "Neither do I."

But the weight of the words sat heavy between them.

They weren't walking toward the end of a prophecy.

They were choosing which shape it would take.

The hearth flared behind them without warning—a sudden whoosh of breathless flame. Not hot. Not destructive. Just present.

Eira turned slowly.

The flame pulsed once. And on the stone wall above the hearth, words formed—etched into the soot by unseen fingers:

You are the first to come this far with your tether intact.

They read it in silence.

Then, smaller, beneath the first line:

If you wish to sever it, walk north at sunrise. If you wish to strengthen it, stay until nightfall.

Eira's pulse raced.

"I don't know what this place is," she whispered. "But it knows me."

Rhys didn't speak for a long moment. He just watched her, the flickering firelight making his expression unreadable. Then:

"If we stay—if we strengthen this—there may be no turning back."

"There was never any turning back," she said softly.

"But there was a choice."

Their eyes met.

The fire between them pulsed again—once.

They chose to stay.

Night arrived like breath caught in a storm.

Outside the watchpost, the wind had stilled entirely. The trees no longer moved. The earth no longer murmured. It was as if the world itself held its breath, watching the flicker of firelight inside the cracked stone chamber, where two figures lingered in the echo of forgotten warnings.

Eira sat cross-legged beside the fire, the journal on her lap, its final page blank and waiting. Rhys sat opposite her, his sword resting across his knees, though he hadn't reached for it once since the words on the hearth wall had flared into being.

Neither of them spoke for a long time.

The silence wasn't empty. It pulsed—alive with the unspoken weight of what staying here meant. Of what it was becoming.

Finally, Eira closed the journal.

"I don't want to see who I was," she said quietly, "but I think I have to."

Rhys nodded, voice low. "The tether... it's thinning the veil between lives. It's not just memories now. It's bleeding. Through us."

She reached for the shard still tucked at her hip. It vibrated faintly in her palm.

"Then let's find out who we were," she said, and touched it to the journal's blank page.

The fire dimmed.

The stone walls shimmered.

And they fell.

Not asleep.

Not awake.

Somewhere else.

They stood in a room not unlike the watchpost—older, darker. Torchlight flickered across stone carved with sigils they didn't recognize, and yet the moment their eyes met, Eira knew—this was not the first time. Her skin burned with it. Recognition. Deja vu sharpened to a blade.

Rhys stood before her, but not as he was now. His eyes were still golden, but ringed in black, ink-stained veins curling across his throat. His chest was bare, marked with sigils carved in ash. The magic inside him was still his—but altered, aligned to something ancient.

She looked down.

Her own hands bore the same markings.

"Do you feel it?" his voice was layered—two voices, overlapping. His and another. Past and present.

"I feel you," she whispered.

The dream shifted.

They were no longer in the room. They stood in a forest of dying stars, where the sky rained silver petals and the ground cracked with every step. And in that forest, she remembered every lifetime they had failed to meet. Every death that had come before the bond had formed.

Every chance missed.

This time, though—this time was different.

She reached for him—not out of longing, but out of knowing.

And he came to her—not as protector, not as sacrifice, but as equal.

Their hands touched.

Magic exploded between them.

A tidal pull of everything they were and were not.

Shadowlight sang in her chest.

Flame bled from his fingers.

And then—

She woke with a gasp.

The fire had gone out.

But the tether was alive.

Buzzing. Thrumming. Loud.

Rhys was already awake, eyes wide, breath ragged, sweat on his brow. He looked at her like he had just seen her die and return all in one breath.

"You felt it," she said.

He didn't answer.

He crossed the space between them in two strides.

And kissed her.

It wasn't a soft kiss.

It wasn't delicate or curious.

It was the kiss of someone who had been made and unmade by her presence. Someone who had died with her in another life. Someone who was no longer afraid of being known.

She answered with everything she had.

There were no vows.

No promises.

Just touch.

Just breath.

Just fire against skin and the thrum of shadowlight pulsing through them both—twisting into something sacred, something chosen.

Clothes became barriers, then memories.

The stone beneath them held their weight, and the bond wove tighter, not with words or prophecy, but with flesh.

They made love not out of desperation, but defiance.

Because fate had asked them to fall apart.

And they refused.

The light that woke them was not sunlight.

It was silver.

Not bright, not harsh—just present. A quiet glow that seemed to hum from the stones themselves, threading through the cracks in the chamber floor, pulsing in slow rhythm with two heartbeats that no longer belonged to only themselves.

Eira stirred first.

The cool morning air brushed over her skin, but she didn't shiver. Her body was warm, not just from the fire that had long since burned out, but from something deeper—within. Magic curled along her spine like breath, steady and sure, and when she moved, it moved with her.

Not alone.

She turned her head.

Rhys lay beside her, one arm still curled around her waist, his face softened in sleep. He looked younger in this moment. Not unscarred—but unburdened.

Or perhaps... finally shared.

Eira shifted, and the moment she touched his bare shoulder, a spark passed between them.

Not pain.

Not alarm.

A message.

He opened his eyes.

For a long moment, they simply stared at one another.

Words felt too small for what they now held between them. Not just memory. Not just magic. History.
It lived in the space between their breaths.

"I can hear you," she said quietly.

He nodded. "Even when you're silent."

They sat up slowly, gathering what remained of their scattered cloaks and clothes, the silence stretching—not awkward, but dense with the recognition of something neither of them could deny anymore.

The tether was no longer a line between two points.

It was woven.

Not a chain.

A braid.

Stronger than before. Living. Listening.

As Rhys reached for his tunic, his hand froze. "Eira—look."

On the floor where they had lain, the stone had changed. No longer smooth and cracked. New glyphs had been burned into the surface, seared not with fire—but with truth.

A single circle. Two figures inside it, mirrored.

And beneath them, a phrase in the same ancient script as the journal:

A bond chosen rewrites the gate.
A bond claimed opens the third path.

She knelt, fingers brushing the warmth still lingering in the stone.

"It responded to us," she whispered.

Rhys crouched beside her. "No—it witnessed us."

Her gaze flicked to him. "And the third path?"

"Not the sacrifice," he said, "not the betrayal..."

"But something else," she finished. "Something never before walked."

A new way.

A new ending.

They sat back on their heels. Both silent. Both changed.

The tether between them pulsed again, once, softly.

And then—
The glyphs flared, and a final line appeared, smaller, fainter, as if it had only waited to be earned:

The last gate awaits the heart that does not break.

Eira reached for Rhys's hand.

And for the first time, he didn't hesitate.

The valley was wrong.

From the moment their boots touched its cracked edge, the air turned heavier—thicker than fog, but weightless like a dream. The landscape below shimmered like oil on water, each rise and fall refracting into variations that didn't align. One tree became three. A stone path wound forward, then backward, then vanished altogether.

Eira reached out with her magic, trying to find a center—a heartbeat. But her power came back blurred, as though it passed through smoke before returning.

"This place doesn't want to be seen," she said quietly.

Rhys walked a step behind, his hand resting on the hilt of his sword though he hadn't drawn it. "It wants to be chosen. That tower in the center—it's trying to become something. And it's waiting for us to decide which version of it survives."

As they walked, the world bent more sharply.

To their left, the path split into a spiral of shallow steps that shimmered with golden light. To the right, a slope descended into mist so dense it swallowed sound. Between the two lay a stretch of ground where no grass grew, only shadowlight—pulsing just beneath the surface, like something buried was trying to remember itself.

And then—

Ahead, a figure appeared.

Eira stopped dead.

Her breath hitched as the shape grew more defined: a woman, cloaked in deep violet and silver, her hair a curtain of black that shimmered like obsidian. She moved with the grace of someone who knew the valley, as if her steps had carved it once.

"I know her," Eira whispered.

Rhys stepped forward, hand lifted cautiously. "Who is she?"

"She was my mentor," Eira said. "Seren."

Her voice cracked on the name.

"She died. Years ago. In the first ritual gone wrong."

But the woman standing before them didn't seem like a ghost. She smiled—softly, knowingly—and gestured for them to follow before turning and disappearing down a corridor of mist and light that hadn't existed a heartbeat before.

Eira looked at Rhys. Her hand trembled where it clutched the shard at her hip.

"She's not supposed to be here."

Rhys's eyes narrowed. "Then we go find out why she is."

And together, they stepped into the veil.

The mist closed behind them like a door without hinges.

There was no wind, no path. Just light. Pale and ambient, as though it radiated from the mist itself. Their footsteps made no sound. Their breaths echoed faintly, warped as if filtered through glass.

The tether between them pulsed erratically—not in fear, but confusion. It responded to the terrain like it was navigating memory, not earth.

"We're not in the valley anymore," Rhys said under his breath.

"No," Eira murmured. "We're in a possibility."

The first shift came without warning.

One moment, they were walking in silence. The next—

—Eira stood alone on a battlefield of blackened stone, her armor cracked and glowing, a crown of shadowlight burning around her head. The world before her was ash and ruin. Rhys was nowhere.

She gasped.

And just as quickly, it faded.

She turned. Rhys clutched her arm.

"I saw it too," he said. "You were… changed. Alone."

They pressed forward.

Another shift.

They stood in a quiet chamber. Their chamber. Lit by candlelight, strewn with scrolls, books, a shared bed. A window overlooked a garden blooming with elderroot and silvervine. They weren't warriors. They weren't mages. Just together.

Eira moved toward it instinctively, a tremble in her steps.

Rhys held her back.

"No," he whispered. "This isn't now. Don't stay too long."

The tether vibrated in protest. The illusion held warmth. Scent. Hope.

But they broke away.

More fragments followed.

Eira cradling Rhys's body as it dissolved into ash. Rhys standing alone at the gates of Vaelwyth, watching the world collapse.

Eira at the head of the Shadowborn, eyes hollow and cruel.

Rhys at a pyre, burning the remnants of her name.

Each vision bled into the next, not like dreams, but memories written into stone.

They stumbled forward, breathless, until the mist finally parted.

And Seren stood before them—unchanged, unreal, waiting.

Her eyes were violet, flecked with shadowlight.

"None of those were lies," she said, her voice low and even. "Only echoes. The cost of every choice not made."

Eira stared at her. "You died. You burned in the ritual. I watched it happen."

"I did," Seren said. "But I did not end."

She lifted a hand, palm glowing with soft light.

"I became what waits between decisions. What lives between endings. I walked into the space prophecy leaves behind. And now... I speak to you not as a ghost."

She stepped closer.

"But as your warning."

Rhys moved slightly in front of Eira.

But Seren's gaze passed through him.

"The tether you carry has changed everything," she said. "You walked a path no one dared before. And because of that, time has begun to unravel itself around you."

Eira's voice shook. "What does it want from me?"

Seren looked almost sorrowful.

"To finish what I could not. To survive what I would not."

The mists curled again, but did not close.

"You must choose what version of you leaves this place," Seren said. "And who you are willing to lose to become her."

Then she turned, and walked into the tower—the tower from her dreams, now standing in full above the mist.

Waiting.

The tower loomed ahead, half-formed yet solid, its walls flickering between architecture and atmosphere. One moment it was stone, veined with black quartz. The next it was silver smoke curling upward into a spire that pierced the clouds. Seren walked ahead of them without hesitation, her form no longer entirely human. Her footsteps left no impression on the ground—only light.

Eira and Rhys followed.

The moment they crossed the threshold, the sound of the world vanished.

Inside, the air was weightless. Not quiet, but silent. Like the breath held at the heart of a spell.

The floor was a mirror. Not glass. Memory. Each step they took rippled with glimpses: Eira as a child, standing at the edge of the Arcanum library, her hands already stained with ink; Rhys training beneath a temple moon, blade in hand, bruises on his ribs. These were themselves—but drawn from deeper places than memory should reach.

Seren's voice came from ahead. "This is not a tower built of stone. It is built of choice. Of what might have been. Of what must still be."

They reached the center chamber—a vast circular hall, with no ceiling, only endless sky above. Pillars circled the perimeter, each carved with glyphs too old to read, too familiar not to understand.

Eira stopped.

At the far side of the chamber stood a monolith. Black stone. Ten feet tall.

It pulsed with faint light, as though it breathed.

She stepped closer—and her knees nearly buckled.

Because carved into the monolith, in perfect lines, was the prophecy.

Not the version she had memorized. Not the one etched in ink or repeated in whispered doctrine.

This one bore her name.

And Rhys's.

And the end it predicted was different than anything they'd been told.

She read aloud, her voice low and steady:

"When shadowlight finds root in the vessel who chooses,
When betrayal is refused, and death is shared,
Then shall the gate unbind its truth,

And time will fracture for the sake of the third path.
But know this: love does not save.
It binds.
And bound things are always broken—
Or reforged."

Rhys stepped beside her. His face was pale, his jaw clenched. "It knew. Even this place... it knew we would change it."

Eira reached out and placed her palm against the monolith.

Her magic pulsed—deep, resonant.

And the stone responded.

Another set of glyphs appeared—ones she hadn't spoken, hadn't read.

Just felt.

"The gate opens when one chooses not to die.
The end begins with refusal."

Seren stepped to her side. "You've walked the path I began but could not complete. You made the tether not a weapon, but a vow. And that changes everything."

Eira turned to her. "Then tell me what this means."

Seren's eyes softened. "It means the final gate will not kill you. It will become you."

"And Rhys?"

Seren looked to him, then back to Eira.

"That depends on whether you let him become it too."

The chamber trembled.

And the tower began to close.

The first crack in the tower came not from the stone—but from the sky.

A deep shudder rolled through the floor beneath Eira's boots, like the world exhaling in pain. The monolith behind her split along a glowing seam. Light—not white, not gold, but colorless—bled from the fissure, pouring upward in jagged arcs that pierced the columns and spiderwebbed across the chamber walls.

Seren's head snapped toward the breach. "It's reacting. The prophecy was never meant to be read by the rewritten."

Eira turned to Rhys, the tether humming wildly between them. "We need to move."

The tower groaned.

Reality bent.

Stone twisted upward in a spiral that defied physics, the walls folding inward like a closing eye. The columns shattered into starlight, each one imploding into motes that whispered as they passed: You are too late. Too early. Too wrong.

"Which way?" Rhys shouted.

Seren raised an arm and tore a rift in the chamber's far wall—not with magic, but with will. The air peeled, revealing a corridor of translucent light that shimmered with movement.

But it wasn't a hallway.

It was time.

Eira and Rhys plunged in.

Behind them, the chamber dissolved in a scream of wind and memory. The tether snapped tight—not in resistance, but in unrelenting need, like it was anchoring them both to each other as the corridor dragged them between fates.

They stumbled down a path that was never the same twice.

To the left: a battlefield littered with bones. Eira stood in the center, her magic wild and radiant, her face broken in grief. She screamed a name that vanished before it reached them.

To the right: Rhys on a throne of shadow, alone, his eyes lifeless. Kingdoms bowed before him. He didn't blink.

Ahead: the two of them burned in silver flame, hands locked, lips parted as if whispering apologies that would never be heard.

They kept running.

Another vision bloomed—

Eira, cloaked in white, her belly round with child, standing before a gathered council. Magic pulsed at her fingertips—but her eyes were cold, her expression carved from ice. She spoke words of law.

Rhys walked at her side.

A protector.

A weapon.

But not her equal.

The tether recoiled. That timeline rejected them.

Cracks formed in the corridor floor.

The air split.

More futures spilled through the fractures like water from shattered glass:

- Eira dead, Rhys immortal, weeping beside her body.
- Rhys sacrificed, his soul bound to the land. Eira ruling alone.
- Both of them erased, replaced by someone else—someone who bore their features but not their names.

Eira stumbled. Fell to her knees.

The tether flared, wrapping her like flame.

"Rhys!"

He turned, reaching back.

The corridor behind him warped—gravity bending, time unraveling.

He grabbed her hand.

The moment their skin touched, the path shuddered—

—and then held.

The images stilled.

Their future—not a future—took shape ahead:

They stood in a ruined city, shadowlight curling from Eira's spine like wings. Rhys was beside her, his blade at her back, his hand in hers. They didn't speak. But they stood united before a rising storm.

And the tower...

It was burning behind them.

This future held.

They stumbled forward.

The corridor sealed behind them.

And the world went quiet.

Eira awoke to silence.

Not the silence of the watchpost. Not the sacred hush of a temple, nor the stillness between spells.

This silence was final.

It blanketed the land like snowfall that had forgotten to melt.

She blinked slowly. The sky above her was ash-gray and veined with fractured light. Not a sun. Not stars. Just a dim, ambient glow that cast the world in soft monochrome. As she sat up, dust slid from her cloak in a cloud of silver flakes, catching in her hair like frost.

Rhys stirred beside her, a hand going instinctively to the blade still strapped to his hip. His eyes flicked open—startled at first, then settling when they met hers. The tether pulsed softly between them.

"Where are we?" he asked, his voice rough with sleep and exhaustion.

Eira turned slowly, taking in the landscape.

They stood at the edge of a plain that stretched for miles in all directions. But this was no valley, no battlefield—not yet.

The earth was scarred.

Deep trenches cut through it like claw marks, glowing faintly with trapped magic. Spires of twisted iron rose in strange intervals, their surfaces blackened and bent by unseen forces. Between them, charred remnants of weapons lay half-buried in ash—blades too long to be practical, broken staves, shattered armor shaped for bodies neither human nor beast.

And yet—there were no bodies.

Only impressions. Burned silhouettes in the stone, as if those who had once stood here had been erased by light, not fire.

"It's a battlefield," Eira murmured.

"No," Rhys said softly, rising to his feet. "It's the battlefield."

Her stomach twisted.

They'd seen glimpses of it before—visions in the sanctum, fragments in the corridor of time. But this... this was real. The soil beneath her fingers was warm, humming faintly with the echo of something unfinished.

"This hasn't happened yet," she whispered.

"And we brought it closer," Rhys said.

She looked at him sharply. "You think this is our fault?"

"I think it's our proof." His voice was steady. "That what we choose matters. That it echoes."

The tether between them shimmered. Eira could feel its awareness now—like a presence leaning forward, listening, waiting.

"This is where the war ends," she said slowly. "One way or another."

She stepped forward, walking into the dust, her boots leaving the first clear footprints in a land that felt paused. Magic surged beneath the surface, like a creature holding its breath. As she walked, the landscape changed—not violently, but subtly.

A tower shimmered into being far across the plain. Not the one from the valley. Not twisted or fractured.

This one was whole.

Waiting.

A monument, or a tomb.

Rhys stepped up beside her, the wind teasing his hair, the glow from the trenches throwing shadows across his face. "This is where we decide how it ends."

Eira didn't speak.

She extended her hand.

He took it.

And together, they walked toward the heart of fate.

They reached the monument just before dusk fell.

Or what passed for dusk here—there was no sun to set, only a slow dimming of the strange fractured sky, as though the world had decided to draw breath inward and hold it. The tower rose from the center of the plain, its walls smooth and seamless, forged from dark crystal veined with shadowlight.

It had no entrance.

And yet it welcomed them.

The tether pulsed sharply as they stepped closer—not in alarm, but recognition. The tower was bound to them. A consequence. A result. And perhaps... a warning.

Eira reached out, fingers brushing the surface.

It shimmered beneath her touch, then cracked open down the middle—not with violence, but grace. The walls peeled back in silence, revealing a chamber carved from mirrored obsidian. The floor reflected them in shifting light, not one-to-one, but in variations.

Rhys stepped past her first. His gaze swept the chamber once. Then froze.

"Eira..."

She followed his line of sight.

At the far side of the room stood a figure.

Clothed in the same armor she now wore. Her hair longer, darker, streaked with white like ash in ink. Her posture was familiar—upright, commanding—but hollow. Her eyes bore the faint glow of shadowlight not controlled, but consumed.

Eira stepped forward.

The figure mirrored her.

No breath.

No heartbeat.

Not an illusion. Not memory.

But an echo—a future anchored into the stone.

The air changed.

The figure spoke.

"You chose the war over the bond."

The voice was her own. Colder. Older. Carved by decisions Eira had not yet made.

"I sacrificed him," the echo said. "Not out of cruelty. Out of necessity. I believed I had to sever the tether to complete the prophecy. I believed love was a luxury."

Eira felt Rhys's presence behind her—silent, steady.

"And did it work?" she asked.

The future-Eira tilted her head.

"The world lived. But I didn't."

Silence.

The echo stepped forward. Her eyes gleamed—brighter now, frantic with memory.

"You win the war that way. You break the final gate. You reshape fate. But you lose yourself. Shadowlight consumes what it cannot share."

Eira felt her stomach twist.

The tether pulsed. Her own magic stirred—not in fear, but sorrow.

"What is this place?" Rhys asked behind her.

The echo turned her gaze on him. And for the first time, her voice faltered.

"This is where I buried the part of me that chose him. The tower keeps it—because even if I severed it, fate remembers."

She turned back to Eira.

"You're different."

Eira stepped closer, feeling her own heartbeat hammer in her ears.

"I haven't made that choice yet."

The echo nodded. "Then listen to this: You don't win by sacrificing him. You only survive."

The chamber trembled.

Faint cracks formed in the obsidian beneath their feet.

The echo reached for her. Their hands did not meet.

But the connection sparked.

A single thread passed between them—energy, memory, truth.

Eira gasped as a flood of images hit her:

Herself, standing alone in this tower, whispering Rhys's name to empty air.
A war won in silence. A world saved by a queen no one could love.
Power unshared. Power unburdened. Power that tasted like ash.

And then—

She saw the other path.

Hands entwined. Tether burning bright. The two of them facing a force not with separation, but unity. A gate opened not by loss, but alignment.

When the vision faded, Eira staggered back.

Rhys caught her.

The echo was fading now. Her edges blurred. Her face softened.

"Your ending doesn't have to be mine," she whispered.

And then she was gone.

The tower cracked once more—and fell into dust.

Only silence remained.

Eira looked down at her hand.

The tether glowed like starlight wrapped around her wrist.

And she understood.

The end wasn't fixed.

It was watching.

Waiting for the shape of her final choice.

The tower was gone.

Reduced to fine gray dust, scattered by the first true wind they'd felt in days. It lifted the ash in curling tendrils that danced around Eira and Rhys as they stepped beyond the last edge of the mirrored chamber and into open air.

But the landscape had changed.

The valley that had once been fractured now lay still—still watching, but quiet. The battle scars were still there: burned soil, trenches of exposed magic, twisted iron. But the light no longer pulsed with uncertainty. It was dim, steady, waiting.

"We've crossed the last threshold," Rhys said, his voice low.

Eira nodded, brushing her fingers through the air where the tether shimmered like a thin flame along her skin. "Whatever comes next... it won't wait long."

They made their way through the quiet, moving with purpose. Not hurried—deliberate.

At the edge of the plain, half-buried beneath the collapsed arm of a stone effigy, they found a ruin—small, old, long forgotten. Its door was shaped like a broken arch, its outer wall marked with glyphs worn smooth by time. But inside, the air was untouched.

This had once been a mage's refuge.

A sanctuary built for those who walked with dangerous magic.

Eira stepped through the doorway and immediately felt the resonance—deep, slow, like an old heart still beating beneath the floor. The tether flared in response. Her magic reached for it instinctively, like muscle memory.

Rhys entered behind her, his steps quiet.

"It's still warded," he murmured.

"Barely," she replied. "But enough."

They moved through the narrow halls, collecting what remained.

There were tomes—sealed in stasis glass, humming faintly with runes older than Vaelwyth itself. There were relics: a blade of clearstone wrapped in red silk; a vial of distilled memory, still warm. A mirror that reflected not the body, but the burden.

And in the final room—a circle of stones etched with a summoning glyph that had never been completed.

Eira crouched at its edge, studying it.

"It was meant to call something," she said. "Not from this world. From beyond the gate."

Rhys crouched beside her. "And they stopped before finishing it."

"Because they knew what would answer."

She brushed her hand across the outer ring.

The glyphs flared—and then collapsed into dust.

She sat back. "No one will call it again. Not through this gate."

They gathered what they could. She took the blade—light as bone, humming with restrained magic. Rhys found a clasped book, its cover etched with a language he didn't recognize but felt in his blood.

They left the sanctuary at dusk, cloaked in shadowlight and memory.

The stars returned that night.

Real stars—cold, sharp, and clear. Not fractured light or memory echoes, but constellations that once guided caravans and kings, long before prophecy became a word whispered in fear.

Eira stood beneath them, her eyes fixed on the horizon, where the ground began to slope downward into the ruins of the final valley—the place where the gate would open.

Rhys approached in silence.

They hadn't spoken much since the ruin. Not out of distance. But because everything between them now felt spoken. Their silence was not the absence of words, but the weight of them, held close like sacred things.

"We do it tonight," she said quietly.

He nodded. "Before the gate knows we're ready."

She knelt in the center of the clearing, where the earth was bare and dark, free of scars or old magic. Just soil. Just stone.

Rhys joined her.

They set the blade between them—flat and silent. No flame. No spell. No blood.

Just the tether.

It pulsed faintly now—visible between their palms, a silver thread braided with strands of violet and gold, the result of everything they'd survived, chosen, refused.

Eira removed the shard from her belt and placed it atop the blade.

It pulsed once.

Then stilled.

"What are we doing?" Rhys asked softly.

She met his eyes. "We're sealing the bond. Not to strengthen it. But to anchor it."

"To what?"

"To ourselves."

They joined hands, palms pressed together, the tether flaring to life.

Their magic responded—not separate forces but one. Rhys's darkness curled in warm shadows around her wrists. Eira's shadowlight rose like smoke from her spine. It circled them both, not in containment—but in protection.

No words were spoken.

But something began to shift.

The stars above them flickered. The tether brightened.

And in the silence, a hum began—low and resonant, not from their throats, but from the bond itself.

It sang.

Like it had always existed.

Like it was remembering itself.

Visions flickered across the ritual circle—not images, but truths:

• Eira, holding Rhys's lifeless body, whispering, not again, not this time.
• Rhys, standing at the gate, refusing to cross without her hand in his.
• The gate, not breaking, but recognizing them.

Not as enemies.

Not as saviors.

But as equal architects.

The tether flared once more—and then settled.

When they opened their eyes, the blade was gone.

The shard had split into two—each half glowing with part of the tether's light.

Eira reached forward and picked hers up.

Rhys did the same.

No longer tools.

Now they were keys.

She smiled faintly, eyes still damp. "No matter what happens on the other side—"

"I won't let go," he said.

"You may have to," she replied.

"I won't."

Their hands found each other again.

And the stars above them did not judge.

They only watched.

The approach to the gate was not what they expected.

There were no ruins. No carved pylons of gold and obsidian. No statues of the Shadowborn. No lines in the dirt or broken banners fluttering in ash. Only a field.

Quiet. Gentle.

Grasses bent in a soft wind, brushing their legs like silk. A warm breeze carried the scent of lavender and stonefire blossoms—scents that didn't belong in a place like this. The sky was clear, the air unburdened. The magic here didn't hum. It lulled.

Eira slowed.

"This is wrong," she said. "Too quiet."

Rhys didn't speak. His jaw was clenched. He recognized the scent too. It matched the grove from the vision in the tower—the place where she had ruled in peace, empty-eyed, alone.

The field rose toward a single hill, and atop it stood the gate.

It did not loom.

It waited.

A curve of stone split down the center by a vein of liquid light, rippling faintly. Not threatening. Not sealed. Inviting.

As they climbed, the world around them began to shift—not visually, but emotionally. The air grew heavier in a way that made their limbs slow, their breath catch. Not with dread.

But with longing.

Rhys froze first.

Eira turned—and saw his expression falter.

"What is it?" she asked, heart skipping.

"I see it," he said quietly. "A life."

And then she saw hers.

To her right: a cottage on a bluff overlooking the sea. Two chairs. A window half-open. Her hand resting on the curve of a stranger's shoulder. Not a soldier. Not Rhys. But someone simple. Gentle.

A voice whispered from nowhere, smooth as wind:

You've suffered enough, Eira. There is no shame in peace.

To her left: Rhys, seated at a table surrounded by books. A child—gold-eyed—laughing beside him. A woman touched his shoulder and he leaned into it. Not her. But a shadow of her.

You are not obligated to the war, Rhys. There are other ways to end.

The tether between them flickered. Not breaking—but quieting.

The gate was showing them peace.

A lie made of wishes.

Eira gritted her teeth. "This is the gate's defense."

"Not fear," Rhys said. "But comfort."

Eira stepped closer to him, placing her hand on his chest. She felt his heartbeat—strong, fast.

"Look at me," she said.

His eyes met hers.

She reached down, took his hand, and lifted it. The tether between them flared—dormant threads reigniting, rejecting the dream.

"I love you," she said. "But I won't trade the world for us."

Rhys's breath caught. His other hand found hers. "Then let's save it—so we have time for everything else."

Together, they stepped through the field.

The images flickered.

Cracked.

The scents faded.

And the gate ahead flared, no longer soft.

It recognized them.

Not as supplicants.

But as threat.

The gate opened with a whisper.

Not a roar of ancient magic or the grinding of stone, but a sound so soft it was felt rather than heard—like silk torn down the middle. The ripple of the tether between them responded immediately, pulsing once with warning, once with memory.

The seam of light down the center of the gate widened, peeling apart into a tall oval of shimmering gray, smooth as glass but deeper than night. There was no inside to see. Only absence—a void that stretched into a place where no light moved and no shape held.

Eira tightened her grip on Rhys's hand.

"I thought it would be louder," she murmured.

"It's not trying to scare us," he said, his voice low. "It's trying to know us."

They stepped forward together.

And passed through.

The void was not darkness.

It was presence.

It had no floor, no ceiling. Only sensation. The air felt warm one moment, freezing the next. Each breath echoed like it had been spoken in a language they didn't remember learning.

And then—
It spoke.

Not in sound.
In being.

The space twisted, and before them stood a shape—not tall, not monstrous, not glowing.

Just... familiar.

It looked like Eira.

And also like Rhys.

And also like neither.

Its eyes were made of light and absence. Its skin shimmered with every color and none. Its voice came not from a mouth, but from the air around them, through them, from within the tether itself.

"You have come to unmake me."

Eira stepped forward. "You're the prophecy."

"I am the echo of every choice that was ever feared. The gate. The sacrifice. The crown. The blade. I was born the moment the first shadow touched the first light. I live in the space where endings are believed inevitable."

Rhys narrowed his eyes. "And what happens if we say no?"

"Then you will leave. And I will wait. For the next pair. The next war. The next heartbreak that makes a world easier to mold."

Eira's hands curled at her sides. "That's all you are? A pattern? A wound repeating itself?"

"I am what you allowed me to be. What you gave your names to. What you carved into stone and whispered to children."

The figure stepped closer.

Its voice softened.

"You do not have to destroy me. You can rest here. You can rule here. Let the story end where it always ends—with choice dressed as sacrifice. One gives. One takes. One lives. One burns."

The tether between them flared—sharper now.

Eira looked at Rhys.

He didn't move.

He only said, "We've made our choice."

The figure tilted its head.

"Then show me."

It lifted a hand.

The void collapsed inward—

—and the final confrontation began.

The void moved.

It didn't lurch or collapse. It shifted—folding inward like a dream turned inside out. One moment, Eira stood beside Rhys, tether burning bright between them. The next, she was alone, on a plain of glass that reflected every version of herself she had ever tried not to become.

The girl who never took up magic.
The soldier who left Rhys to die.
The queen who embraced the prophecy and burned the world to save it.

Each reflection turned its head to look at her.

Each one whispered the same words, in her own voice.

"You were always meant to be alone."

Eira's magic surged in her chest, but it didn't lash out.

It listened.

Across the glass, she saw Rhys—trapped in his own storm. He was surrounded by shades of himself: the zealot with bloodied hands, the scholar who begged for peace, the broken man who never escaped the Shadowborn's hold.

They circled him. Not attacking. Tempting.

And the figure—the prophecy made flesh—watched from the center of the void.

"You do not kill me with blade or light. You end me by refusing to become me."

Eira took a step forward. The glass didn't crack. But her shadowlight pulsed beneath her feet, blooming outward in concentric rings.

She lifted a hand.

The tether flared, casting a silver arc from her palm through the space between them—through the void itself.

"Rhys," she called.

He turned. Their eyes met.

And something broke.

The void trembled.

Their magic—joined by the tether—leapt from their bodies, no longer threads but roots, piercing through the floor of the void, reaching beneath the prophecy's foundation. The glass began to melt, the reflections fading into steam. The illusions screamed—not from pain, but from being denied.

The prophecy-being stepped forward again.

"You think love is enough to undo me?"

"No," Eira said, her voice steady, power curling through her bones like fire taught to dance. "But truth is."

She reached out.

The shard in her hand—now fused with her magic—responded.

Rhys stepped to her side.

Together, they raised their hands. The tether, burning between them like a living river, wrapped around the prophecy's form—coiling tighter, tighter, not to strangle but to rewrite.

They didn't speak the spell.

They became it.

Their joined voices echoed through the void, not as incantation—but as declaration:

"We are not your end.
We are what comes after.
We refuse your order.
We accept your chaos.
And we bind it to choice."

The prophecy's form shattered—not in agony, but in release.

The void collapsed around them—

and became light.

Eira woke beneath a sky that felt new.

It wasn't the brightness that startled her—it was the stillness. Not silence, not emptiness, but peace. The kind born not from absence, but from aftermath. The kind no one could fake.

She blinked up at a sky swept in gold and pale violet, clouds drifting lazily across a sun that hung lower than memory said it should. The horizon shimmered—not with heat, but with possibility.

The ground beneath her was soft. Not grass, not ash. Something clean. Unscarred.

Rhys lay beside her, one arm draped over his chest, the tether between them a faint silver glow running up his forearm. It pulsed once—calm, content.

Alive.

She reached for him gently, fingers brushing his cheek. "Rhys."

His eyes fluttered open. And when they met hers, he didn't speak. He just smiled.

Not relief.

Not triumph.

Just truth.

They sat up together.

The land around them was unfamiliar—not torn, not ruined, not untouched—but rewritten. The tower was gone. So was the void. The gate now stood as a simple arch of root and stone at their backs, moss growing along its sides like it had always been part of the earth.

There were no signs of war.

No remnants of prophecy.

Only choice.

"Is it over?" Rhys asked, his voice low.

Eira didn't answer at first. She rose to her feet, breathing deep. Her magic pulsed beneath her ribs like a sleeping heart. Not hungry. Not fractured.

Whole.

"I think," she said slowly, "it's just begun."

He joined her.

Together, they stood facing the path ahead—rolling hills lined with trees in bloom, skies streaked with a quiet storm forming on the far edge of the world. Not one of destruction.

One of becoming.

Because the prophecy was gone.

But the gate had not closed.

Something else would come.

And this time, it would not be fate that decided who stood against it.

It would be them.

Epilogue:

Whispers in the Dark

Night fell gently over the unmarked land.

The stars above were unfamiliar—brighter, somehow wider. As if the sky itself had been waiting to stretch. A soft wind stirred through the trees, brushing the tops of the grass with a sound like pages turning.

Eira sat near the low-burning fire, cloak slipped from her shoulders, skin still cooling from the heat of the day. Her hands were clasped in her lap, fingers relaxed, unarmed.

For the first time in what felt like lifetimes, she was not watching for enemies.

Beside her, Rhys moved quietly—kneeling to stoke the fire, his hair damp with sweat, eyes shadowed by reflection rather than fear. The tether between them no longer pulsed in warning. It hummed like a distant lullaby, as if even the magic had settled into the rhythm of breath and presence.

Their glances met—not charged with urgency or confession.

But with invitation.

Rhys came to her wordlessly, settling on the furs beside her, his hand resting over hers. The contact was warm. Familiar. But not casual.

They sat that way for a long time—shoulders brushing, silence stretching like silk between their pulses.

Then Eira leaned in, her lips brushing the corner of his mouth.

A slow, curious pressure.

His fingers slid to her jaw.

And in that simple touch, something ignited.

No prophecy guided them now.

There was no ruin at their backs, no war waiting just beyond the ridge. Only heat blooming between skin and breath—slow, deliberate, and unguarded.

She moved into his lap, knees pressing to either side of him, her hands sliding over the curve of his shoulders. His arms encircled her, not as a shield, but as an answer. Their mouths met again—deeper this time. Hungrier. Not desperate. Certain.

Their bodies remembered each other.

But this was different.

This was not tether-driven, not magic-laced need.

This was choice.

Her tunic slipped from one shoulder. His fingers traced the line of her spine beneath the folds. The firelight caught on the arc of her collarbone, the sheen of sweat at his throat. Their breathing deepened—matched. Built.

Clothes peeled away—not torn, but undone, reverent.

The fire crackled.

The furs shifted.

They lay together, limbs interwoven, heat rising between them like a tide drawn by gravity alone. The air turned damp with breath and closeness. Her body molded to his, skin to skin, heartbeat to heartbeat.

Every motion was slow, deep, known.

Their gasps became rhythm.

Her back arched, his hand anchored at her waist. The world narrowed to sensation—the pressure of his hips against hers, the shiver of her thighs curling around him, the quiet sound she made when he kissed the base of her throat.

They moved together—not seeking release, but recognition.

A crescendo rose—gradual, consuming.

Their magic didn't spark or flare.

It melted.

Heat built, spreading like honey along her spine. His jaw clenched beneath her lips as her breath stuttered against his shoulder. They held nothing back—not the tremble, not the rise, not the quiet cry swallowed into skin.

And when they reached it—together, trembling, undone—it was not an end.

It was a beginning.

After, she lay draped across his chest, fingers trailing patterns along his ribs. The night pressed close but did not intrude. His hand cradled her hip. Their legs remained tangled, warmth shared like breath.

Neither spoke.

They didn't need to.

Their tether glowed faintly, no longer a bond of magic.

But of intention.

Eventually, her voice broke the quiet.

"Whatever comes next... we go together."

Rhys turned his head, brushing a kiss into her hair.

"Always."

She closed her eyes.

But before sleep could take her, the wind stirred again.

This time, it carried more than air.

A whisper wound through the trees—soft, low, intimate.

Not warning.

Not threat.

A knowing voice.

"You've unmade the prophecy."

"But not what waits beyond it."

Eira didn't lift her head. She only let her hand find Rhys's.

"Let it come," she whispered.

And in the dark, the world held its breath.

A Note from the Author

Dear Reader,

If you're here—eyes lingering on the final pages, brain fogged with magic and feelings—thank you.

Truly. From the deepest corner of my ink-stained heart.

You've journeyed through ruins, tangled with fate, clutched a few emotional daggers (hopefully metaphorical), and emerged on the other side of Eira and Rhys's story a little more entangled than you were when you began.

I see you.

This book tested me in all the best and worst ways. Writing it felt like herding emotionally complex cats across a battlefield of collapsing timelines, all while dodging unsolicited opinions from shadow-gods and that one character who refuses to stay dead (you know the one). And yet—I loved every minute. Because you were here. Reading. Holding space for these broken, brilliant people to choose each other in a world that demanded sacrifice.

So yes, we made it to the end.

But also—plot twist! This was never the end.

Book Four waits just beyond the gate, quietly sharpening its teeth. What comes next is… more. Higher stakes. Stranger echoes. Even softer moments between sword swings (I'm sentimental, not sorry). And the return of some long missed characters from the first book (you gotta go back and read it because you should never start reading a series in book three). And no, I still don't know who survives. Ask me again at 3 a.m. when I'm crying into a scene rewrite and questioning my life choices.

Until then, thank you—for every page turned, every gasp stifled, every time you nearly texted a friend just to scream "OH NO."

You're part of this now.

Stay strange,
stay soft,
and let your tether burn bright.

"Never trust a prophecy that doesn't flinch when you call it a liar."

— Probably Rhys, definitely me

With endless gratitude and a whisper of chaos,